The Amish Schoolmarm

A Historical Romance

NICOLE CRONE

D1521915

The Amish Schoolmarm

Copyright 2024 Nicole Crone

Subject: Historical Romance; Amish-Fiction; Romantic Fiction

Author Information: **https://www.nicolecrone.com**

Chapter One

Deer Springs, Montana

August, 1920

An involuntary cough flew through Levi Hilty's lungs as dust from the forgotten bed sheet drifted through the small Amish school *haus*. Giving it a final shake before folding it in two, his gaze resting momentarily on the solid, wooden desk which the cotton fabric had been protecting during the too-hot summer. His guarded heart flinched. Levi could almost envision his old *aldi* Rhoda sitting behind the piece of furniture, her face tanned a golden bronze from the unforgiving Montana sun. He felt his expression sour as he ran his fingers across the brim of his hat before crossing to the chalkboard which graced the full-length of the adjacent wall.

His worn hands reached down into a galvanized bucket brimming with suds, and he removed a cloth in order to begin washing the board clean. After it had been thoroughly scrubbed, he turned to the window to check the time based on the sun's position in the clear sky. Levi winced once realizing the sun not only streamed through the thick panes of glass dotting the cabin, but through glaring cracks in the structure as well. A deep sigh blew through his lips. He would need to apply fresh chinking to the joints shortly, but it would have to wait for another day. As the schoolmaster, he was expected to introduce the new schoolmarm to her classroom this very afternoon.

A frown filled Levi's jaw when a soft rap sounded at the door. While meeting the new schoolmarm was the last thing he wanted to do, it would be best to get the task behind him. He plopped the rag into the bucket hastily, sending a spray of lukewarm water across the plank flooring. Sighing, he wiped his hands across his gray pants before quickly striding to the door and swinging it open a bit too forcefully.

To his surprise, a waif of a girl stood meekly on the porch, gazing at him shyly with hollow eyes the color of spun caramel. Her black mourning dress had seen better days, and the *kapp* perched on top of her head was darkened with soot. He spied the worn carpet bag resting by her side in concern, wondering who this young girl might belong to. She was surely new to the small Amish community of Deer Springs.

Levi cleared his throat while sinking down to the girl's level. She was small and lanky, and his heart went out to the young stranger who reminded him so much of himself at that age. His brown eyes caught on hers. "What can I help you with?"

The girl's eyes widened in a mixture of fear and concern. "I…I'm looking for Hattie Fisher. She's the new schoolmarm. The stagecoach driver told me I could find her here."

Levi tried his best to keep his composure as he rose to his feet. The new schoolmarm didn't say anything about bringing an extra mouth to feed. While the runt of a child surely wouldn't eat a large supply of food, any amount was scarce in these parts. "*Ja*, I'm planning on meeting Hattie any minute now. Feel free to take a seat until she arrives."

The girl didn't hesitate, and after looking over the '

school room, she slid into a desk on the first row of the cabin. Unsure of what to do next, Levi decided to get back to work cleaning the area. While many questions swirled through his mind concerning the young girls' identity, the disgruntled schoolmaster figured it would be best to ask Hattie Fisher for the facts herself.

As Levi wiped the desks clean of the dust which had accumulated over the dry summer, the young girl's eyes began to droop. In five seconds flat, her head and arms were draped across the desk, and a loud snore erupted from her mouth. Raising an eyebrow, he continued tidying the room while wondering where the schoolmarm could be. She wasn't putting her best foot forward, and he couldn't help but think that the young girl who was currently drooling across the hand-hewn wooden desk top had put a big wrench in his plans for the day.

Levi's stomach began to growl as he quietly stepped outside near dinnertime. A sense of alarm began to fill his chest with worry for the new schoolmarm's safety. What could be keeping her? His ears perked as a soft bleat sounded from his nearby pasture. As a sheep farmer, he knew that his time at the school *haus* must draw to an end. His flock would need to be tended to shortly, and he wasn't one to leave them waiting.

He took his job seriously, never taking for granted how the passage of the Enlarged Homestead Act of 1909 had allowed him to purchase quite a large spread for near to nothing. But what was he to do with the girl? He removed his straw hat to scratch his head full of dark hair as a patch of red fabric caught his eye around the side of the school *haus*.

"Have you...have you seen a young Amish girl? She's ten years of age, and her hair is brown, much like my own. She's been traveling for days, and is liable to be quite the sight." A young woman of medium height dashed to the front of the school building before clutching her abdomen and leaning downward to catch her breath. Perplexed, Levi studied the woman's garment carefully. The crimson frock was bunched and pleated. Much too fancy in his opinion. The beige lace trim which accented the high neckline and sleeves mirrored the fashion of the modern world perfectly.

His gaze traveled to the woman's face, her piercing caramel eyes locking onto his as she raised her chin while catching her breath. Small tendrils of chestnut hair which had escaped from her loose bun curled around her face, drawing attention to the lift of her chin and rosy cheeks. Levi's chest clenched when he looked her over, feeling both uncertain and compassionate.

"Answer my question, please! Have you seen my *schweschder*?"

With that, Levi quickly made the connection between the woman standing before him and the girl snoozing inside of the school room. The surname and caramel eyes were a dead giveaway. But why was the young Amish girl related to the very worldly woman standing next to him? Was this the new schoolmarm he had hired? Instead of asking any of the questions at the front of his mind, Levi stepped aside and motioned for the woman to enter the school *haus*. "*Ja*, I have. A girl matching your description is waiting for you just inside."

"*Ach, danke* ever so much!" A faint citrus scent drifted to Levi's nose as she rushed past him quickly, her skirt brushing against his pant leg in her haste.

Curiously, Levi turned away from the choking heat and rested his gaze back inside of the schoolroom. With trepidation, the young woman approached the girl and gently touched her shoulder, shaking it slightly. She awoke with a start, her back suddenly ridged while staring wide-eyed at the woman.

"Hattie? Is that you?"

"*Ja* dear girl, it surely is."

With that, Leah squealed with delight and rushed into Hattie's outstretched arms. The two began to cry as the woman rocked her slightly while stroking the hair which had escaped from the girl's *kapp*. She brushed a stray piece behind her ear before pulling away and holding her at arm's length.

"You gave me quite a fright. We were supposed to meet at the Train Station in Bozeman hours ago. What caused you to ride on the stage coach to Deer Springs without me?"

Leah shrugged slightly, her light brown eyes clouding over. "I...I don't know. After so many days of traveling after *Mamm's* death, I was confused, I guess. I'm sorry."

Hattie scooped the girl back into a hug, sighing deeply while her eyes squeezed shut in relief. "That's understandable, Leah. The important thing is that we are together now. I don't believe that I've ever been as scared as I was this afternoon." She shuddered violently. "My mind began to run away with imaginations of what might have happened to you. After searching for hours the stage coach returned to the depot after its run to Missoula, and the kind driver let me know that he had just dropped off a young Amish girl in Deer Springs."

"Jonathan Philpot?" Leah's eyes brightened at the thought. "He sure was nice. Much nicer than the people running the train."

Hattie smiled. "*Ja*, Jonathan Philpot. I jumped on the coach and came here myself as quickly as he could carry me. I hope you weren't too frightened."

Levi leaned against the door frame, trying his best to understand the scenario unfolding before him. He had obviously made a grave mistake hiring this woman sight unseen. He had hoped a woman who fit the definition of an aging spinster would be gracing his presence this afternoon, and instead, a fancy young woman arrived in her place.

While the sisterly reunion was touching and he felt sorry for the young orphan, Levi couldn't allow a woman who had most assuredly left the Amish faith teach the local *kinder*. The school year was due to start in mere days, and he wasn't sure what step to take next. The families of Deer Springs were counting on him...and Hattie...to teach their children after Rhoda abruptly left before the school year officially ended three months ago.

The other girls in the community were either too young, or simply not interested in the position given the disproportionate amount of men to women. As soon as a girl reached courting age, she had her pick of at least a dozen suitors and was usually betrothed within one year's time. He had made a promise to the community that a qualified teacher was on her way, which was enough cause for several families skeptical of the harsh Montana climate to stay put. But now? He had no desire to hire a worldly teacher who was destined to leave when the going got tough.

Levi shook his head in embarrassment, ridged as his fence next door. The few families which held the small Amish settlement together were likely to be on the first train heading East as soon as they caught sight of her. Hattie's letter stating that she was of Amish descent and had taught for six years had been quite convincing. She had fooled him but *gut*.

Hattie and Leah jumped when Levi took a few tentative steps into the schoolroom. Hattie stood to her full height and quickly wiped her eyes dry with an embroidered handkerchief. After tucking it into a fold of her skirt, she pulled Leah to her side. She smiled brightly at Levi, giving him her full attention. He sucked in his breath as her face shined with a sense of gratitude. Turning Hattie and Leah Fisher away wasn't going to be easy.

"I take it that you are Levi Hilty, and that this is the Deer Springs School *Haus*?" She looked around the room, drinking in her surroundings. "I've been looking forward to starting my job here as the schoolmarm. My Leah and I are ever so grateful to *Gott* for the opportunity."

Levi frowned, confused at her use of the *Deitsch* along with a tone that he wasn't used to hearing. She sounded...highly educated. Her words were soft and delicate, in a very appealing kind of way. He licked his parched lips and took a step backwards.

"And I'm guessing you're Hattie Fisher?"

"*Ja*. I surely am."

Levi sucked in his breath, while noticing the pure kindness which radiated from Hattie's smile. "Well then, I'm afraid that we have a problem. I can't hire you to be the teacher in this school *haus*."

Hattie gasped as her heart rate quickened. While she was counting on this job offer to give Leah a buffer of protection, the thought of returning to an Amish community after many years spent away while supporting her *mamm* and *schweschder* had filled her heart with happiness. After her mother's death Hattie's inheritance was released, freeing her from the burden of working amongst the *Englisch* for a paycheck. Now the simple security a quiet and safe town offered was all Hattie was after. Her love of teaching propelled her to apply for this position, and she hoped to continue working as a schoolmarm for a long time.

She turned, her wide eyes focused on the man whose warm correspondence had put her mind at ease about choosing to accept the teaching position at the Deer Springs Amish School. His chiseled jaw looked grim, which besides pointing out the gravity of her predicament, indicated that this man was a bachelor. Levi's raven black hair poked out from under his straw hat with the slight hint of a curl, and his strong arms were a *gut* indication that the man wasn't afraid of hard work. A strange sensation wrapped around her insides. Hattie hadn't been around an Amish man in nearly six years, and she was surprised by the way standing next to Levi made her feel.

"Pardon? I thought all the details of my employment have already been decided. We…we are counting on this position."

"With all due respect, it's clear that you weren't truthful while filling out your application. So I can't be hiring you."

Hattie's eyes flashed as she thought back to the day when she had sat inside of her small rented room in downtown Bozeman, neatly answering every question which Levi had asked of her concerning her training by the light of her desk side lamp. She had been nothing but truthful and accurate. Hattie reached down and rubbed Leah's back, who was currently leaning against her hip. This surely wasn't the way she had hoped to reunite with her *schweschder* after six years' time. "I'm sorry, but I disagree. I need more details please."

His eyes traveled over her body, making her toes curl. "How can I hire a woman who isn't Amish to teach at an Amish school *haus*? The local families would be fit to be tied." He wrung his hands together, looking anxiously out of the window. "If you need a place to stay for the night, you're welcome to sleep in the small home behind this building. But you'll have to leave in the morning. Now if you don't mind, I must be on my way."

Hattie shook her head fiercely while looking at her crimson frock. Of course Levi had come to the conclusion that she wasn't Amish. What else would he think while she was wearing such clothing? She had intended on changing into the Amish cape dress which she had carefully sewn only one week ago after finishing her last tutoring session with a troubled youth in Bozeman this afternoon.

Even after nearly one year, news of her *mamm's* death was still fresh, and she needed to change into her proper Amish mourning clothing as quickly as possible. There should have been plenty of time for her to change before catching the stage coach with Leah, but her sister's unexpected disappearance had put a wrench in her intentions. Hattie's plans to make a *gut* first impression in Deer Springs flew out the window while searching for dear Leah. She thought she had lost her.

"I understand your concern." Hattie motioned towards her dress. "But I'm truly Amish. Six years ago, I accepted a job in Bozeman as a teacher's assistant after my *daed* passed away. You see, he made many poor decisions, and left my *mamm* with a rather large debt to pay. I saw a flier advertising teaching assistant jobs at an ice cream shop in Lancaster, and decided that I would do whatever I could to help my family."

She bit the inside of her lip, trying her best to fight back tears. The debt would have been non-existent if it were not for her scoundrel of a father. His trickery had caused her once-wealthy *mamm* to place her entire dowry into a trust for her daughters which could only be payable to them upon her death. The family had lived in near poverty due to her *daed's* negligence. "My previous schoolmaster did not approve of my Amish clothing, so I was asked to dress like the local townspeople. Otherwise, I would never be caught in such worldly attire."

Levi rubbed his jaw, which was beginning to show a slight five o'clock shadow. "Your story just doesn't make sense. Why would a girl travel across the county in order to support her family? Besides, I thought you had real teaching experience. A teacher's assistant doesn't count in my book."

"I know my story seems odd. And surely it is. But I'm telling you the truth. Shortly after arriving in Montana, I took my teacher's exam and received my full certification. I am more than qualified for this position. I've been teaching a normal class as well as mentoring troubled youth in Bozeman for quite a while now." Her hands shook as she clutched them behind her back. There was more to her story. So much more. But could this man be trusted? His chocolate brown eyes shifted to the window as he impatiently tapped the toe of his work boot. Hattie quickly decided that she didn't know enough about Levi to tell him more of her story. Leah's safety depended on their whereabouts remaining unknown.

"Have you been baptized?"

"*Nee.*"

"Well then, my decision stands. Your connections outside of the Amish community are too strong, and I ask for you to be on your way shortly."

Hattie stood her ground as Leah tightened her grip around her abdomen. Levi was right about one thing. Her relationship with the outside world was strong. Stronger than this man would ever realize. Hattie's connection to the *Englisch* was in fact the root of her and Leah's problems. But she needed this job like she needed oxygen. She couldn't give up so easily.

"If you are certain about this, I will need to speak to the Bishop."

Levi raised an eyebrow, a half smile exposing a dimple on his right cheek. "Do you intend to go over my head?"

She tilted her chin defiantly. "That's exactly what I plan on doing."

He huffed underneath his breath. "I'm afraid you'll be wasting your time. Since I'm the schoolmaster, Bishop Graber will likely agree with me."

Levi's prediction might prove to be true, but Hattie knew she must try. While she wasn't willing to share confidential information with him, surely the Bishop would be trustworthy. He was her only hope if she and Leah were to remain in Deer Springs. They most certainly could not return to Lancaster. She put her hand inside of the hidden pocket within her pleated skirt, and ran her fingers against the thin piece of paper which she had folded neatly before placing it by her side at the beginning of this warm Montana day. She would need to share this bit of information after all.

Truth be told, there was much that she needed to share with Bishop Graber, and Hattie would do well to pick up her forgotten suitcase from the stage coach station before meeting with the man. "With all due respect, I ask that you take me to the Bishop. Immediately. I must get this sorted out."

Levi blew out a puff of air. "And I must get back to my flock. They are expecting supper shortly."

"Are you planning to forego your duties as the schoolmaster in order to feed a few sheep? I'm sure they won't starve." Hattie regretted the words as soon as they flew through her lips. In fact, she had much respect for the farmers who had not given up and moved their herds during the severe drought. But fear of the unknown coupled with her empty stomach was causing Hattie to become overwhelmed. She felt like she might snap.

Levi clenched his fists by his side. "I own more than a 'few' sheep. They are my responsibility."

"As am I." She pushed a stray tendril of hair behind her ear, wishing that she had at least been conscious enough to wear her head covering on this day. The two adults locked eyes, and Hattie continued to meet his glare for all it was worth until she felt a slight tug on her skirt.

"Hattie, I'm hungry." Leah's voice wavered as she

clutched her stomach in demonstration. "I haven't eaten since the train."

She looked down at the child sympathetically, sorry that their reunion was going so poorly. "Of course you are, dear. We'll find something to eat in just a few minutes." Hattie returned her gaze to Levi's face, surprised by the flicker of concern which drifted across his eyes.

"Surely there is a woman in this church district who sells baked goods from her home. Right? Perhaps we can purchase a snack on our way to the Bishop's home. That is, after we pick up my valise from the stage coach drop off location." Hattie sucked in her breath, surprised at her gumption. She had learned a thing or two since moving West. One of her lessons was that women, and not only men, needed a certain amount of strength to survive. This lesson along with her faith in *Gott* had caused her to acclimate to her surroundings over the past six years. Living alone in the frontier wasn't for the faint of heart.

"Hattie…"

"I won't take no for an answer."

Levi sighed deeply, scuffing his toe across the wooden floorboard. "All right. Greta Miller sells baked goods from her home. We'll stop by on our way to Bishop Graber's." He took long strides towards the entrance of the school *haus*, pausing momentarily to motion the Fishers to follow. "*Schnell*. We must be on our way. If one of my sheep falls ill, I'm planning on holding you accountable."

Hattie hid the smile which threatened to tug on her lips. "Fair enough. Come Leah, let's make our way to Levi's buggy."

Leah grabbed Hattie's hand and began to pull her to the door. "Okay. Hey, did you see the automobiles driving around Bozeman? Do you think we'll ever travel that way?"

"I suppose not. We much prefer the simple life, *ja*? There's no need to travel around town any faster than a horse and buggy can carry us, right?"

"Right. They did look exciting though, didn't they?"

"That they did." Hattie patted her *schweschder*'s head, thankful that she seemed comfortable with her after a six year absence. Why, she had just turned four when Hattie had traveled to Montana as a frightened sixteen-year-old, desperate to find a way to provide for her *mamm* and *schweschder* after her *daed's* death.

Hattie didn't realize she would never see her dear mother again after stepping on the train headed West. Her absence shadowed her days. Thankfully, Leah was fortunate enough to have never felt her father's strong hand. After his passing, Hattie thought that Leah would be safe forever. Unfortunately, it appeared like the frail girl had taken after her mother. And she had no idea that an even greater threat would someday loom over the horizon.

Hattie stifled a cough as she stepped outside, a hot wind blowing a puff of dust to her nostrils. Instinctively, she covered Leah's face while stepping towards the waiting buggy. Hattie glanced across the parched valley, which was once covered with lush greenery. The drought that began last year had changed things. When she had first arrived in Montana, the promise of beginning a new life with a large tract of land was evident. Now only the strong remained.

She looked curiously at Levi, who was propped up against his rig. His broad shoulders and strong arms were evidence of his physical strength, while his simply being there proved the strength of his spirit. He could surely be an ally if only he would believe her...

"Don't forget your bag." Levi motioned towards

the porch, pointing out what Hattie assumed was Leah's belongings.

"I'll be back in just a minute." Leah's voice was soft as she quickly bounded back up the porch steps to retrieve her things.

Hattie continued towards Levi, while praying that her impromptu meeting with Bishop Graber would go well. When she reached his side she gasped in surprise as his arms encircled her waist, and he hoisted her into the buggy as if she weighed next to nothing. Her heartbeat quickened slightly as she felt a warm blush rise to her cheeks.

"*Danke* for the help."

His lips twitched slightly. "Don't thank me. You've given me no choice in the matter, remember?"

Hattie bit back the childish urge to stick out her tongue, and instead, tightened her lips in exasperation. He had her there. She scooted over, allowing Leah room once she returned to the buggy, carpet bag in hand. While Hattie normally tried to exhibit the meekness that she was painstakingly taught as a *kind*, desperate times called for desperate measures. She gazed at the nearby mountains, their tall peaks offering a welcome change to the otherwise bleak landscape. Her heart began to pound when she began to think about what was really at stake if the Bishop turned them away as well. Returning to Lancaster County would be disastrous to her Leah.

Chapter Two

"Are we getting close to Bishop Graber's home?"

Levi turned one eye towards Leah and Hattie, before swallowing hard and training his gaze back on the rutted road, which weaved through clusters of both tidy cabin-style and clapboard homes and businesses within the small Amish community. Hattie's unassuming beauty was getting the best of him, and he vowed to hurry on to the Bishop's as quickly as his ebony mare, Dolly, could carry them. They had already purchased a sack of baked goods from Greta. The new schoolmarm would get no sympathy from him. "*Ja*, he lives right up ahead. We will arrive shortly."

He wondered what Bishop Graber might think of the fancy woman sitting on his bench seat. Jonas Beiler and Zachary Beachy had certainly raised an eyebrow as his rig had passed by the local dry goods store after picking up Hattie's luggage, and they didn't have any children who attended the Deer Springs School *Haus* unless Jonas' nephew turned charge, Luke, was taken into consideration.

He had thought that Greta Miller would certainly have voiced her opinion about the new schoolmarm, since she had several *kinder* under the age of fourteen. Fortunately for Hattie, Greta was known for her kind and merciful spirit, much unlike his *Aenti* Katie who had taken him in when he was a youngster.

"*Gut.*"

Leah leaned into her sister's side, the smile on her face a sure sign that she was thankful to have filled her stomach after a long day of traveling. Her face lit up like a warm summer's day as she tugged at his shirt sleeve with urgency. "I had such a *gut* time meeting Greta's *kinder*. I haven't had a playmate in so long."

Levi swallowed hard while clutching the reins a bit tighter. Greta's Abigail would have been the closest to Leah's age. While Greta did have a passel of children, Abigail, along with her husband, had passed during the influenza pandemic of 1919. But instead of turning her nose at Leah's presence, she offered warm acceptance. Incredulously, she had allowed her children to play with the child who was related to the likes of Hattie Fisher.

Levi decided it would be best to ignore the girl, and continued staring straight ahead at the Bridger Mountain Range, which peaked above the grove of pines near the next bend in the road. Feeling a slight prick in his conscience, he silently petitioned God to send the Fishers away gently and quietly. Being an orphan himself, Levi couldn't help but feel a measure of compassion towards tiny Leah.

His parents had died in a barn fire, leaving three-year-old Levi in the care of his *aenti* and *onkel*. As soon as he saved enough money working the nearby fields as a hired hand, he left Holmes County, Ohio in search of a new start. In search of a family of his own. His face twisted as anxiety pinched his stomach like the vice at the nearby blacksmith's shop. Since Rhoda had left, his dream had died.

"Are you enjoying your food, dear one?" Hattie opened the satchel and offered a second potato roll to Leah. She then reached inside and retrieved a piece of cinnamon bread before delicately taking a bite. She closed her eyes as she chewed. "This is heavenly."

Levi smirked while leading his mare towards Bishop Graber's farm, which was just next door. "Greta is the best cook around."

"I understand how you've come to that conclusion." Hattie took a second bite, and then another, before washing the bread down with lemonade. "I feel so much better."

"*Gut.*" He kept his focus on the Bishop's home as he made his way up the lane. For a moment, he wondered if he was doing what was best. Why not give Hattie a chance to see if she really was who she said she was? Levi glanced at his companion once more, and quickly realized that he was doing the right thing. After Rhoda's betrayal, an outsider surely could not teach the *kinder* of Deer Springs.

"Are we at the Bishop's home?" Hattie's eyes grew as wide as saucers as she looked the tall clapboard home over.

"*Ja.*"

The buggy lurched to a stop, and Hattie reached down and clutched her valise. "Leah, please be a *gut* girl and stay with Levi Hilty while I speak to the Bishop for a few moments. Alright?"

Leah nodded her understanding while taking a large gulp of lemonade.

Levi rose to his feet. "Don't you want me to introduce you?"

Hattie tilted her chin while a beam of sunlight spilled over her dress, brightening it all the more. "*Nee.* I need to do this myself." With that, she swung herself from the enclosed buggy and began taking long strides towards the home.

"Why are you bringing your possessions with you?"

She turned, her eyes begging him to say no more. "Please, Levi. You have been no help to me thus far, and as I said before, there is something I must bring to the Bishop's attention. Then we will allow him to decide my fate." Her voice cracked as she spoke her last word. She pulled up her skirts and took yet another tentative step towards the Graber home.

Levi twiddled his thumbs, feeling completely confused. And curious. He couldn't help but wonder why Hattie was so insistent on keeping this job. With her credentials, she surely would be offered employment in another location quite easily. What could she be hiding?

"*Nee*, I'll need to be the one who introduces you. I'm the one who was in charge of hiring you after all." Hattie's eyes lingered on Leah as she stole back to the buggy to quickly motion for her to follow.

Hattie bristled slightly. "Very well. Let's make this quick."

Levi chuckled underneath his breath. She appeared to be back to her normal, bossy self.

She abruptly turned to him as they began walking towards the homestead. "Here, take this as payment for our food. I apologize for not offering it to you earlier." Hattie reached towards Levi, her gloved fingers gently prying his weathered hand open. After placing a few coins into his palm, she closed his fingers back around the money, and gave his hand a soft squeeze in insistence.

Levi clumsily took a step back, surprised by the way her touch left his fingers quivering. Against his *gut* sense, his confusing emotions tugged him towards her, and he gently placed his hand on her back to lead her towards the sprawling home.

After leading the way to the front porch, he rapped on the door and took a step forward, ready to introduce the new schoolmarm to Bishop Graber. Slow and steady footsteps sounded behind the door, and Levi winced slightly imagining the chastisement soon to follow once the Bishop realized his own mistake. What a fool he had been.

The door swung open, and Levi sucked in his breath as he stood eye to eye with the Bishop. The man's kind eyes widened as he took in Hattie and her now permanently-disheveled frock.

"Levi…what is this about?"

He lifted his broad chin as his teeth clenched. "Bishop, I would like you to meet Hattie Fisher. She is…I mean was, to be our new schoolmarm."

"*Is* to be your new schoolmarm." Hattie stood to her full height and eyed him meaningfully before shooting a pleading glance towards the Bishop. "If I could just have a moment of your time, please. I desperately need to speak to you."

Bishop Graber stood silently for a time before motioning them inside. Hattie clenched Leah's arm tightly before stepping inside of the home. The barren whitewashed walls shone as beams of sunlight rushed through the windows. Levi cordially pulled out a chair, stiffly motioning for Hattie to take a seat. Pushing out a breath, he leaned against the wall as Hattie shot him a condescending look.

"Pardon my slowness. Old age is beginning to wear on my bones." Bishop Graber shuffled into the room, wincing slightly as he settled onto a wooden bench. "Now then, I would like to get to the bottom of this. Quickly. I promised my *frau* I'd check to see what the Beiler boy was up to after supper."

Levi clenched his fists as he thought of the orphan who was basically left to take care of himself. His parents died when influenza wrapped its arms around Deer Springs last year. He was miffed at the Bishop's gentle treatment of *everyone* in the community, including those who deserved some sort of punishment, or even *the shun*.

A few church members treated those truly needing assistance poorly, like Luke's *Onkel* Jonas, and Levi couldn't understand the reasoning behind the Bishop's silence. "We are still getting on our feet here, and I've been allowing some leniency. However, I'm not sure that I can allow an *Englischer* to teach our *kinder*. Levi, please explain."

He pressed his heels into the floorboard while avoiding eye contact with Hattie. "I made the mistake of hiring the new schoolmarm sight unseen. Her application led me to believe she was Amish, and I'm so sorry for making this blunder."

"But I *am* Amish." Her caramel eyes widened as a single tear slid down her face, washing the trail of dust which had saturated her skin clean. She rose quickly to her feet and crossed to Bishop Graber before clutching his hand earnestly. "We are in a big predicament since our inheritance has been released. My *mamm* was once quite wealthy, but she locked her money up tight, only to be touched by my sister and me upon her death. I have much more to share with you, but I ask that I do so privately. I would like to protect my *schweschder*'s young ears."

The lilt of her voice caused his breath to catch in his throat. Levi's curiosity peaked once more as he turned to young Leah. Her back had gone ridged and she tucked her chin to her chest while listening to Hattie's plea.

"Levi, please step outside with the child." Bishop Graber's eyes offered a measure of compassion to Hattie. "It is only fair that she be able to share her side of the story."

"Are you certain? Truly, we can simply send her on her way now…"

"Do as I bid."

Levi ushered Leah outside as the Bishop's curt words rang through the room. He gently squeezed the child's shoulder as they stepped outside before swinging the door closed. Leah trembled slightly as a dry wind brushed against her cheek. At a loss for words, Levi settled onto the top stoop while hoping the Bishop would see through Hattie's scheme…whatever it may be.

After what seemed like an eternity, the door swung open. Hattie's tear-stained face remained somber as she rushed to Leah. "We can stay, sweetheart."

A scowl darkened Levi's face as he turned to the Bishop who was close behind the maddening woman. Deep lines creased his face. "Hattie has been through much, Levi. She seems sincere. You are to welcome her into the community with open arms as she completes her baptismal classes. I also expect you to keep a close watch on both of the Fishers…to be their protector. Do you understand?"

He froze as the Bishop's request registered in his mind. He nodded mechanically as Hattie swung Leah off of the front porch and they began walking towards his buggy. Bishop Graber didn't know what he was asking.

"*Schnell.* It is growing late and I have much to do on my farm before turning in for the night."

Ignoring Levi's rough tone, she pushed her valise back into the rig before lifting her skirts and pulling herself to a seated position. She squeezed Leah's hand in happiness as he encouraged Dolly to step onto the path which led through town.

Relief pressed through her. *We can stay.*

Hattie closed her eyes as Levi's buggy rocked her to and fro after leaving the Bishop's driveway. Her nerves had almost gotten the best of her only a few moments ago, but thankfully, Bishop Graber had kind eyes and a warm smile which put her at ease immediately. A tremor raced through her body as she remembered pulling the court order from the pocket in her gown before handing it to the aging man. While the Amish usually did not use the court system to have their way, her *onkel* had petitioned the Lancaster County District Court first. She just did what she must in order to keep her and her *schweschder* together. Hattie had determined that the document would do well to remain by her side during their reunion, in case her wretched *onkel* had somehow found them and attempted to interfere with her rightful custody of Leah once she stepped off of the train. She could never relinquish her sister to the man who was only after their inheritance.

She had swallowed the bile which had risen in her throat while unfolding the documents placed neatly in her valise before handing them to the Bishop. His eyes showed sympathy while he read the newspaper clipping regarding her mother's death.

Hattie glanced once more at Leah, who needed to put a *gut* bit of meat on her bones in her opinion. Her sister's frailty reminded her of their *mamm's* sad state before she passed.

While her mother's frailty had caused Hattie to seek employment in Montana, it hadn't caused her untimely demise. She had been found dead several miles from home, in an *Englischer's* field no less, which is why the story made it to the paper. The cause of death was ruled to be a blow to the head. Hattie had reason to believe that her *daed's* twin *bruder*, Henry Fisher, caused that blow. And now he had his sights set on Leah.

Hattie shivered despite the lingering warmth of the day while looking over at Levi. His lips were tightened in a straight line, the compassion which she had seen in him at Greta's having quickly passed with the Bishop's firm decree. *As long as she completed baptism classes and*

24

became a member of the Deer Springs church come
November, she was to keep her job. As the schoolmaster,
Levi was expected to not only act as an advisor to Hattie
and Leah, but as a protector.

Hattie's mouth had fallen agape when Bishop
Graber had asked Levi to protect them. This was surely
outside of the realm of Levi's normal duties, but he
obviously felt it necessary due to the documents she had
provided. He respectfully accepted the Bishop's decree,
but all sense of propriety had now left the man.

Deciding to ignore Levi's scowl, she turned to the
young Amish girl who was clinging to the side of the
buggy. "How are you holding up, Leah?" Worry for her
sister glazed over Hattie's features.

"Just fine. Just trying my best to take a *gut* look at
our new town, is all."

Hattie squinted as the buggy jostled over a few
rough spots in the road. Against the dwindling twilight,
the small Amish community was delightfully charming.
Both clapboard and log homes dotted the landscape. She
admired patches of wildflowers growing freely, seemingly
oblivious to the drought.

Not many Amish settlements sat west of the
Mississippi, and Deer Springs appeared to be her
schweschder's quickest ticket to safety since she had been
residing in nearby Bozeman. Most people would not
suspect that she possessed a large inheritance if she kept a
teaching job. Unfortunately, it looked like her place of
refuge included dealing with an ornery employer. While
Hattie found Levi to be quite handsome, his brooding
tendencies were wearing thin on her nerves. Hattie
silently mourned the fact that marriage was forever to be
off of her table, before biting her lower lip and turning to
the schoolmaster.

"Where are we headed now, Levi?"

His back stiffened at her words, and he urged his black mare ahead a bit faster than necessary. "I'm going to show you around your home before I head back to my flock. I apologize for not giving you a *gut* tour of the school *haus*, but that will have to wait until tomorrow. The school's having an open *haus*, you know. Members of the community will stop by to meet you."

She stifled a giggle behind her gloved hand while holding tightly to Leah with the other. "Might I remind you, it was strictly by your choosing that I wasn't given a tour today."

"Enough."

Levi's soft and steady word sliced through the air and straight into Hattie's heart. But the small pinch of compassion she'd felt for the man didn't last long since he had just tried to rid Deer Springs of her Leah. He didn't seem too happy that she had gone over his head to speak with the Bishop, either.

"I'll say we've all had a long day, let's do our best to finish it quickly. Your new home…for the time being…is directly behind the school *haus*. "

He trained Dolly back into the school yard, and then urged the horse towards the rear of the building. Hattie gasped as a small white clapboard house peeked out from behind a thicket of pine trees. Its charming front porch made her heart sing, and the trees behind and in front of the home would surely offer ample shade to the Fishers in the middle of the long hilltop which encompassed most of Deer Springs. Her eyes lit up when she realized the home's most promising feature was its privacy. It was completely hidden behind the school *haus*. Surely Leah would be safe there.

"Here we are."

"It's lovely." Hattie sprung from the buggy as soon as it made a complete stop. She stopped short from running to the structure to gently help her *schweschder* to the ground. "It looks so charming and new."

"New it is. I, along with other able-bodied men, built it for our previous schoolmarm." Levi's dark eyes grew cloudy as he pulled the Fisher's bags from the floorboard. "Your valise weighs next to nothing. You sure don't own much."

A blush stained Hattie's cheeks. Truth be told, she actually owned many lovely dresses, all of which she bequeathed to her friend from town, Marjorie Allen. She had no use for them here. All of her mother's prized possessions remained in Lancaster County for the time being.

"I just have one dress, one night gown, and a few other necessities in my bag. Oh, and some fabric I picked up in Bozeman before leaving." She bit her lip before spilling the beans about the documents which outlined her family's tainted history folded neatly in the bottom of her valise. Levi surely didn't need to be privy to such information.

He smiled wryly while eyeing her meaningfully. "If you ever need more fabric, I'm happy to tell you that the local dry goods store carries all that an *Amish* woman needs."

Hattie sighed, while hearing his emphasis on the word *Amish*. The maddening schoolmaster surely didn't believe her story. "I do not need your assistance in regards to where I should purchase fabric."

He matched her gaze, and Hattie forced herself to swallow yet another giggle when he missed a stair and tripped wildly onto the front porch. Righting himself, she heard an unintelligible grumble leave his lips before he pushed open the door. "Here is your home. Please take a look inside."

Hattie and Leah brushed past Levi and stepped into the main living area. It was sparsely furnished with pale blue walls, and Hattie clapped her hands together in happiness when she spotted a treadle sewing machine in the corner. She then stepped into the kitchen, which had a small counter top, basin sink, a table with chairs, and cookstove. The wooden boards beneath her feet creaked with each step she took as she made her way towards the two bedrooms to her right. Each room contained a bed complete with a tick mattress, and a bureau. She then returned to Levi, who was standing stoically in the living area with his arms crossed.

"Oh, it is just perfect. It reminds me of home...of Lancaster County."

"Why didn't you return to Lancaster, then? Why Deer Springs?"

Hattie cleared her throat while walking purposefully to the front door, determined to avoid his question. As her employer or not, he wasn't entitled to her personal business. She inspected it carefully. "Where's the lock?"

"There's no need for locks in Deer Springs, Hattie."

She raised her eyebrows, not so sure that Levi was correct. He surely wasn't in the same predicament as Leah was.

"You can get to the root cellar through the kitchen, and I filled it up with necessities donated by local families before you arrived. I hope it'll be enough, since I was expecting one person, and not two." He tilted his eyebrows skeptically, before motioning to the wide, picture window. "And the outhouse is right out back, along with a well pump. Please use the water sparingly. You see that fence? My property backs up to yours, so don't hesitate to call on me if you need anything. My home is right beyond that tree line."

Hattie's worry over the lock lessened slightly when she realized that Levi would be close by. She shook her head, confused by the comfort Levi's presence obviously brought her…all while he had made it perfectly clear that he wished she would be well on her way come morning. "That's *gut* to know." Her voice raised barely above a whisper as she shied away from his gaze.

"I must be going now. My sheep are hungry and it's getting near dark, which is prime time for a mountain lion attack."

Hattie took a shaky step backwards while grasping the edge of the settee, her knuckles turning white from fear. "Did you say mountain lion attack?"

"Mountain lions have been more of a threat to livestock in Deer Springs since the drought. Their primary food source of deer and elk have moved on to more fertile lands. Hopefully this predator will follow them shortly." He gave her a gentle yet measured look while slowly turning the door handle. "*Guten nacht,* Hattie Fisher."

"*Guten nacht,* Levi Hilty." A shiver raced up her spine as the door handle clicked when Levi exited the small residence. Her new home had more dangers lurking close by than even Hattie had anticipated.

Chapter Three

Levi's chest burned with determination and the muscles in his back tightened while he corralled his Corriedale sheep to the far pasture with the help of his sheepdog, Amos, the next day. "*Gut* job, boy." He rubbed the mop of a white dog behind his ears for a job well done as the animal's tongue lolled to the side. Purchasing Amos was one of the best decisions Levi had ever made. He had taken a chance on the runt of the litter, and the dog never disappointed. The close eye that he kept on the flock was priceless.

When Levi had returned home terribly late the day before, his flock had remained untouched from harm. Nonetheless, he had spent the rest of the evening counting his sheep carefully, and making sure they were properly fed before turning in himself. He was thankful the deep well on his property was still providing an adequate amount of water for himself and his flock. Not all of Deer Springs could say the same.

Unfortunately, his night had ended the same way it started. Terribly. When Levi blew out the last lantern and had turned into bed, sleep eluded him as images of Hattie twisted and turned through his mind. When the Bishop sided with the schoolmarm, Levi had almost lost his composure. Why did the Bishop insist that he be the schoolmaster if he was unwilling to listen to his opinion? Just because his mother, aunt, and a number of cousins had taught in their Amish church districts didn't mean that Levi was qualified to direct one.

While he *had* been more than willing to take on the role after he'd laid eyes on the beautiful Rhoda Greenloe, now he wished to put all of this school business behind him. Far behind him. Rhoda had made it clear in her letter that she had never truly been one of them. He puffed out his breath in frustration. *Why would Bishop Graber insist on allowing another beautiful outsider to teach the kinder of Deer Springs? Did he not learn his lesson with Rhoda?*

Leaving Amos with the flock, Levi turned and began taking long strides towards a nearby stream. He needed to cool off before the open house, and turn his mind back to reason. A frown tugged on his lips. Thinking poorly of the Bishop was wrong, and Levi knew he needed to repent of it quickly. He reached the stream which used to rush through his property with roaring force, and had now been reduced to a slight trickle. He removed his hat, raking his fingers through his dark hair before cupping his hands into the slow moving water. Once filled, he splashed the water directly into his face, inviting water droplets to snake down his jaw.

He rose to his feet and began walking towards his home with slow and steady steps. His residence was similar to the schoolmarm's house, since Rhoda had made her opinion known while he was working on both buildings. The main difference between the two homes was that his was built much larger, in anticipation of the many children which would come over the years. While Rhoda had requested the grand home to be built to suit her expensive taste, its enormous size was important to him only because he wanted ample room for their future *kinder.* Now with all hope of having a family lost, Levi really had no use for the spacious home. He thundered inside, the anticipation of laying eyes on Hattie again building with each step. She could definitely be considered a distraction to any man with a pulse, with her wide eyes which shined like liquid gold, and her chestnut hair which had curled beneath the heat of high noon just so. Levi shook his head in exasperation while he quickly changed out of his work attire and into a fresh set of clothes. After strapping on his suspenders, he exchanged his straw hat for a black one before heading towards the front room.

A floor plank groaned underneath his weight as his gaze rested on a forgotten piece of paper lying on a side table. Hattie's application. His brow furrowed as he looked it over, irritation once again rising in his chest while thinking about how she had fooled him. Her answers had led him to believe that she was a perfect fit for the scholars of Deer Springs, but he had been wrong.

Levi gently ran his fingers across her distinct lettering when an idea popped into his head as his heart began to pound. *Wait a minute…an application might be the answer to my problem with Hattie Fisher. A different application.* Determined, Levi sat at his kitchen table and carefully began to draft yet another employment advertisement. *If I could hire another schoolmarm quickly and quietly, Deer Springs'…and my…problems would be solved.*

His conscience pricked slightly at the thought of sending an advertisement to the paper without the blessing of Bishop Graber and the rest of the community, but surely there was nothing wrong with taking matters into his own hands. *I won't tell anyone else about this for now. One day, the town will thank me.* Levi continued writing until it was nearly time for the school's open house. He then folded the piece of paper neatly and slipped it into an envelope before rising to his feet and heading to the front door. The *kinder* of Deer Springs, many of whom were orphans like himself, deserved better than Hattie Fisher could ever hope to give them.

Levi had a new spring in his step while he crossed the field towards his fence line, despite the impending problem of introducing Hattie in Rhoda's old school *haus*. Before long, Hattie Fisher would be a thing of the past. Hopefully, it would be two months, tops, before an adequate replacement was found. Maybe…just maybe, he could survive.

After jumping over the fence with ease, he stepped around a small grove of cypress trees and into the schoolmarm's backyard. Leah stood at the well pump, her scrawny arms trying to push the metal handle down with all of their might. He glanced towards the clapboard home, and noticed Hattie staring out of the window, her hair pulled back tightly, making her beautiful eyes all the more noticeable. Her face was pinched with concern.

"Do you need any help?"

"No, I've got it. I told Hattie that I could do this all by myself."

Levi stood aside and watched Leah's intense struggle for a few more minutes, before discretely stepping behind the child and pushing the handle down ever so slightly. A gush of water erupted from the spout, filling the metal bucket quickly.

"See? I knew I could do it!"

Levi looked sheepishly at Hattie, who had clapped her hand over her mouth while stifling a giggle. He shrugged his shoulders. Levi just couldn't stand to watch the child struggle any longer.

Leah picked up the bucket and began staggering towards the house, her bare feet shuffling through the dirt, causing puffs of dust to fill the air.

"Do you want me to carry it?"

"No! I really want to do this for Hattie."

Levi cringed as the child once again denied his help. She was almost to the front porch when she tripped over a small rock and lost her footing. Water splashed onto the ground, causing the surrounding dust to turn into mud which caked the bottoms of Leah's feet.

Large crocodile tears filled her eyes. "I'm sorry. Hattie has been teaching me how to sew almost all day, and I really wanted to fetch some water for her all by myself. I wanted to help her, too."

Levi sighed as he pulled Leah to his side in an awkward hug. He didn't appreciate the wasting of water, but he couldn't fault the child for her kind heart. The front door slid open, and Hattie stepped onto the porch, her small feet delicately stepping towards the porch railing. She looked down at the two, a smile twitching her rosy bow-shaped lips upwards.

"*Hullo* again, Levi. Have you come to fetch us for the open *haus*?"

Levi momentarily lost his voice while looking Hattie over. She was wearing a crisp black apron layered over a traditional black Amish mourning dress. On top her head sat a white heart-shaped *kapp*, which was starched to perfection. A sunbeam touched her head, causing streaks of gold to shine through her chestnut hair. She was a sight to behold, and Levi lowered his gaze before his heart betrayed him.

"*Hullo*. That I did. Are you ready to go?"

"Almost. I'm afraid Leah will need to clean her feet before we are on our way."

Levi lifted the child over the mud pit which was swimming directly beneath the porch steps, and sat her on the decking boards. "I'll fetch some water for her to clean her feet." He frowned at the use of water before turning once more to the well pump.

"And I'll grab Leah's socks and shoes, along with a bar of soap."

After Levi returned with the pail of water, Hattie cleaned Leah's feet before the child slipped on her practical black shoes. Hattie locked eyes with Levi as the child tied her laces, a question mark dotting her features.

"*Ach*, I'd rather not step in the mud before meeting the scholars at the school *haus*. How do you suggest I...?"

Before Hattie could finish her question, Levi had placed his strong hands around Hattie's waist and lifted her across the mud. She squealed in surprise as her hands gingerly touched his shoulders. He slowly lowered her to her feet, and the two locked eyes before Hattie slowly pulled away.

"My turn!"

Levi took in a gulp of air before turning his attention towards Leah. She leaped into his arms and he spun her around before setting her to the ground, a good distance away from the mud puddle.

"That was fun!"

His cheeks burned as he ran his hand across the back of his neck. He couldn't help but feel like he was deceiving the Fishers by being so friendly when he had plans to dismiss them shortly.

They began walking towards the school *haus*, Hattie keeping a good distance from Levi as they trudged forwards. He hoped he hadn't made her feel uncomfortable a moment before. Surely she realized that romance was the farthest thing from his mind.

A long row of buggies were parked along the school yard, causing Levi's brows to wrinkle with concern. It appeared as if the entire community had turned up for the open house instead of just the families with children.

Hattie's eyes lit up when they peeked their heads inside. "Look at all of the people! I didn't know my class would be this large!"

Levi took a step back, his expression grim. Most of the folks inside did *not* have *kinder* who attended this school *haus*. Judging by the expression on everyone's faces, word had gotten around that he had inadvertently hired a worldly schoolmarm. He prepared himself to enter the lion's den as he swung the door open and ushered the Fishers inside, a twinge of concern for the young woman's well-being tugging at his insides.

Hattie ignored the butterflies dancing in her stomach as she stepped into the Deer Springs School *Haus*. She couldn't wait to meet the scholars and their families, and she hoped to make a good impression. Hattie put a protective arm across Leah's shoulders, while stepping towards the front of the room. A freckled girl who was wearing a sky blue frock scooted over to offer Leah a seat next to her on the floor. The room was full to the brim, and most of the children were sitting quietly in the front of the room, while the woman squeezed as best as they could into the too-small desks. It was standing room only, and the men stood stoically along the outer walls, with their stiff backs mimicking their facial expressions.

"Hattie, this is Mary Miller. I met her when we bought a snack at her *mamm's haus*."

The young woman smiled down warmly at Mary, thankful that Leah's new friend was seated directly in the front of the room, within plain view of Hattie when she addressed the crowd. "It's nice to meet you, Mary. I'm your new schoolmarm."

The girl smiled shyly beneath her auburn hair, which was tucked neatly underneath her *kapp.* "I'm glad that you are our new teacher. Rhoda Greenloe wasn't too nice."

"Is that so? I take it that Rhoda Greenloe was your previous teacher?" Hattie tried her best to hide her amusement.

"*Ja.* And you look much nicer than her!"

"I'm sure she wasn't too bad, Mary. I'm looking forward to getting to know you better later, but now, I must address everyone before the open *haus* begins."

Hattie rose to her feet, while winking discreetly to her *schweschder.* She was thrilled that they had seemed to pick up right where they had left off six years ago, despite Leah's young age. The girl had followed her around all day, and Hattie had explained the process of sewing a cape dress in detail while she made three of her own, in anticipation of the new school year. Leah's mother's frailty before her death had caused her not to teach her daughter herself, and the child's excitement about learning this new skill had been contagious.

Hattie walked demurely towards the front of the room, eager for the meeting to begin. Levi was already standing close to the chalkboard, and she hurried to his side. In her haste, her arms brushed against his, and he shied from her touch. A blush stained Hattie's cheeks as she stepped away quickly.

Levi's tenderness only moments earlier had stirred her spirit. But surely Levi knew that she had no interest in him. Besides the fact that he usually made his dislike of her clear, Hattie was well aware that with her large inheritance in hand, men couldn't be trusted. Like her mother, she would never know if a man truly loved her for her, or for her deep coffers. There was no way that she could risk entering into a loveless marriage, like her *mamm* did. She was destined to be a spinster for the rest of her days.

Levi cleared his throat, and the low din echoing throughout the room quieted. Hattie noticed that he swallowed hard before raising his voice above the crowd. "*Hullo* neighbors. As you all know, we are here today to greet our new schoolmarm, Hattie Fisher. She has come to us from Bozeman, and I hope that everyone will give her a warm welcome."

Hattie opened her mouth to take the floor, as a man stepped forward. His lanky build and beady eyes made her squirm as he looked her over in disapproval. "I saw you driving this woman through town yesterday, Levi, and we don't need the likes of her teaching our *kinder*." He nodded his head towards a group of young folks towards the back of the room. "This is the young woman I told you about. She was as fancy as can be only twenty-four hours ago." He chuckled loudly. "You didn't do too *gut* of a job choosing a schoolmarm, did you Levi?"

Whispers began to zig-zag through the crowd, and Hattie kept her eyes focused on Leah to keep from trembling. What trouble her silly dress had caused. The frock now sat in a crumbled mess in the corner of her bedroom, ready to be disposed of permanently.

Slowly, a woman rose from a desk. Greta Miller stood to her full height as she motioned towards Levi. "May I speak?"

"*Ja*, go ahead Greta."

"I met Hattie yesterday, and she seemed like a fine young woman. Now, it's true that we don't know her whole story. But shouldn't we give her a chance? Life in Deer Springs is hard, and at least she is willing to teach our *kinder*, instead of abandoning us in favor of an easier life."

Levi reached out, gently squeezing the back of Hattie's arm while holding her steady. Leah's warm smile offered her a measure of comfort as she replayed Greta's encouraging words through her mind.

"I've spoken to the Bishop, and as of right now, Hattie Fisher is to stay. I might not agree with the decision, but I expect the community to welcome her kindly. We must take the Bishop at his word, and respect the man and his position. If you have any problems with Hattie Fisher's background, I expect you to come to me, and not to her directly." Levi leveled his gaze on the man who had questioned his judgment. "Is that clear, Jonas?"

The man didn't answer, and instead stormed out of the school room.

"*Gut* riddance."

Hattie looked up at Levi in surprise as he mumbled quietly underneath his breath. If she didn't know any better, she would think that he was standing up for her. But one look into his uncertain and annoyed eyes told her differently.

"Now, I would like to turn over the floor to Hattie."

As Levi stepped to the side, Hattie trained her gaze on Leah. After the child flashed her an encouraging smile, she felt the strength to begin. "*Hullo,* everyone. As Levi said, my name is Hattie Fisher. I was raised in an Amish home in Lancaster County, Pennsylvania. When I was sixteen-years-old, I headed West, and I received my teaching certificate in nearby Bozeman." She licked her parched lips as Leah nodded, urging her to continue.

"I taught in Bozeman for six years, and I'm so grateful that I have been given this opportunity to now teach in Deer Springs…and to fully return to the Amish church. My ten-year-old *schweschder* Leah has joined me, and she will be a new classmate to your children. I believe that hands-on learning is the best way to teach, and I utilize that method whenever possible. I also believe in allowing the older scholars to mentor the younger *kinder*, much in the same way that our young people apprentice underneath various vocations around the community. Again, I'm so happy to be here, and if you have any questions, please let me know."

Levi once again stepped to her side. "Please feel free to come to Hattie personally and ask any questions that you might have about her teaching methods. I'm sure she'd like to meet the scholars, too."

"*Ja*, I surely would." Hattie's eyes shone with unshed tears as she looked down at the sea of tiny faces looking up at her. Her students were so important to her, especially since she would never have any *kinder* of her own.

Most of the parents and children rose and cautiously took their turns speaking to Hattie at the front of the room, while the church members who were there out of pure curiosity shuffled outside. Hattie kept a close eye on Leah as she spoke to each family in turn, but after two hours, her feet began to ache and the stuffiness inside the room was nearly unbearable. Levi had slid open the windows, but the slight breeze did little to combat the heat which had taken hold of the small cabin.

Hattie approached Levi, who was talking warmly to Greta Miller in a low baritone. "Could you keep an eye on Leah for a minute? It's awfully warm in here, and I'd like to step outside for a moment."

"*Ja*, that's no problem." He eyed her curiously as she motioned towards her *schweschder*, who was playing with a faceless doll with Mary Miller.

"I'll be right outside if you need me." She pushed away from the maddening schoolmaster and stilted environment inside of the school *haus* as quickly as possible.

Hattie smiled as the cool breeze kissed her parched skin once she stepped foot outside of the school *haus*. She welcomed the change in atmosphere, since almost all of the adults in attendance had turned up their noses at her. The one bright lining was the *kinder* in this Amish church district. They were enchanting, and overall, seemed eager to learn. She closed her eyes while she leaned onto the railing, allowing herself to daydream about the first day in her new classroom.

"Well, *hullo* there, girly."

Fear gripped Hattie's stomach as her eyes snapped open. The gritty voice sounded painfully familiar. Sure enough, Jonas Beiler stood before her, grinning like a cunning cat. His beady eyes looked her over in admiration as he leaned closer, his greasy blonde hair broadcasting a foul smell in her direction.

"Is there anything I can help you with?" Hattie stepped back slowly, mentally planning her escape back into the school *haus*. She had encountered a handful of ranchers in Bozeman who reminded her of Jonas' mannerisms to a T. They hadn't taken kindly to her rejection, and she suspected that Jonas Beiler wouldn't either.

"Well, when I saw you with Levi yesterday, you looked like the kind of girl who liked to have a *gut* time. What do you say?" He grinned while sliding his hand around her arm.

She stifled a scream while trying to pull away from his ever-tightening grasp. "Jonas, please leave me be. You have no business being here. You don't have any children, do you?"

He leaned his head back and chuckled loudly. "Well, not exactly. But I am the guardian of my nephew, Luke Beiler. He's six. His *mamm* and *daed* died during the influenza outbreak last year. So I'll be around."

She felt bile rising into her throat before a deep voice resonated behind her.

"Let her go."

Hattie felt a strong form brush into her side as Jonas dropped her arm like a hot potato. She looked up to see Levi next to her, his expression grim.

"You best be on your way, Jonas."

The man scowled at Levi. "I was just about to fetch Luke and head home. See you later, girly." He slinked away, calling for a small towheaded boy to follow. He ran after the man barefooted and hopped into a buggy, his clothing noticeably too small, stained, and dirty.

"Are you alright? Please pay no mind to Jonas Beiler. He isn't *gut* for nothing."

She brushed a strand of her hair back into place, while staring wistfully at the departing buggy. Shame squeezed around her. "I'm fine. I had to reject the advances of several ranchers while in Bozeman. No harm done. I just worry for Luke…I didn't get to speak to him, or Jonas for that matter, while inside about his education."

"I'm sure the furthest thing from Jonas' mind is his nephew's education. I've felt terribly for the boy, and would take him in if I could." He locked eyes with her as grief laced his face.

Levi straightened and motioned for Hattie to follow him off of the porch. "The open *haus* is over. I'd say it's time to get you home."

Hattie called for Leah, and the three plodded through the dry grass towards the back of the property. Once they pushed through the grove of trees Leah ran ahead to the clapboard home, leaving the adults behind.

"Hattie…I think someone was here while we were gone!"

She quickened her steps, and joined her *schweschder* at the base of the porch. Hattie gasped, while covering her mouth with both hands. Muddy footprints

42

lined the length of the porch, stopping in front of every window. Levi reached the Fishers, his brow furrowed in confusion.

"What is this? Did someone stop by during the open house?"

"It appears so."

"Those are cowboy boots, surely from an *Englischer*. Could have it been Jonathan Philpot? Did you leave a bag behind in his stagecoach?"

"*Nee*, I did not." Hattie sank to the ground, wondering what this could mean. Her *Onkel* Henry was as Amish as they come, so he couldn't have anything to do with this. Could he? Hattie rubbed her pounding head.

"You mentioned that in Bozeman there were some would-be suitors interested in you. Could it have been one of them?"

Her eyes flashed as she leveled his gaze. "Certainly not. I didn't show one ounce of interest in any of those cowboys. Besides, they wouldn't know about my whereabouts now."

Levi removed his hat before raking his hand through his hair, his gaze focused on her wide-eyed stare. "I just don't know then. Maybe it is a *gut* idea to put a lock on your home. I'll look into it tomorrow."

Hattie's stomach twisted as Levi wished them well after looking the property over and verifying that no intruders were lingering nearby. She had a sinking suspicion that Henry did have something to do with the mysterious boot prints. She had been careful to keep their location private…but could he have found out somehow? Hattie pulled Leah close as they stepped foot inside. She would need more than a lock to keep Henry Fisher at bay if he was behind this.

Chapter Four

"What can I do for you?"

Levi looked the portly shop owner over after he ducked into the Bozeman Mercantile, the bell located directly over the door still ringing in his ears. "I'm in need of a simple door lock. Do you have what I'm looking for?"

The man shifted his comfortable bulk. "Locks are on the far wall over there. Let me know if you need anything else."

With a polite nod, Levi lumbered towards the hardware section, hopeful that he would find what he was looking for quickly. A surprise trip to Bozeman wasn't in his plans for the day, and he was forced to complete his afternoon chores hastily in order to fit it in. Of course, the trip wasn't just for the new schoolmarm's benefit.

Levi had been sure to bring his newest want ad to the bustling settlement, since handing the employment advertisement directly to Jonathan Philpot, who served as both stage coach driver and mail carrier in Deer Springs, would never do. What if one of the church members saw what he was up to? He had promptly slipped it into the local Post Office before walking towards the mercantile.

The twinge of guilt he felt while handing over the letter could not compare to the relief that washed over him when he realized that Hattie might soon be a thing of the past. While the fear in her eyes last night was troublesome, he knew he must rid the school district of her as quickly as possible. His conflicting feelings concerning the new schoolmarm warred inside of him as he clumsily clutched a smooth metal lock and turned towards the checkout counter.

"I didn't expect to see you here. What are you needing that lock for?"

Levi looked up and realized that he was face to face with Jonas Beiler. The man pulled his straw hat over his crooked nose as he motioned for him to follow him into a corner. Levi balled his fist as he complied. Seeing his skinny fingers wrapped around Hattie's arm last night had almost caused him to lose his composure. He somewhat understood why Bishop Graber had lightened his censure of the families affected by death over the past year, but enough was enough. He hoped the man of God would confront Jonas about his wrongdoing…and soon.

"I'm picking up something for the new schoolmarm. What are you doing in Bozeman? And where is Luke?"

Jonas crossed his arms across his lanky frame. "I have some business to attend to, which is none of your concern. And Luke is back at the homestead. It's *wunderbaar* to have him out of my hair for a few hours, let me tell you."

Indignation welled up inside of Levi at the thought of the young orphan being left alone at the Beiler place. "Isn't six a little young to be left by oneself?"

"*Nee*. I leave him as much as I can. He just slows me down."

He had heard that before. After his parents died, Levi was left alone while his *aenti*, *onkel*, and their *kinder* made house calls within their small community in Ohio. Levi's *aenti* had long ago pined after his *daed,* but he never showed any interest in her. Katie married his brother after her first choice turned her down, simply out of spite. She never cared for Levi, and acted like she blamed him for his *daed's* dismissal, never truly allowing him to become part of the family.

Levi pulled his attention away from Jonas, hoping to leave the conversation before saying something he would regret later. "I need to head back to Deer Springs now, and I suggest you do the same. Little Luke is surely lonesome."

"I'll return home when I'm *gut* and ready. But I'm glad I ran into you today. Do you need any help with your sheep? My wheat crop is all but lost this year, and I could really use some extra cash."

Levi sucked in his breath. Jonas had proved to be a sorry worker when he helped shear his sheep the previous spring. But if he took him up on his offer, he might be able to keep an eye on Luke…to make sure that he was being properly cared for and fed. When he was at his home, at least. The young child was in need of desperate help, and Levi would do almost anything to give it to him.

He reluctantly pried his lips open in agreement. "I could use some help. I have to spend a *gut* amount of time getting the schoolmarm settled and all, and I'll be observing her in class from time to time too. I would like for you to bring Luke along when he's not in school if you accept my offer. Leaving the child alone for long periods isn't *gut* for him."

Jonas grunted, beady eyes shifting. "*Ja,* I guess I could do that. I'll tell him to come by your place when he's done with school instead of heading home. I must say that I feel sorry for you, having to spend so much time around Hattie Fisher and all. She looks to be nothing but trouble."

Levi's stomach tightened. Jonas had been very eager to become cozy with the schoolmarm last night. He decided to let well enough alone, and offered a curt nod. "She's not who I was expecting to arrive in Deer Springs to teach our *kinder,* but it is what it is. For now, we must accept her appointment. I'll see you tomorrow at my farm, if that agrees with you."

Levi barely waited for his instructions to register across Jonas' features before swiftly heading to the counter and purchasing the lock. He then strode out of the store, ignoring the riotous crowd of ranchers and trappers stationed outside of the saloon. While many areas of town weren't quite as rowdy, he could hardly imagine Hattie teaching for six years in such an environment.

He jumped at the sound of a backfiring automobile before heading towards the stagecoach which would take him back to Deer Springs before continuing on towards Missoula. After waiting for ten minutes, he hopped into the coach along with a few travel-weary *Englischers.* He carefully chose a seat near the driver, hoping to question Jonathan Philpot about the mysterious footprints found on the schoolmarm's porch.

"*Gut* afternoon."

A smile crinkled the eyes of Jonathan's creased face. "Hello again Levi, I didn't expect you to be back so soon. Why, you're on the first scheduled coach back to Deer Springs."

"My business in town was quick today. I'm glad to have caught you."

"Well, you Amish are a punctual bunch. I'm sure you were keeping up with the time."

Levi nodded, while leaning a little closer towards the driver. "I was indeed. If you don't mind, I have a question to ask. Did you by any chance stop by the new schoolmarm's home yesterday evening? Or did you drop off any *Englischers* in Deer Springs?"

Jonathan scrunched his brow while tipping his cowboy hat backwards. "I'm afraid that I didn't leave my coach while in Deer Springs yesterday, and my memory is slipping in my old age. I carry so many folks back and forth across these parts along with keeping up with mail that I usually can't remember who gets off where. Is there a problem at Hattie's? I do recall her and Leah. She was beside herself with worry when she couldn't find her sister earlier in the week."

Levi figured as much to be true, but he had to ask. "*Nee*, there likely isn't any problem. *Danke* for your cooperation." He sank back into the wooden seat, and closed his eyes for the remainder of the two hour journey. He hesitantly agreed with Jonathan Philpot on one count. With Hattie's features, she wasn't easily forgotten. He had never laid eyes on such a beauty.

When the stagecoach jolted into the Deer Springs station, Levi stretched his long legs before disembarking. The blazing sun cast shadows through the rocky mountain peaks above him as it made its journey to the West. He took quick strides towards the schoolmarm's home, a warm glow shining through the windows and enticing him inside.

While the time was growing late, he resolved to go ahead and install the lock tonight. He had barely slept a wink the night before since the look of fear in Hattie's eyes spilled into his mind while he tossed and turned on his mattress. Telling himself that he was working later than necessary for his own benefit and not hers, he stepped onto the porch and gently rapped on the door.

A loud scratching sound erupted from the other side of the door before it was flung open. Leah stood before him, in a white nightgown which gently brushed the floor. Her mousy brown hair was pulled back in a neat braid which trailed down her back, and it swished to the side when she turned her head to call for her *schweschder*.

"Hattie! Come quick!"

Hattie rounded the kitchen corner as quick as a wink, her eyes widened in surprise. Levi drank her in before quickly turning his gaze to the plank flooring. She was wearing her night clothes, much like Leah. Her chestnut hair spilled over her shoulders in gentle waves, causing his breath to catch in his throat. He backed further away from the door while his heart hammered in his chest. It was a mistake to stop by so late unannounced.

"*Ach* Levi, I thought that you'd forgotten about adding a lock to the door and we've readied ourselves for bed. I'm so sorry that you're seeing me in such a way."

He raised his eyes to hers. "*Nee*, it's my fault for not coming earlier. I had to tend to my sheep before heading to Bozeman for a lock." He held up the paper bag which was within his grasp. "But I'm here now, and I intend on fixing your door for you before turning in for the night."

Hattie's shoulder's visibly relaxed. "I will sleep a bit easier tonight, then."

As will I. Levi shook his head as he took a tentative step into the home. His eyebrow raised as he wiggled around the settee, which was blocking his path. "What's this all about?"

A blush rose to Hattie's cheeks. "It's what I used to block the door until a proper lock was in place." She turned to Leah. "And *schweschder,* it is imperative that you do not open the door to anyone unless you know who it is. Is that clear?"

Leah nodded sheepishly while taking in Hattie's gentle admonition. "I'm sorry, Hattie."

"I accept your apology, dear one. Now please head to bed while Levi fixes the door, and don't forget to say your prayers. You have a big day tomorrow."

"I will, Hattie." She leaned up and placed a quick kiss on her cheek before leaving the room.

Levi examined the door closely, and then shuffled back onto the porch. "Give me just a minute, I need to get a few tools from the shed out back."

"Take your time."

Hattie's soft voice shot pain through his heart as he walked to the back of the property and rummaged through the building for his toolbox. He quickly reminded himself that her charm and kindness was no match for his tough exterior. Why, at the open house even the gentle members of the community eyed her with caution. Firm resolve to keep her at arm's length marred his thoughts as he trudged back towards Hattie's cottage.

Levi sank to his knees and got to work on the door. The room was silent, and Hattie was nowhere to be seen. He shrugged his shoulders as he screwed the lock into place. Perhaps the schoolmarm had decided to turn in for the night with young Leah. It was just as well, and he decided to finish his work as quickly as possible.

The sound of soft footsteps resounded across the floor, and Hattie entered the living area. Her hair was pulled back into a tight bun, and the strings of her *kapp* brushed against her slender shoulders. Her black cape dress sat primly against her thin waistline. She pushed the settee into place against the wall, and took a seat.

"You didn't have to change on account of me."

"*Ja*, I did. It wasn't proper for you to see me in my night clothes."

Levi nodded in understanding as he focused his concentration back on the lock as he quickened his hands. "I'll be gone in a few minutes."

"Take your time." Hattie stifled a yawn as she motioned towards the kitchen. "I've been working on my lesson plans for tomorrow, and I'll probably stay at it for another hour or two at least. Earlier today, Leah and I visited the school *haus* and decorated it for tomorrow. The first day of school calls for a celebration!"

Levi raised an eyebrow. Hattie decorated the classroom? Rhoda had never done such a thing.

"I know I'm not your first choice as a schoolmarm, but I'm still very thankful for this job. I cannot tell you what joy teaching and being around *kinder* brings me."

"Well then, hopefully you will become a mother one day."

The sparkle in her eyes grew dim. Hattie's expression darkened progressively as she rose to her feet. "Unfortunately, that will never happen. I, um…want to express my gratitude again for your help, but…I believe I will retire for the night after all."

Levi shook his head as the door to Hattie's bedroom shut firmly. He figured she was just like Rhoda, and she was quickly proving him right…running away at the first mention of family, instead of wanting to settle down. Levi let out a grunt as he gathered his tools and began to walk towards his own home. A feeling of dread clutched his midsection while thinking about observing Hattie in the classroom the following day.

Leah shoveled a bowl of oatmeal into her stomach as Hattie stood behind her, carefully coiling her braid into a tight bun. After inserting a few pins, she placed her *kapp* onto her head and patted it gently.

"Are you ready for the first day of school?"

"*Ja*, I can't wait to see Mary Miller again. After my nightmare, I hardly slept a wink just thinking about it!"

Hattie stifled a yawn as she began securing her own hair into place. She'd hardly slept a wink, either. The lock had done little to ease her peace of mind, and Leah's incessant night frights had caused her to rush into her

schweschder's room more than a time or two. After Leah
fell asleep while talking about her mother, Temperance,
Hattie's thoughts had turned to her own woes. Levi had
unknowingly stirred her heart while mentioning that she
would hopefully become a mother someday.

Hattie knew that these hopes were dashed, and she
washed the morning dishes with a little more force than
necessary before instructing Leah to meet her at the front
door. Hattie cautiously peered outside before motioning
for her *schweschder* to follow. Surely she was being
overly cautious…the footprints left on her porch must
have a simple explanation. She straightened her shoulders
while stepping carefully towards the school *haus*. She
needed to make a good impression on Levi today. If she
didn't, he would find a reason to send her on her way,
despite Bishop Graber's instructions. She enjoyed
teaching so, and had lavished attention on her students in
Bozeman except for when the influenza pandemic insisted
the normal school close its doors for months on end the
year prior. She had full intentions of showing the scholars
of Deer Springs the same care and consideration.

"*Hullo* Hattie."

Her hand flew to her mouth in surprise as the
mystery voice reached her ears after stepping foot inside
of the school room. She turned, and in a darkened corner
stood Levi. She let out her breath in relief as her gaze
washed over his features. He scrubbed his hand across his
jaw while his eyes revealed a hurt…a deep hurt which
Hattie had never noticed before.

"*Hullo* Levi. Are you feeling alright this
morning?"

"*Ja*, I'm fine. I was just looking over your
handiwork from yesterday. It's quite impressive, although
it looks like you wasted a lot of supplies."

Hattie's gaze swept across the room as she bit
back an ugly retort. She had raided the art cabinet the day

before, and had made welcome banners with Leah's help. Colorful paper chains draped from the ceiling, and each desk had been outfitted with a handwritten note from the new schoolmarm. She eyed him suspiciously. "I was just trying to make the day special for the scholars. Is that a problem?"

"*Ja*, it is. You must learn not to be wasteful in Deer Springs."

Her shoulders tensed while she turned to Leah. "Why don't you go ahead and place your bonnet on a peg on the back wall and choose a seat. Your classmates will be arriving shortly."

While Leah skipped away to do her bidding, Hattie slid into the desk closest to Levi as tightness filled her chest. "I must admit, I'm a bit nervous for you to watch my teaching like this. What I mean to say is, I hope you enjoy your time here, and don't find me lacking."

"As the schoolmaster, watching you is my job. I used to observe Rhoda often. If you have a problem with it, you can be on your way. In fact, I believe the next stage coach to Bozeman leaves shortly."

Her mouth fell open as irritation ate at her insides. "I suppose you did observe the previous schoolmarm. Mary Miller mentioned that she didn't care for the woman, so I hope you'll find my teaching methods to not only meet, but exceed what you've seen in the past." She forced a smile, while hoping Levi would realize that she earnestly wanted to teach at this school. Her eyes grew wide as a scowl swallowed his features whole.

"Rhoda wasn't only our schoolmarm, she was also my *aldi*. This entire situation isn't what I expected when I agreed to be the schoolmaster. Now if you don't mind, I suggest that you prepare for your class to arrive, and leave me be."

Hattie felt about two inches tall as she slinked from the desk and walked to the front of the room. She realized what a mistake it was to bring up Rhoda Greenloe, but how was she to know that Levi used to court her? She had already made the worst impression possible on her first day as the schoolmarm, no less. The way Levi looked at her reminded her of her father...just one look at his features would reveal if he should be avoided. The faded scars which ran along her back bore witness to the many times she stood in her *mamm's* stead during his anger. He blamed his wife for all of their financial woes, since after they married and she found out he was a scoundrel, she quickly removed his access to her overflowing coffers.

Hattie ordered the tears which burned through her lashes to stop their flow. She jumped when the door slammed open. Who could that be? She relaxed into her chair when a pair of brothers jogged through the door, talking merrily before hanging their straw hats on the pegs next to Leah's bonnet. Of course, her class was arriving. She vowed to remove her father and *Onkel* Henry from her mind for at least the remainder of the school day. Hattie didn't want memories of her first day to be marred with the fear that easily stirred inside of her.

The school *haus* steadily filled with youngsters over the next twenty minutes. Squeals of excitement ran through the room when the *kinder* slipped into their seats and read their welcome notes. A smile widened the almost-late Luke Beiler's face when he stepped into the room. Hattie hurried to greet him with a hug and introduced herself before he took a seat. Feeling much better now that she had properly introduced herself to each of her students, she glanced out the window at the lawn which was now littered with pony carts before returning to the front of the room.

"*Welkom* students! I'm so happy to have you all here!" Hattie decided to ignore the scowling Levi while looking over the sea of beaming faces. Much like her *onkel*, she wouldn't allow him to ruin her day. "In a few minutes, I will explain more about what you can expect from me this year. But for now, let's open our day in prayer."

After Hattie asked God to bless their studies, the students looked at her expectantly, wondering what was next.

Her eyes smiled, with hope that the school day might encourage the wide-eyed scholars who were dealing with so many hardships at home. They sang songs in both German and English, Hattie being ever mindful that her youngest students had not yet been taught English at home. Hattie leaned back against her desk, resting her fingers across the wooden surface as her eyes sparkled with excitement.

"I hope everyone enjoys my class this year. I expect everyone to work together. We are going to learn new things and investigate many topics. I hope that we can take a few trips within our community to watch skilled craftsmen and farmers, since many of you will fill these positions one day."

A hand shot up and Hattie nodded at a lanky thirteen-year-old boy. "Go ahead, Jacob."

"Most of the nearby farms have gone belly up, with the drought and all. It really is too bad."

Hattie agreed silently, wishing that better days would arrive in Deer Springs shortly. "I know, but there are some in the community who are able to keep small tracts of land watered by their wells and underground springs." She noticed another raised hand. "Yes, Caroline."

"How about we visit the sheep next door? I spent all my time watching them out the window last year, and I would love to learn more about them."

Hattie raised an eyebrow at Levi, who was still scowling for all it was worth. "That could possibly be arranged. In fact, Levi Hilty is the *gut* shepherd who owns this piece of land. How about we ask him?"

Twenty pairs of eyes zeroed in on Levi. A smile twitched his lips as he nodded in agreement. "*Ja,* that would be alright."

Several girls squealed while turning back around in their seats. Hattie quietly clapped her hands to regain everyone's attention. "Okay class, now that that's settled, let's get back to work. First up, reading and literature!"

The class broke into groups, and Hattie asked for each group to write their own short story about Deer Springs while she gave her youngest students their first English lesson. The room erupted into giggles as each group told their story while acting it out in the front of the room. After a short mathematics lesson, complete with a multiplication competition, Hattie recessed the class for lunch. She approached her *schweschder* by giving her a quick pat on the shoulder. "If you don't mind, please stay close to the building and with a group of friends at all times, *ja*?"

"Okay, Hattie."

And just like that she was gone, laughing amongst a small group of girls.

Hattie breathed a sigh of relief as she retrieved her own lunch sack and headed for the door. She welcomed the brush of fresh air as she sat on the top stoop. Her gaze swept over the school yard as she devoured her sliced meat and cheese. She noticed Levi speaking quietly to Luke near a tall oak tree, his arms crossed across his small frame. Frowning, she realized that he hadn't eaten anything for lunch. Hattie grabbed an apple and snitz cookie from her satchel, and hurried across the yard.

"Have you eaten, Luke?"

"*Nee, Onkel* Jonas didn't send a lunch sack with me."

"Well, here you go then." Luke's eyes widened in appreciation as Hattie plopped the remainder of her lunch into his outstretched hands.

"*Danke* Hattie. I wish I could live with you like Leah does."

Hattie's heart sank to her feet as the youngster slinked away. She turned to Levi as a tear slid down her cheek.

"It's hard to watch, isn't it?"

"I just don't understand how someone can take such poor care of a child."

He clenched his fists. "It happens every day. Believe me, I know. But don't worry, I hired Jonas Beiler so I could help keep an eye on Luke. He'll be coming home with me after school, and I'll feed him dinner."

She nearly fell into his side with gratitude. With burning cheeks, she swayed in the opposite direction, surprised that such an unkind man would do such a thing. "I hope you've found my teaching abilities to be adequate. I've learned quite a few new techniques in extended learning practicums in Bozeman."

Levi removed his hat, and ran his fingers through his thick hair. Hattie admired its texture and slight curl before warmth rose from her neck.

"It wasn't what I expected to say the least." With that, he turned on his heel and returned to the school *haus*.

Worry filled Hattie's abdomen. Levi's words were a far cry from the glowing review she had hoped for. She bit her lip as she rang the bell, signaling the end of the lunch hour. Her feet felt heavy as they trudged back inside of her class room. Would she ever be able to impress Levi Hilty?

Chapter Five

"Hattie, may I finish my homework outdoors?"

"*Nee* Leah, I need you to stay in my sight for now. It's almost twilight."

The youngster huffed as she slid into a chair. "I don't understand why you keep me on such a tight leash. *Mamm* allowed me to walk through our fields whenever I liked."

Hattie's lips tightened into a straight line as she concentrated on grading her spelling papers. Until she was absolutely certain that Leah hadn't been followed by their *mamm's* likely killer, then she must not be left alone. Letting her *schweschder* in on her fears would likely only worry the child, so Hattie kept her mouth shut. "Please just trust me, dear one."

Leah's lips formed a pout. "*Ja,* okay."

The room grew silent as both sisters worked on the papers laying in front of them. Hattie finished grading the quizzes just as the dinner hour rolled around, and she pushed her chair back to start their cook stove.

"I'll be right back, I'm just going to grab a few logs so I can start our supper." Hattie brushed past Leah, whose eyebrows were scrunched in concentration. She couldn't help but smile at her *schweschder* as she unlocked the front door and continued towards the woodpile which Levi had cut for them. When she reached her destination, a twinge of uneasiness settled over her like a blanket as she loaded her arm full of dried logs. She trained her gaze over the nearby field, looking for something…anything, out of the ordinary. She spied Levi on a nearby hill, surrounded by sheep.

Attributing her uneasiness to his closeness, Hattie turned back towards her home. Levi was a mystery which she didn't care to solve. His steady dedication to his community and flock, strength of both body and mind, and rugged attractiveness was all that Hattie had ever hoped to find in a husband. Now that her dream of marrying was dashed, her senses also warned her of his critical eye, which was a character quality of her *daed's* which she remembered all too well. Pushing these feelings aside, she rushed to the house, at least grateful that for the time being that she and her *schweschder* were together, despite the maddening schoolmaster.

Locking the door behind her, Hattie returned to the kitchen and promptly began a fire in the cast iron stove. "Leah, would you grab some potatoes from the root cellar and pull the shoofly pie from the ice chest? I'll grab the leftovers from church, and we shall have a fine feast tonight."

A warm happiness spread over Hattie as Leah ran to do her bidding. They had now lived in Deer Springs for three weeks, and had had the privilege of attending church meetings on two different occasions. She felt like she had truly returned home while raising her voice in song along with the rest of the Amish community, despite the church member's scowls in her direction. She wondered if she would ever gain their trust after Jonas' outburst at the open *haus*.

Besides Greta, Hattie had made one new friend in the Bishop's daughter, Rose Graber, during their baptism instructions. The young woman with blonde hair and glowing cheeks had taken a liking to both Hattie and Leah immediately despite her tainted reputation, and she had insisted that as the town's schoolmarm, Hattie bring home leftovers from after-church dinners as a form of payment for her services. Hattie yearned for a garden of her own, and hoped that come the spring she could convince Levi to plow a small spot for her to use if the drought wasn't so severe at that time.

Apparently the previous schoolmarm hadn't been interested in a garden, and most of Deer Springs was currently sustained on a large community plot which was located near the largest river in the area.

After boiling, peeling, and mashing the potatoes, Hattie spread the food across the table and the two sisters said a silent prayer. They ate in happy silence until Hattie's keen ears perked when a soft *thud* drifted from the front of the home. She clutched Leah's hand, and motioned for her to remain still while her heartbeat almost drowned out her ability to listen to the sounds surrounding them. A moment passed, and then a large crack preceded the sound of shattering glass in the front room. Had their *onkel* found them?

"*Schnell.*"

Leah rose to her feet with wide eyes as her *schweschder* pulled her towards the window overlooking the wide sink. A surge of adrenaline allowed Hattie to open the thick wooden window with ease, and she stared into the dimming light with glassy eyes. Each shadow looked ominous and foreboding, and yet Hattie knew that the growing darkness would most likely be safer than their home. She motioned for Leah to stay quiet while lifting her out of the window and setting her feet on the dust outside. She then quickly followed, trying her best to ignore the fear which threatened to swallow her whole.

Her eyes darted to the left and the right, before focusing straight ahead to Levi's fence line. Swallowing hard, she realized there was only one place they could go. Circling around to the front of the house where the window shattered was not an option. The frustrating schoolmaster's farm appeared to be their only ticket to safety. Clutching Leah's hand, Hattie stumbled through the darkness to Levi's fence. She hoisted Leah over the barbed wire, and then tried her best to cross the barrier herself. Hattie winced in pain as her leg caught on the wire just as she was about to clear the hurdle.

Choosing to ignore the burning throb, she grabbed Leah's hand once more and ran over the first hill. She sighed with relief as a large clapboard home came into view. A warm glow radiated from a window, indicating that Levi had finished his farm chores and was inside of his *haus*. The sisters rushed to his home, and Hattie straightened her *kapp* before she rapped on the door with as much civility as she could muster.

A few moments passed before a confused Levi opened the door wide. A wave of panic descended on his face as he looked at Hattie's leg. "What in the world? Hattie, are you alright?"

She gulped back her fear as Levi led them into his home. Besides watching him in his fields, she'd hardly seen hide nor hair of him since his classroom observation. Despite bringing them to church in his buggy, he always had gone out of his way to avoid her after the service. He had brought necessary items, such as food stuffs and firewood to her home while she was teaching in the school *haus*. Would he send them on their way without offering his assistance?

Levi led her to a chair and took hold of her elbow to slowly ease her into it. He rubbed his thumb across her cheek, wiping away the dirt which had smudged her face after her tumble across the barbed wire. Subconsciously, she leaned into his comforting touch before he slowly pulled away and reached for an oil lamp. She once again felt consumed by fear as the sound of breaking glass rang in her ears. "Do you mind filling me in on how you were hurt?"

"I...I fell across your barbed wire fence."

He raised an eyebrow. "And why did you do that?"

She sighed in exasperation. "While we were finishing up dinner, I heard a thud on our porch, which was followed by the sound of shattered glass from our window flying through the room. We narrowly escaped through the kitchen window before fleeing to your home." She rubbed her head in trepidation. "I did feel uneasy when I fetched logs earlier, but I thought...

"You thought what?"

I thought it was just the effect you have on me. Hattie shook her shoulders in a shrug, unable to speak any further.

"Hattie, most likely a ball from the schoolyard flew through your window. You could have investigated it further before hurting yourself on my fence."

"*Nee,* what if it was..."

"What if it was what?"

"*Ach,* never mind." Hattie bit her tongue as Levi left the room before returning with a bowl of warm water and antiseptic. He gently took her leg in his hand and washed the wound before dressing it properly. She shuddered as his hand gave her calf a gentle squeeze before lowering it to the floor.

"It appears like you've done this before."

"I must tend to my sheep if they are injured. It comes with the territory."

"So now, you are comparing me to a sheep?"

A low rumble of laughter sounded from his chest as he rolled his eyes. "*Nee,* actually you are the farthest thing from it."

Hattie blushed as his tender gaze caught hers. What was Levi saying?

"Everyone, I'm really scared over here and I would like to know what's going on."

Leah's quiet request pierced the air, pulling Hattie away from his commanding stare. "I'm not sure Leah, but just in case trouble was coming our way, I wanted to get us out of there quickly."

"Trouble? What kind of trouble?"

"Nothing for you to worry about, dear. Levi is probably right. I acted in haste."

He rose to his feet in agitation. "You just did what you thought was best. I'll leave you ladies here while I check out your home if you'd like."

"*Nee.*" Hattie swayed from side to side after rising to her feet a bit too quickly. "I would rather not stay here alone. If you don't mind, we would like to come along." Hattie realized that she had not been very stealth-like in her escape, and if her *Onkel* Henry was involved, he could have easily followed them here. Staying close to Levi would unfortunately be the safest option for them to take.

"Alright then, come along." Levi stepped into the other room and returned with a rifle draped over his arm. Hattie gasped in fright.

"You aren't intending to shoot the intruder, are you?"

"Of course not. I would like to have some form of protection against the wildlife which plagues my sheep under the cover of darkness, however."

Levi reached for Hattie's elbow as she began to sway once more. She had been fooling herself to believe that she could keep Leah safe in the Montana wilderness by herself.

"Hattie...it will be alright."

His carefully measured words soothed her spirit as she took a deep breath. "You're right...come Leah."

The trio stepped into the darkness, with Levi leading the way by the light of his lamp. Hattie gave her sister's hand a gentle squeeze as they tentatively stepped away from the large home. She glanced back a final time before turning her attention to Levi. The size of his home had been surprising. While she knew he had once had an *aldi*, a young couple starting out surely didn't need anything of this magnitude, and without a *dawdi haus* no less. Hattie kept taking one step after another until their home was once again in view. She froze in place as Leah tried her best to pull her forward. If her *onkel* had something to do with this, what was she going to do?

Levi set the lamp on top of a stump before using his strength to hop the fence leading towards Hattie's home with ease. He offered a warm smile at Leah as she grabbed the lantern from its resting spot before he lifted her across. His face pinched when Hattie's golden eyes caught the flicker of his lamp's warm glow. He had tried his best to avoid the new schoolmarm over the past few weeks, but it was becoming increasingly difficult.

Observing Hattie in her school room had brought back memories...all kinds of memories that were directly related to Rhoda. Except, his past fiancé hadn't shown the same spark of excitement while teaching as Hattie had. Her teaching methods had been rote and ordinary, while Hattie's had been anything but. The way that she seemed to really care for the *kinder* of Deer Springs, many of whom were orphans, made his heart smile to his chagrin. And as time went on, Levi realized that he was drawn to her more and more. Which is exactly why he stayed close to his farm for most of the month, while keeping a sharp watch on Jonas and Luke Beiler as applications to replace Hattie continued to roll in. He paid no mind to the fact that he would likely never find a teacher as kind and giving as Hattie ever again. All that mattered was that she left Deer Springs as quickly as possible.

"You're next. Grab hold of my shoulders, please."

Hattie looked him over shyly before following his instructions. He could feel a tremor race through her hands as she clutched his shoulders, digging in her fingers. Levi lifted her gently over the fence, while his hands rested on her waist a bit longer than necessary.

"There is no reason to be afraid, Hattie. Nothing is going to harm you while I'm around."

"I don't know how you can be so sure. There is no telling what, or who, caused my window to shatter."

He cocked his head as he looked down at Hattie's hair, which was for the most part tucked neatly into her prayer covering. While as an Amish man Levi didn't believe in violence, he knew that any danger trying to reach Hattie or Leah would have to tear through him first.

"Well, there's nothing for us to do but to check out the situation. You can hang back if you'd like."

"*Nee,* I plan to stay right by your side, and I won't be a hindrance to you. Come along, Leah."

Levi felt his back tighten in annoyance as she dug her fingernails into his bicep. She must really be scared. He raised his lantern as the three cautiously rounded the home, being careful to look deep into the shadows for signs of movement. Satisfied that they were alone, Levi gently nudged Hattie towards the front porch.

She put one trembling foot in front of the other, until she reached the top stoop, where she stifled a scream. Levi stepped in front of her, careful not to tread on the mixture of shattered glass and wood. Whatever had done this had used a tremendous amount of force to crash through the majority of the large picture window. Written across the front of the home were the words, *LEAVE*

NOW. Levi did his best to steady Hattie as she clutched Leah and sank to her knees.

"Do you believe me now, Levi? I don't think this was the work of a misguided ball from the schoolyard. I was outside just a short time before we heard the glass shatter. The schoolyard was clear, and I felt like something wasn't quite right. I thought I was just distracted, because you were…oh, never mind."

"Because I was what?"

"That isn't important now."

Levi's eyes narrowed. "Is there an *Englischer* who is out to get you? I highly doubt someone in our community would do this to your home despite their avoidance of you, and the strange footprints would fit into this puzzle."

The only Amish man he knew of that could possibly pull this off was Jonas Beiler. And while the man was troubled, Levi highly doubted that he would do such a thing to Hattie's home, especially with Luke in tow. The man had left his home with the boy only minutes before Hattie and Leah arrived on his doorstep, not giving him enough time to do such a thing.

"*Nee,* not that I know of. And Levi, I'm sure that you've had many *gut* interactions with *Englischers* around town, as have I. In fact, my *mamm* used to be one."

The blood left Levi's face as he ushered Hattie and Leah out of harm's way. Hattie's *mamm* was an *Englischer?* Had he been right about her all along? "What are you saying?"

"My *mamm* was Temperance Portsmouth, from Philadelphia. Her family owned a large and quite profitable lumber company, and her parent's pushed suitors towards her against her will. When she could, she would get away to the Lancaster County farmland, just to think…just to breathe. That is where she met my *daed,*

66

Joshua Fisher, who was an Amish man. He promised her a simple life, and she accepted, thinking that he truly loved her. Unfortunately, it was all a lie."

Hattie looked up at him, a spark in her eye visible beneath the tear threatening to spill down her cheek. "Don't you dare hold this against me, Levi. I've given you my word that I'm Amish, and I am a woman of my word."

Unsure of what to think, he took a step away while clearing his throat. Resentment curled around him as he remembered his dream of a family had been lost to the *Englisch* way of life. "I'm going to make a sweep of the house to make sure the intruder is gone. Then we will figure out what we can make of this."

Hattie shuddered as Levi pushed through the door after unlocking it with his key. He surveyed each room carefully, looking for anything out of place. He smiled wryly when he came to the dining table and noticed the stack of spelling papers stacked neatly just so. Hattie was obviously a dedicated teacher who cared deeply for her students. In fact, almost all the words that flew through Luke Beiler's mouth while he was at his farm involved the attractive schoolmarm in some form or fashion. Why would anybody wish to hurt her?

He poked his head through the front door, frustrated by what his position as schoolmaster called him to say next. "It looks to be all clear. I don't feel safe leaving you ladies alone tonight, though."

"You can't expect to stay in our home. It wouldn't be proper. I just don't know what we should do."

"I wasn't intending on staying in your home, Hattie. Sleeping under the shade of your porch will do just fine."

She lowered her lashes as she contemplated what Levi had to say. "*Ja*, I suspect this would be the best thing for Leah and me, considering the circumstances. Are you sure you don't mind?"

"I don't mind." Levi's throat constricted as he said this half-truth out loud. He could easily capitalize on the threat, and encourage Hattie that the best thing to do would be for her to leave town. But he couldn't do it when she looked so small and afraid. Levi wished that he could pull her to his chest and convince her that all would be well as long as he was around.

Hattie traced the hem of her apron, deep in thought. "Levi…I think that coming here might not have been wise. You see…I'm afraid that trouble has a way of following me, and I would hate to put Deer Springs in danger."

He pressed his lips together as he looked Hattie over. Her golden eyes were framed by a few haphazard curls which had escaped from her *kapp*. Though her expression was crippled with fear, he could still see a sense of strength and determination lined across her cheekbones.

She pulled her trim frame towards Leah as she leaned into her side. Trouble? While he was certain she spelt trouble to Deer Springs, why would an angry intruder follow a woman such as this? Perhaps Hattie wasn't what met the eye underneath her sweet exterior. Levi knew who she really was. An *Englischer* ready to turn on both him and Deer Springs as soon as she saw an opening.

He bit back his callous, yet realistic, thought. "I don't think you are in any real danger, Hattie. This is likely an empty threat from someone who isn't sure of your teaching credentials, or from an old beau."

"As I've told you before, there haven't been any old beaus. What will it take for you to believe me?"

He shook his head at her taut words as he walked back into the schoolmarm's home by lantern light. Believing that Hattie had never had a beau was akin to believing Rhoda was still a devout Amish woman. He chuckled underneath his breath while carefully cleaning the shards of glass and splintered wood from Hattie's plank flooring. The frustrating schoolmarm was as intriguing as she was beautiful.

"It's all clear, feel free to return inside. I'll keep watch over your home tonight, and if I see any new signs of trouble, we'll figure out where to go from there. Amos is guarding my flock tonight, and I'll relieve him in the morning."

"I didn't know that you had a hired hand...other than Jonas that is."

A deep laugh rumbled in Levi's chest. "I don't. Amos is my sheepdog, but I do tend to think of him as my right hand man."

"You have a dog, Levi? Oh, can I meet him soon?" Leah's eyes brightened from the shadows of the living room. He felt a sense of relief, glad that talking of Amos had lightened the poor girl's troubles, if only for a short time.

"*Ja*, I do. Luke enjoys playing with Amos whenever he stops by my home when his *onkel* is helping me with the sheep."

"Luke comes over to your *haus*? I help him all the time in school. He's a sweet little boy."

Levi smiled when small Leah regarded someone as *little*. He guessed that one would regard someone who was four years younger as little if you were merely ten-years-old. "Luke talks about you and Hattie all of the time. You seem to have made quite the impression on him. You are welcome to stop by to play with Amos and Luke anytime."

"Hattie and I try to help Luke out as much as we can. It's so sad that he lost both of his parents, just like us."

He awkwardly patted the child's shoulder as Hattie slipped out of the room. She returned moments later with a pillow and brightly colored quilt in a double wedding ring pattern. "Here you go. I hope you'll be comfortable through the night. Please holler if you need anything." She gently pressed the blanket into his midsection as he felt like he had been punched in the abdomen.

He mechanically accepted the quilt and took a tentative step outside. "*Guten nacht*, Hattie." Levi pushed against his frustration as he settled in for the night on the exact quilt which the women of the community had created for Rhoda as a bride to be...his bride to be. She must have left it behind during her flight. A prick of pain tugged at his heart as he rolled over on the unforgiving flooring, reminded once again how incompetent of a prospective husband he must have been.

Chapter Six

Hattie brushed a piece of lint from her for-*gut* apron while waiting on Levi to pick her and Leah up for church services the following Sunday. Taking a tentative step on the porch, she watched her wash sway in the wind before glancing at the new window that Levi installed two days prior. It had been nearly one week since the unsettling window breaking incident, and so far there were no new signs of trouble on the horizon.

Levi had begun watching Hattie's place much more carefully, which very well could have detoured the mischief-makers. She had been touched by his offer to stay the night when she was frightened. Under Levi's watchful eye, Hattie had forced herself to finally relax and try her best to take each day in stride. His insistence that he bring them to church today after painstakingly replacing the broken window and repainting the front porch was the continued evidence she needed that Leah was being watched out for, albeit by an irritating Amish man.

The faint clip-clop of horse hooves reached Hattie's ears. "Leah, please grab the chow-chow and meet me outside. Levi's come to fetch us."

"I'll be right there!" Leah's singsong voice drifted outside, and Hattie smiled, thankful for her good attitude amongst the trouble. Levi had stuck to his word, and the two sisters had already had three *gut* visits with Amos and Luke after the school day ended in the past week. Being around the endearing sheepdog had made Leah light up like nothing else, and Hattie was determined to purchase a pet for her *schweschder* once all signs of mischief had passed.

She had also taken a liking to Luke, and Hattie wished she could save the child from his poor fate. She hadn't turned a blind eye to the fact that Levi had tried his best to keep Jonas occupied in a far field whenever she was around, which in turn allowed her to dote on Luke freely while inside of his sprawling home.

"Here you go!" Leah interrupted the silence which had settled over the porch as she plopped the covered dish into Hattie's outstretched hands.

"*Danke,* Leah. Now let's hurry along."

The sisters dashed towards Levi's buggy once he ordered his mare to come to a stop. He jumped out of his buggy and pulled the food from Hattie's arms. "Let me take that. Give me just a second, and I'll help you into the buggy."

She shuddered slightly despite the warmth in Levi's voice. Hattie wondered what he could be hiding beneath his cordial exterior, since she had learned as a young child that men couldn't be trusted. Levi was surely only putting up a kind front, and would one day let her down. She was also beginning to think that despite the relatively calm week, Leah wouldn't remain safe there for long. Hattie would hate to invite trouble to Deer Springs, which had begun to find a place in her heart. After watching many of the struggling *kinder* in her classroom, she had slowly devised a plan to help. Would she be around long enough to put it into action?

After assisting the Fishers into his buggy, Levi jumped up and with a flick of his wrist pushed his raven black horse forward. They were lulled into an uncomfortable silence before Hattie found the courage to voice her thoughts.

"So…the Yoders are hosting church today?"

"*Ja*, they are. Have you met Reuben?"

A smile twitched her lips. "Of course I have, he's in my class."

"That's right."

"He lost his younger *schweschder* last year, right?"

"*Ja*, just like many others in Deer Springs."

"Well, I have an idea. I would love for my class to complete a project of sorts, and I was thinking we could have a town festival to benefit those affected by sickness and the drought. I honestly think it would be a great idea to begin a Deer Springs Aid Fund. The class would host a bake sale, along with fun and games for both those in our community and the surrounding Bozeman area. What do you think?" Hattie held her breath as the breeze teased the strings of her *kapp*. She hoped beyond hope that Levi would approve, and the truth be told, Hattie planned to anonymously donate a good portion of her inheritance to the cause.

For a moment, Levi stared thoughtfully to the road, as a variety of businesses rolled by. "I think that's a *gut* idea, except for the inviting *Englischers* part. But are you sure Deer Springs is the place for you? After the break in, I would completely understand if you decided to be on your way. I can even help make the plans for your departure if you'd like."

Anger rolled through her. "*Nee*, I plan on staying on for the time being."

"I'd take a closer look at my offer if I were you." He frowned in disappointment while gazing at her injured calf. "And by the way, how is your leg healing? There isn't any sign of infection, is there?"

A blush rose to her cheeks as she thought of the way Levi had carefully tended to her leg earlier in the week. When he was near, a sense of comfort settled over her like a blanket against her *gut* sense. "It's doing well."

"I'm happy to hear it."

Hattie coiled back in trepidation as the Yoder home place came into view. While she enjoyed attending the church meetings, she knew she hadn't been accepted into the community. Most families eyed her every move suspiciously, and their actions couldn't help but put her on edge.

Hattie bit her lip as Levi tenderly settled her to her feet after tying Dolly to the hitching post and offering her a snack of apples and oats. His arm brushed against her side while handing her the covered dishes left on his floorboard.

"Please take it easy, *ja*? I want your leg to heal but *gut*."

Ignoring Levi's pleading eyes, she turned from him and motioned for her *schweschder* to follow her to the wide, white clapboard home. "Come Leah, let's find our seats before the service begins."

Hattie hobbled slightly as she rushed to keep up with her younger *schweschder*, who had quite the spring in her step. She needed to escape Levi's lingering stare. Quickly. She hastily pressed herself into the bench designated for unmarried women after she slipped through the door.

"*Hullo* Hattie, how are you doing today?"

She forced a smile while turning towards Rose Graber. The young woman eyed her gently, her bright expression showing a measure of delight that Hattie had taken a seat beside her. The two had become fast friends, but Hattie couldn't help but wonder if this was because her father had shared all of the secrets which she had laid out to the kind Bishop not so long ago. Rose's teenage *schweschders*, Adaline and Ruth, were a different story. They pushed her aside like a hot potato.

"*Gut.* How about you?"

"Oh, I couldn't be better." She lowered her voice as her blue eyes widened. "You can keep a secret, *ja*? Elias came to call yesterday, and though I know it is not our way to discuss such things, I feel like my heart might burst if I kept it to myself for a second longer."

"I'm so happy for you. I just knew it would happen sooner or later." A tight smile filled Hattie's rosy lips as she thought of the way the two love birds shot glances at each other during their baptism instructions. While she was truly happy for Rose, she couldn't help but feel a pinch of sadness since her own turn to be courted would never come.

"Hattie, why don't you accompany me to the singing tonight? Oh, we would have so much fun, and it would be a *gut* time for you to become better acquainted with the young folks."

"Singings aren't for me. I hope you have a fine time with Elias tonight, though." Pushing aside her self-pity, she squeezed Rose's hand and lowered her own voice. "I want to hear every detail you're willing to share about your new beau after the service is over."

Rose's eyes shone. "You've got it."

The women settled into silence as the Bishop and deacons filed into the room. The partitioned walls had been removed from the large farmhouse to create a wide open space to accommodate all of those who belonged to the Deer Springs Church District. Hattie stiffened her back as she prepared herself for the three-hour service.

After singing a few songs in High German, she eyed Leah, silently admonishing her to stop her fidgeting. She pushed aside a feeling of worry before staring straight ahead once more after not only Levi, but Jonas too, caught her eye. Her cheeks burned as she felt the scoundrel's stare focused on her features.

After the service came to a close with the benediction and a closing hymn from the *Ausbund*, Hattie rose to her feet while stretching her aching back. She kept her focus on Leah as several women passed her by, their chins tipped in arrogance. Stumbling into the aisle, she turned to Rose.

"I'll be counting on those details soon, *ja?*"

"After the noon meal."

Nodding in satisfaction, Hattie moved towards her *schweschder* and motioned for her to follow. After stepping into the sweltering kitchen she pushed towards Greta, who was hard at work pouring beverages for the men.

"Let me help you with that."

"*Danke* Hattie. Here's a pitcher of root beer, this will be sure to quench the men's thirst on such a hot and humid day. It was always my Jeremiah's favorite." She stared into space wistfully. "I would do anything to see him one more time. Jeremiah was a *gut* man, husband, and father...there was truly none greater."

With sympathy lacing her eyes, Hattie stepped closer to Greta and enveloped her in a warm hug. "I'm so sorry for your loss, Greta."

The older woman tucked a strand of graying blonde hair back into her *kapp* as her blue eyes widened in understanding. "It's alright. It is *Gott's* will for things to be as they are." She motioned towards Hattie's black frock meaningfully. "Besides, it looks like you are in need of some comfort too. You're wearing a mourning dress, *ja?*"

Hattie's throat constricted as she nodded stiffly. After laying her troubles out to the Bishop such a short time ago, she realized she most definitely wasn't ready to share her predicament with others just yet. While Greta's face mirrored compassion, she could easily turn on her, much like the rest of the town.

After mechanically pouring a good number of beverages, Hattie slipped towards where Rose was organizing a variety of cold cuts onto a platter. "Can I help you with that?"

"Sure, go ahead and take this to the men if you don't mind. I bet Levi will be happy to see you fitting right in with the rest of us. He's a *gut* man, you know." She winked discreetly.

Hattie blushed as her skirt brushed past Rose, eager to exit the conversation. She surely had gotten the wrong idea when it came to her and Levi. Any thoughts of romance were the furthest thing from her mind, and besides, Levi obviously wasn't too enthused when it came to her employment.

Hattie kept her eyes trained on the floor as she walked into the expansive great room. She quietly slipped to the buffet table outfitted with a bit less food than normal, trying her best to remain unnoticed. Too little too late, she realized that Jonas was sauntering towards her.

"*Hullo*, girly. I've had my eye on you, and it's mighty nice of you to bring me something to eat. I've tried my best to be neighborly and all while working for Levi, but he seems mighty keen on keeping me from you. How 'bout we spend a little time together at the singing tonight?"

Repulsed, Hattie took a step towards the exit. "*Nee*, I have no interest in singings. I have no business attending."

"I disagree."

Afraid of what might come out of his crude exterior next, Hattie turned in haste. Her mouth hung open as she nearly ran smack dab into Levi's strong chest.

"Jonas, have a seat please."

"You might be my boss in your fields, but you certainly aren't now."

"If you would like to keep your job, I suggest you keep your mouth shut."

Hattie's mouth grew dry as the men stood toe to toe. After what seemed like an eternity, Jonas backed down, and headed towards his chair.

"Are you alright?" His quiet voice blew through her.

She squirmed, unsure of how to answer as she pushed the strings of her prayer covering away from her flushed face. Hattie wanted to thank him…to tell him how grateful she was for his comforting presence…but she just couldn't. She surely wasn't alright, but then, was Jonas anything more than a small annoyance compared to her other troubles? Her lips pressed into a tight line. "I'm fine."

"Would you like for me to take you home?"

She shook her head vehemently. The last thing she wanted to do was to cause the church members to dislike her more by leaving early. "*Nee*. I'll head back to the kitchen to see if I can be of any more help."

"Sounds *gut*. You know where to find me if you need me."

Hattie rolled her eyes as she turned from him. She would like to believe that she could trust his motives, but she knew exactly where he stood. Against her. Wiping her hands against her skirt, she rushed back to Rose, eager to hear her *gut* news. The sooner she could take her mind off of Levi, the better.

Levi wiped the sleep from his eyes as he sauntered into his kitchen the next day. He was discouraged that the Bishop had put him in such a predicament…with both

Hattie *and* Jonas. If his leniency continued, he wasn't sure if he could bear it. Besides being forced to accommodate Hattie, taking it upon himself to keep watch over Luke had put him in quite a bind. Levi would like nothing more than to tell Jonas to take a hike after his continued mistreatment of Hattie. But then what would come of the boy? He was stuck between a rock and a hard place, and he didn't care for his plight one bit. As soon as a new schoolmarm was hired, he planned to leave his position as schoolmaster. No matter what the Bishop thought.

Levi drank a sip of strong *kaffi* as he thumbed through the growing stack of applications piled on the kitchen counter. More women than expected had applied for the schoolmarm position, and he would make his decision shortly. After he narrowed the field down to two or three candidates, he decided to ask for a recommendation from their Bishops. He didn't plan on making the same mistake twice.

Of course, he would also wait to hire a replacement until after Hattie's community festival was over. Surprisingly, Levi thought the fundraiser was a very good idea, but he hoped that the plans would be made quickly. He wanted to have a replacement for Hattie willing and waiting by that point after all. He squashed his feelings of guilt by reminding himself of all the trouble Hattie had already caused him. She would continue causing more as long as she stayed in Deer Springs.

He had just finished his brew when a loud knock sounded on the door. With a sigh, Levi pushed the applications aside and rose to answer his visitor. Swinging the door wide, he scowled when he realized that he was face to face with his sorry excuse of a worker.

"How's it going boss? What do you need me to do for you today?"

"You're late, and you should know the protocol by now. Are you meaning to tell me that the flock hasn't been led to the stream yet?"

"Nope. I'll get to it when I can."

Annoyance surged through Levi's veins. He was ready to fire Jonas then and there when he remembered little Luke. At least now he knew the boy was fed and taken care of every day after school. He clenched his teeth. "My flock is used to visiting the stream before they eat what they can from the parched pasture. I expect you to follow my instructions to a T. Do you understand me?"

"*Ja*, I guess so." Jonas shrugged nonchalantly as his eyes shifted listlessly. "By the way, I noticed a bunkhouse in the far field the other day. You don't plan on using it, do you?"

Surprised by the question, he leaned against the heavy door frame in thought. Levi had planned on using the soddy structure…he had wanted to hire a *gut* bit of hard workers to assist him with his daily farm operations until the drought hit and he was forced to sell off a large portion of his flock. For now the bunkhouse had remained empty, but Levi was hopeful that one day things would make a turn for the better and it would be filled with willing farm hands.

"*Nee*, it remains empty. You aren't in need of a place to stay, are you?"

Jonas shuffled his feet as he backed off of the porch. "No…curiosity just got the best of me, is all. I'll get right to work, boss."

Levi sighed as he turned back to his home, hoping for a few minutes of quiet before heading to the fields himself. Keeping a cool temper while around Jonas was becoming more difficult by the day. Besides his poor work ethic, the man seemed to try his best to linger near the fence line closest to the schoolmarm's home…and Levi knew no *gut* could come of this.

To his dismay, the feelings of anger and jealousy he'd felt when the man cornered Hattie at the Yoder's home yesterday was almost too much to bear. He prayed that he would be reminded of the heartache Rhoda caused him whenever he looked into Hattie's wide, caramel eyes. This would certainly squash his unwanted attraction.

After gathering a sack lunch for both himself and Jonas, Levi shuffled towards his flock. He set the lunches onto a table within his expansive barn before meandering towards the adjacent field, hoping to check on the nearly-healed wounds of one of his younger ewes.

"How is she doing?"

"She's looking *gut*. Her leg healed right up."

Levi narrowed his eyes as he examined the small sheep, while gently pushing aside her growing wool. Jonas' negligence had caused the coyote attack in the first place, and he wondered what had possessed him to leave the flock while Amos was occupied with Luke and Leah near his home. Thankfully, Levi had been near enough to hear the pitiful bleating before the animal had managed to pull her away from the flock. It was a *gut* thing that a larger predator wasn't after the young ewe.

"She looks to be fully healed. I expect no more mishaps to occur with my flock. Do you understand?"

Jonas shrugged his shoulders while his mouth held an angry jeer. "Whatever you say."

Levi pulled away from the man before he said something he would regret later. The two spent the remainder of the day herding the sheep while Levi tallied a number of young lambs ready for a buyer in Bozeman. When it was nearly time for the school day to end, Levi decided it was time to do the usual and turned to Jonas.

"How about you herd the flock to a far field for grazing with Amos? I'm sure they wouldn't mind a change of scenery."

Jonas' eyes lit up. "Sounds *gut* to me. I'll take them towards the bunkhouse if you don't mind."

Levi waved him away as he began lumbering towards his home, eager to intercept Luke. He thoroughly enjoyed spending time with the young boy, and had already created somewhat of a bond with the youngster. Despite all of his troubles with Jonas, if it meant Luke would regain some sense of normalcy, then the hassle of dealing with his *onkel* was well worth it.

The tinkle of children's laughter drifted towards Levi's ears as he neared his porch. Despite his desire to be annoyed, he smiled once he realized that Leah was accompanying Luke up the slight incline. He was growing fonder of Leah with each passing day, against its foolhardiness. As soon as he hired a new schoolmarm both Hattie and Leah would be well on their way, hopefully never to show their faces in Deer Springs again.

He did his best to crush the burning sensation in his abdomen once he realized that Hattie was following close behind the youngsters with a large basket of laundry. What was she doing here? While she *did* normally follow Leah whenever she came to visit Luke and Amos, after her run in with Jonas the previous day he had hoped that she would have the *gut* sense to stay home. His frown deepened, hoping she didn't expect him to take care of her laundry. Couldn't the woman do anything for herself?

"*Gut* day to you. I hope you don't mind Leah and me following Luke to your home today. I have something that I need to give you."

"Don't you want to stay far away from Jonas after the way he treated you yesterday?"

Hattie threw him a dismissing wave as she set the basket on her hip. "*Nee*, it will take more than Jonas to frighten me away. Underneath his threatening demeanor, I believe he's harmless."

82

"I'm not so sure about that. And what do you have there? I know I'm to watch out for you, but that doesn't include doing your laundry."

A soft giggle escaped Hattie's mouth. "Silly, I'm bringing back your clean laundry to *you*. I noticed that you had quite a pile of soiled garments when Leah was over the other day, and I thought I would wash them with our own. It must be hard on a bachelor to tend to household chores as well as run a business. Besides, after all you've done for us, it's the least I could do."

Levi's voice choked in his throat as he looked down at his neatly pressed and folded clothing. Even Rhoda hadn't taken the time to care for this need in such a way. Gentle feelings of care for Hattie washed over him before he quickly pushed them away.

She pried open his front door with the tip of her boot. "I'll be back in a jiffy. Just let me set these inside."

Levi's eyebrows rose in alarm as he realized that he had left the new schoolmarm applications in plain sight on his kitchen counter. He needed to have a replacement ready before Hattie learned of his plan, otherwise, it would be ruined. She surely would tell the Bishop what he had been up to before the new arrangement was settled. Levi rushed into the home behind her.

"Just set the clothing down here. Now." Levi sighed at the curtness of his voice as he entered the foyer. She had paid him a favor, and then he returned it with rudeness.

Her eyes widened at his request, just steps away from the kitchen. "Of course. I apologize for taking your clothing in the first place. I shouldn't have."

She turned up her chin as she stepped quickly out of the room. Levi followed her meekly, while wondering if an apology was in order.

"Come Leah, we have no business here today."

"But we just got here, and I want to play with Luke."

"I understand dear, but I truly think it's time to go. Say goodbye to Luke and Levi, please."

Levi's heart twisted as the young girl gave him a half-smile before trotting after Hattie, who was already nearly out of his sight. He realized he had made a mistake, but didn't know the means to fix the problem. It was best to continue to keep the Fishers at arms length, no matter how kind or accommodating they may be. Women like Hattie were nothing but trouble. He frowned while being reminded that the large home he had built for Rhoda and their future *kinder* would always remain empty.

Chapter Seven

Sweat pressed against Levi's brow as he carried the bucket of chinking towards the school *haus*. He had put off the task long enough already, and wished to be done with it quickly. Working inside of Rhoda's, and now Hattie's school room was the last thing he wanted to do. The porch steps groaned underneath his weight on the bright Saturday morning. He hoped that the northerly winds would usher in autumn, but at the same time, he dreaded the harsh Montana winters he'd grown accustomed to.

Levi had purposely waited until Saturday to repair the school *haus*. Surely Hattie wouldn't be around. The tension between them had grown since the unfortunate laundry incident. He hoped to avoid her unless it was absolutely necessary to be around her. He would much rather Hattie's coolness towards him be linked to laundry rather than the pile of schoolmarm applications sitting on his counter.

"*Gut* day." A soft voice rang from the front of the room as Levi swung open the door. There sat Hattie, as pretty as a picture.

He bit his bottom lip while nodding curtly. "What are you doing here?"

"Well, what a kind welcome that was Levi. I imagine you are pleased to see me."

He groaned at her sarcastic undertone as guilt pricked his conscience. "I just figured you wouldn't want to work on your day off."

"A teacher's work is never done. After grading papers I will begin working on lesson plans for the week. My *schweschder* and I are also beginning to throw around ideas for our town fundraiser, and will be heading to Rose Graber's home shortly to work through a few details with her. Isn't that right, Leah?"

"*Ja*, that's the plan."

Levi's eyes shot to the corner, where young Leah was doodling on a piece of paper. He hadn't even noticed her...Hattie's presence seemed to fill the room whenever she was around.

"Well, don't mind me. I plan on repairing the cracks in the wall today." He held up the bucket of chinking by its handle.

A pout framed her lips. "I rather liked all of those cracks. They allowed a lovely breeze to flow through the building."

Levi smirked, realizing how Rhoda would have been the first to notice when the school *haus* needed repair. Each day, he realized how different the two women really were. "You will thank me when winter sets in. Your 'lovely breezes' will turn into frigid gales."

"Fair enough. Don't believe that I'm afraid of winter though, mind you. I survived many cold spells in Bozeman."

Levi sank to his knees, as he reached into his bucket with a trowel, using more force than necessary. He wondered if Hattie missed her time in Bozeman, where she lived as a common *Englischer* with a large bounty of suitors.

The two worked in silence, the air thick with tension. After nearly an hour, Hattie closed her book with a *thud* and motioned for Leah to follow her out of the room. "Let's go Leah, it's time to head to Rose's home."

Levi looked up as sweat dripped down his brow. He removed his hat while eyeing her curiously. "How do you expect to reach Rose's *haus*? Walking such a distance is hardly practical."

"She's picking me up. However, I'm in need of a mare and buggy of my own. I do not wish to depend on you to take us around town any longer."

He memorized the curve of her chin as he swallowed hard. It would be foolish to secure a horse for her if she was to be leaving town shortly. "We'll see about that. For now, I don't mind driving you wherever you need to go."

Her eyes shot arrows in his direction. "Fine. *Kumme*, Leah."

The door slammed shut as the two made their exit. Levi sighed, happy that at least now he could work in comfortable silence. Hattie made concentrating difficult, and he struggled to make decent time on his chinking project.

After completing his repairs, Levi leaned against Hattie's desk. He looked down at her scrawling notes, thankful that the lettering looked so different from his previous *aldi's*. Seeing Rhoda's delicate handwriting would have been painful. Too painful. After his girl had left the community with only a simple farewell note, Levi had decided he was destined to be a bachelor for the rest of his days.

With a pen in hand, Rhoda had explained her reasons for leaving before vanishing into the night. *She wasn't 'strong enough' to survive the West. The long dry spells and influenza outbreak of the year prior proved to be too much for her to handle. She had decided to leave the Amish faith altogether.* But Levi could read between the lines. She hadn't trusted in *his* strength to carry them both through the difficult times the state of Montana was sure to dish out. This realization shook him to the core, and he felt as if a knife was twisting deep inside of his abdomen whenever he thought of Rhoda perched on a plush seat inside of her new fancy school room in the heart of Chicago.

With a push of determination, he locked away his dream of a future family as he read Hattie's words. A long list of supplies needed for the town fundraiser was at the top of the massive pile of paper. Compassion for the woman came crashing down on him as he realized the care she was showing to a town which had rejected her. Why would Hattie love if it was not returned? He turned from her paperwork and headed towards the exit.

He was nearly to the door when he heard a strange noise coming from the rear of the school *haus.* Levi paused, wondering if he was imagining things. The loud thud sounded again, and this time, it appeared to be coming from the schoolmarm's residence. With his heart beating fast, he rushed from the building, hoping to catch the mysterious intruder once and for all.

Shadows pressed around him as he stepped onto the dry ground. A warm breeze ruffled his hair as the limbs of a nearby cypress tree tapped against the building in a sinister rhythm. He hastened his steps as he rounded the school *haus* and the small clapboard home came into view.

A tall shadow disappeared behind the back of the home as Levi broke into a jog. If he could determine who was at fault for the mishaps at Hattie's his job would be so much easier. Levi longed for the day when he no longer needed to worry about the Bishop's instructions to protect the maddening outsider.

Adrenaline rushed through his veins as he rounded the corner. The crash of brush could be heard in the distance as he hung onto the side of the home. The intruder had escaped. Again. Levi raised his eyebrows as he noticed a cowboy hat laying on the ground. He traced his fingers along the upturned brim, wondering just who could be so intent on bothering the Fishers. The thought of school children being at fault flew from his mind as he realized an *Englischer* was likely behind this.

A billow of dust wafted from the road through the dwindling twilight as the sound of clopping horse's hooves sounded in the distance. Instinctively, Levi rushed to his fence line and tossed the hat behind a grove of trees at the edge of his property. There was no need to worry Hattie more than necessary. A feeling of protectiveness propelled him forward, hoping to meet her at the front of her property if it was in fact Rose's rig meandering down the rutted road.

Feminine laughter met his ears. "*Danke* for picking me up, Rose. I had such a *wunderbaar* time working through the details of the town festival with you."

"The pleasure was all mine. I appreciate all that you are doing for our community." Rose threw her hand up in a wave as the strings of her *kapp* danced in the growing breeze. "*Hullo*, Levi. What are you doing here?"

"I just finished up closing in the cracks of the school *haus* with a fresh batch of chinking."

"I'm sure the scholars of Deer Springs will be mighty appreciative once winter sets in. Your kindness matches Hattie's. I can hardly believe her kind heart regarding the upcoming fundraiser, especially considering the town's poor treatment of her."

Hattie forced a smile as she jumped to the ground. "It's nothing really, I'm happy to do it. See you later, Rose."

Hattie turned to Levi as Rose departed into the impending darkness. "Now that you've completed chinking the school *haus*, you have no business here. If you'll excuse me, I need to fetch a stack of logs for the cook stove before retiring for the evening."

He caught her arm as she took a tentative step towards his fence line. Her *kapp* fell to the ground as she turned to him with questioning eyes. Levi quickly turned his gaze from the coil of hair on Hattie's head. He fought back the urge to reach for a curl which had loosened and fallen across the young woman's cheek.

"What are you doing, Levi?"

He loosened his grasp as she continued to eye him curiously. "Since I'm here, I don't mind fetching the firewood for you. Just wait on the porch and I'll be back in a moment."

"Fine. Leah, why don't you step inside and ready yourself for bed? I'll join you shortly."

Levi matched his strides with the youngster until she turned towards her home and he continued on behind it. He was thankful that so far he had been able to hide evidence of the intruder from Hattie. His heart twisted as he remembered the worry which had crossed her face during the other strange occurrences.

After loading his arms with wood, Levi took a few tentative steps towards the Fisher's home. The light of an oil lamp at the kitchen window pierced the darkness. His ears pricked once more as a slight rustle sounded from the brush. They might not be alone after all.

"Here you are." He gently deposited his load into Hattie's outstretched arms while using his body to shield her from a strong gale of wind. "If you need anything else, please just let me know. The Bishop has made it clear that I'm to help when needed."

She wrinkled her nose as she looked right through him. "We'll be just fine, thank you very much. You have enough to worry about without burdening yourself with Leah and I. Please head home Levi, I'm sure you had a busy day and need some sleep."

Levi sighed as the door shut in his face. A shiver raced up his spine as he stared into the darkness. He was almost positive they were being watched. He squinted his eyes, hoping to find some type of evidence of the prowler. He stepped off of the wooden porch as a puff of dust blew into his face. The cracking of tree limbs along with the rustling of leaves indicated that despite the drought a storm was brewing.

Levi pushed his way through the nearby brush, hoping to see a sign of the intruder. Nothing. A crack of thunder groaned as lightning lit the distance. Against his better judgment, Levi continued his search to no avail.

He walked into his entryway sopping wet a *gut* two hours later, satisfied that the threat had passed. Why did he let Hattie get to him? Why did he care? Despite his better judgment, he realized the thought of harm coming to either Hattie or Leah caused pain to pierce his heart.

A shallow groan erupted from Hattie's lips as she sat up in bed. The smell of *kaffi* drifted into her room, notifying her that Leah was already awake and in the kitchen. She stretched her aching back while remembering the meeting she had with Rose the day before. The young woman couldn't hide the piteous look on her face once the discussion turned to the ailing town members who so desperately wanted her to leave. Nonetheless, Hattie was determined to press on and do the right thing no matter what others might think.

She swung her legs over the bed side and allowed her feet to rest on the cool floor. Her thoughts turned to Levi, and she wondered yet again why he was so insistent for her to stay out of his home. She thought he had warmed up to the idea of her stopping by his *haus* to help keep watch over young Luke, but apparently not.

Hattie quietly pulled her weight to her feet, and then tiptoed across the floor, hoping to catch sight of her *schweschder* unnoticed. She peeked out of the room, watching Leah's nose scrunch in concentration as she lifted a batch of biscuits from the old cook stove. The young girl meant ever so much to her. She was a spitting image of her beloved *mamm*.

"*Gute mariye*, Leah."

The girl smiled widely as she turned to her sister. "*Gute mariye* to you, too. I hope you don't mind, but I've taken it upon myself to make some biscuits for breakfast."

Hattie nodded, pleased at her industrious spirit. "I don't mind at all, dear one. I'll grab some jam from the root cellar and we'll be ready to eat in a jiffy."

She slid open the heavy wooden door and held a candle in front of her in the darkness. After finding a jar of apple preserves supplied to her by the Bishop's family, Hattie rose back into the kitchen. Her eyebrows lifted once she spied a mess of batter and dirtied spoons spread out across the counter.

"You plan to clean up your mess from making biscuits, right?"

"Oh, I've already done that. I have some cookie batter ready to pop into the oven in a few minutes. I thought it would be nice to bring some over to Levi, since I've had such fun playing with Amos and Luke at his house lately. It's a new recipe that *Mamm* taught me right before she died."

A wave of compassion overcame the sinking feeling of dread which had clenched onto Hattie's stomach. "Are you sure you want to bring the cookies over to Levi? We could enjoy them just the same."

"*Nee,* I really want to take them to Levi. If that's alright with you."

Hattie caught the disappointment mirrored in Leah's caramel eyes. There was no need to involve the child in the very grown-up emotions she was now experiencing. She had been through enough during her tender ten years. "*Ja,* it's alright with me. We must tend to a few chores first, though."

Leah grinned from ear to ear as she eagerly plopped the biscuits onto a shiny platter before placing it on the center of the table. The two sat down and bowed their heads, giving a silent prayer of thanks. Hattie was very grateful that although food was scarce, they had never gone hungry. She took an extra moment to express appreciation to her Maker regarding the home they had found in Deer Springs. Thus far, her dear Leah had been kept safe.

"Are you ready to eat, Hattie?"

Her eyes flung from her plate as a sheepish grin broadened her cheeks. "*Ja,* let's dig in."

After eating their breakfast, Hattie tied an apron around her waist and got to work tidying the small home. Her hair loosened and curled slightly from beneath her *kapp* as she washed several cape dresses underneath the scorching noon day sun. She shook her head in disgust while the thought of washing Levi's clothes just the week before flew to her mind. She hadn't expected much of a thank you, but the negative reaction concerning the favor was almost too much for her to bear. After finishing her task, she decided to work on grading the papers her scholars had completed during the previous week to keep her mind off of her frustrating neighbor.

"Hattie, would it be okay if we walked over to Levi's? It will be getting dark soon. If it would be easier, I can just walk over myself."

She glanced out the window, realizing that Leah was right as fear gripped her insides. She couldn't put off walking next door forever, and she certainly wasn't about to allow Leah to walk alone. "Grab your bonnet, and we'll be on our way. *Danke* for your patience with me today."

"Of course. You've been so busy. I hated to interrupt you."

Hattie groaned inwardly while taking in her sister's sweet words. In all honesty, Hattie had feigned her busyness to an extent while hoping Leah would forget all about the cookies. "I obviously needed the reminder. I apologize for not walking you over sooner."

After slipping her bonnet over her *kapp,* Leah scooped up the platter of ginger snap cookies from the counter. The Fishers began their trek towards Levi's home, carefully avoiding the barbed wire which had trapped Hattie once before.

Her ears perked at the soft sound of a bleating sheep in the nearby field. "Levi should be home by now, and either Amos or Jonas are probably watching over the flock."

"Well, what are we waiting for? Let's hurry!"

Hattie laughed at the child's exuberance as she frolicked through the field. Her excitement was infectious. She decided to lift up her skirts and follow suit. The cool air licked across her cheek, a very welcome change from the blistering heat only a few hours ago.

Leah clomped onto the wide front porch and knocked hard on Levi's door. Gasping for breath, Hattie leaned into the shadow of the overhang, hoping beyond hope that Levi would be in a *gut* mood.

The door swung open and his piercing chocolate eyes caught on hers, avoiding Leah entirely. "What can I do for you?"

Hattie cocked her head to look past her bonnet's wide, black brim. She motioned to her *schweschder,* who was standing plainly in front of her. "Leah made a batch of cookies for you to enjoy. She is grateful for the time spent here with Luke and Amos, and she wanted to show her appreciation."

Her breath caught in her throat as a wide smile crinkled the corners of Levi's eyes. He leaned down and accepted the platter with a surprising amount of tenderness. Hattie stepped back, wary of the emotions brought to the surface of her heart. More than anything, she yearned for a family...for a strong man who would lead her and their children by his kind words and actions. Unfortunately for her, the actions of both her *daed* and *onkel* made Hattie believe that such a man did not exist.

Not that she was interested in marriage or men, or even Levi's impression of her...no, now that she was in the same predicament as her *mamm*, she would never know if a man was truly interested in her, or her bank account. She had vowed to never enter a union like the one between her parents when she was but a young *kind* walking through the corn fields of her old farm in Lancaster County, trying desperately to escape her father when he raised his hand in anger.

"I'm looking forward to eating your cookies, Leah. Why don't you and your *schweschder* join me inside so we can eat them together?"

"*Ja!* Come on, Hattie!"

She turned to him with her head cocked to the side. "Are you sure, Levi? Not too long ago, I was absolutely certain that I was not *welkom* in your home."

He sighed deeply. "If you'd rather, we can forget the whole thing."

"*Nee*, please let's stay for a while." Leah looked pleadingly at Hattie, and then Levi. "I would enjoy it ever so much."

"Fine." Hattie remained tight-lipped as she stoically waltzed into Levi's home and sat stiff-backed in the chair closest to the exit. She managed a smile when Leah offered the platter to her, while thinking of the best way to leave as quickly as possible. For a few minutes, they ate the treat in silence. "So, is Jonas with your sheep now?'

"He's usually gone by this time of day, but Luke fell asleep in the back room and he figured he'd stay on a little longer. He'll probably leave shortly."

Hattie nodded while swallowing a bite of ginger snap. Despite trying her best to ignore the man, just the thought of Jonas being nearby made her toes curl.

"We'll be leaving as soon as possible, then. Come, Leah." Hattie rose to her feet, while her chair scraped against the wooden floor. An angry yowl followed by a few sharp barks from the open window drifted inside, causing her to lean against the wall in fright.

Levi rose to his feet, taking a few quick strides to the door. "Stay inside. I need to check on my flock."

"Do you think there is a problem?"

He nodded grimly. "There very well could be. Now stay put, you hear?"

With that, he flew from the door while holding his straw hat to his head.

Hattie fidgeted, wishing there was something she could do to help. Jonas or no Jonas, she felt compelled to make sure the flock she had grown to care for was in one piece. "Leah, I'm going to check on Levi. He might need an extra hand. I need you to stay in the house with Luke in case he wakes up, alright?"

"But, didn't you hear what Levi said? He asked for us *both* to stay put. What if something dangerous is lurking outside?"

She pulled together every ounce of courage she could muster before heading to the door. "Don't worry Leah, everything will be just fine."

Hattie stepped out of the house and scanned the darkening horizon. A guttural growl seeped out from the western hills. Swallowing her fear, she began to jog in that direction. She slowed when she caught the first sight of the flock peeking out from behind a rise in the landscape. Carefully, she stepped closer, wondering what was going on.

She gasped when she noticed a lanky figure crouched down against the fading grass. The creature's amber eyes turned into slits as it reached its mouth down and clenched a small ewe before trotting away. Levi stood nearby, throwing a handful of large rocks and shouting in its direction. Hattie rushed to his side.

"Levi, what was that?"

He turned to her, and she could see frustration smoldering in his eyes. "What are you doing here? A mountain lion just picked off one of my sheep. Don't you understand he could have killed you, too?"

Her mouth turned dry as she felt her stomach attempt to empty its contents. "I just wanted to help."

He pulled her towards him as she began to sway with nausea. She leaned into his chest, unable to do anything else as her feet nearly gave way. His arms circled around her, and Hattie breathed in his scent.

"Now look at what you've done. I have an injured sheep that I need to tend to, and I will have to carry you back to my home first. You are in no condition to be left in this field."

She forced herself to stand on wobbly feet as she pushed away from him. "Another sheep is injured? I thought the mountain lion took his prize."

Levi shook his head grimly. "He had his eye on a larger animal before I made my appearance. He decided to go after a young sheep once I arrived."

"Where is Jonas? Wasn't he watching the flock?"

An irritated breath blew through his lips. "He was supposed to be, but he's nowhere to be found. I would have secured my sheep inside of the barn if I would have known he planned on deserting them. Amos tried to scare the predator off, but he is no match for a mountain lion."

"I'll be fine. In fact, I want to help you."

Levi walked purposely towards the sheep lying in the tall grass. "I don't know what help you can be."

"I'll do anything I can."

He nodded curtly. "If you believe you can keep your wits about you, come along."

Levi scooped up the sheep in his arms and Hattie matched his strides to the nearby barn. "I need you to light a lantern and gather a few supplies for me. Do you think you can do that?"

"*Ja*, just point me in the right direction." Hattie's voice softened as the ewe bleated pitifully. She hoped with all of her heart that she would pull through.

After following Levi's sharp instructions Hattie kneeled by his side as he gently set the sheep down on top of a mound of hay. Absent-mindedly, she patted his back in encouragement as he tried his best to stop the bleeding near the sheep's neck and then stitch the wound. Levi stiffened briskly and she quickly pulled her hand away.

"I don't need your help any longer. Feel free to head home with Leah."

"But what about Luke and the rest of your flock? Will the ewe make it?"

"We won't know for a few days at least since she lost a large amount of blood. I've got everything under control, and I would like for you to return home while the lion is still occupied with his meal. *Schnell*."

Hattie rose clumsily to her feet as she backed away from the ewe's resting place.

"Hattie?"

She turned at the sound of her name. "*Ja*?"

"You have helped me more than you'll ever know. If I was forced to leave the ewe to gather the needed supplies, she might have already passed."

Hattie tucked Levi's words into her heart as she headed towards his *haus* to fetch Leah. They would need to hurry to their home while praying that another predator wasn't lurking nearby.

Chapter Eight

The muscles in Levi's back tensed as he wiped a coat of stain over a wooden beam next to the school *haus*. He had worked steadily as the clip-clop of horses announced the arrival of the festival committee, one by one. Several women-folk had met to discuss the upcoming town festival while he worked on constructing a large welcome banner just outside.

He rubbed the wood with a bit too much force as a bleat sounded over the nearby barbed wire fence. Frustration with Jonas pricked his conscience nearly day and night after the latest mountain lion attack. What was the man thinking, leaving his sheep unattended in a field far from the safety of the barn? When Jonas strolled back to the barn an hour later, Levi had nearly fired him. If it wasn't for Luke, he would have sent him on his way in a hurry.

"Can we eat our dinner now?"

Levi looked down at the small orphan who was currently helping him by sanding the next beam. He had insisted that Luke accompany him back to the school *haus* once his lessons had come to an end. Jonas wouldn't have worried about the child's whereabouts if left to himself, let alone his supper.

"*Ja*, let's take a break and have a bite to eat. Afterwards, we can check on the ladies and see how the fundraiser plans are coming along."

"I can't wait until the festival. I heard that it was going to raise money for orphans like me. Maybe then, *Onkel* Jonas will be able to give me more to eat."

Levi bit the inside of his cheek while looking down at the tot. Jonas would likely squander any money given to him for Luke's care away in a hurry. But talking forthrightly to the child would do nothing to help the situation. "Maybe so."

After the two finished off their sandwiches with a few swallows of root beer, they made their way to the school *haus*. Levi ushered Luke through the open door and took a seat in the rear of the room. His ears perked as criticism rushed towards him.

"I don't think Hattie knows what she's talking about. How 'bout we take over the preparations ourselves. What do you say, ladies?"

His eyebrows raised as he watched Hattie's shoulders slump at the front of the room. She took a deep breath as a blush darkened her cheeks. "I've planned benefits such as this before, and I truly believe my strategies would work if implemented properly. Inviting the public of Bozeman to the festival would likely increase the profits we can donate to the families affected by the influenza pandemic."

"*Nee*, you are just wanting to invite the people of Bozeman since you're one of them. I can see right through you." Annie Zook turned her pert nose up in Hattie's direction. She shook her head, with her dark hair pulled back harshly underneath her *kapp*. "Excuse my tact, but I think you are no *gut* for our *kinder*. Even the schoolmaster thinks so. I see the way he looks at you in disgust."

Levi hung his head as his cheeks burned. He hated to think that his own sour attitude had caused others to dislike Hattie. But isn't this what he wanted all along?

Hattie straightened her back as her countenance sank. "I'm doing the best I can for both this town and the scholars who attend this school *haus*."

Annie turned with wide eyes as Levi lumbered into the building. "Your schoolmarm isn't very agreeable. She thinks she knows what is best for our *kinder*, when she surely does not. What are you going to do about it?"

He took a step back, shocked by the way Annie spoke to him. Most women in the community exhibited a certain level of respect for the men, whether they be unmarried or not. "This is none of your concern, Annie."

Annie's cheeks turned a shade of pink before she huffed and exited the school *haus*. His heart pinched when both Greta and Rose rushed to her side and placed gentle hands on her shoulders. He fought the urge which tugged him to do the same.

"Are you all right, Hattie?"

"*Ja*, I'm just fine."

Greta tucked a stray strand of graying hair back into her *kapp* as she squeezed her shoulder. "Don't worry about Annie, dear. I believe your plans for the town festival will work well for our community."

"I'm glad that you think so, but I really don't want to cause any more trouble. It seems like everything I attempt to do for Deer Springs is met with opposition."

"Hattie, most folks around here have endured a great deal. They are just wary of you since you've yet to be tested."

"I've been tested alright. And I fear I've failed."

Levi frowned as his ears perked on Hattie's whispered words to Greta. What could Hattie be hiding behind her hushed tone?

"At the end of the meeting I would like to let you in on why people around here feel the way they do. I believe inviting the *Englischers* from Bozeman would be the best way to make the festival a success. Please carry on with the meeting and let us know what we should do next." Greta pressed her gentle hand on Hattie's shoulder once more before shuffling away.

Hattie delegated several tasks to the handful of ladies gathered before turning to Levi with a cautious, tight-lipped smile. "Do you come with *gut* news or bad?"

He shrugged while shooing Luke to play with Leah who was sitting quietly at a desk. "I guess I came with no news at all. Luke and I just wanted to check on the committee to see how the festival plans were progressing."

She hung her head. "Not well. I was hoping the town's folk would be agreeable since I'm trying to help them." Hattie raised her gaze, while unshed tears shined across her caramel eyes. "But even in this, they show not even a small sign of trust. Yesterday, Jonathan Philpot brought a letter from my old friend Marjorie Allen. She will be visiting soon. What will the church members think when they notice an *Englischer* stopping by my home?"

Levi scratched his head, his thoughts muddled with confusion. Could Marjorie hold a clue concerning the troubling occurrences at Hattie's place? Maybe he should drop in when she arrives to get a better idea if this could be a possibility.

"I don't think Marjorie's appearance will stain your reputation any more than it already is."

Her face grew white as she clutched the nearest desk. "I truly don't belong here, do I?"

Silence grew between them as Levi shuffled his feet. He hadn't meant to hurt Hattie's feelings, but he wouldn't speak against the truth. She didn't belong in

Deer Springs, and the sooner she accepted this idea, the better.

Levi cleared his throat, breaking the tension which had crept in. Determined to change the subject, he nodded towards Luke and Leah. "Those two seem to get along wonderfully, don't they?"

She smiled wistfully. "*Ja*, they do. Leah always says that she feels like Luke is her little *bruder*. It's too bad she will never experience living in a large family."

"If you marry and have children someday, she will have the chance."

Hattie wrinkled her nose. "I will never marry. Seeing the trouble my *daed* caused was enough for me to…"

The couple were interrupted when both Leah and Luke rushed in their direction. Leah bumped into her *schweschder*, and Levi's face grew hot as Hattie lost her balance and pressed against him. He gently guided his fingers around her shoulders and made sure she was steady on her feet before stepping away.

"Hattie, Luke wanted to know if we could stop by and see Bessie after school tomorrow."

Levi's heart warmed once he realized the youngsters felt comfortable enough to invite themselves to his farm without his permission first. More than anything, he wished he could take over guardianship of Luke. But with Jonas in the picture, this seemed to be out of the question.

"Tomorrow I'm expecting a visit from an old friend, dear one. Maybe we can visit the ailing ewe the next day."

Hattie, Leah, and Luke had insisted that the sheep hurt during the mountain lion attack be given a proper name. Levi rolled his eyes at first, but upon their insistence, he agreed. After a rather lengthy meeting, a consensus was made. The ewe would be named Bessie.

Both Leah and Luke stopped by her barn stall any chance they could, and he couldn't deny that the sheep seemed to enjoy being around the two youngsters.

"I can pick up Leah and bring her by the barn tomorrow if you'd like." He nodded hopefully, realizing that this would give him the chance to take a closer look at Marjorie. Possibly he could even ask her a few questions. Yes, this would be a *gut* plan.

Hattie's lips pursed as her hand tightened protectively against Leah's shoulder. "I'm not sure if this is the best idea. I'm not very comfortable with my *schweschder* being around Jonas without me there. Would you keep a close eye on her? She mustn't leave your sight, even for one second."

Levi sighed, wishing Hattie would understand the measures he took to keep both her and Leah out of harm's way. He'd never allow Jonas to hurt Leah.

"You have my word."

She nodded curtly. "Okay, then. Leah, you may visit Bessie with Levi tomorrow."

The youngster jumped with delight and hugged her sister's waist. "Did you hear that, Luke? We'll both get to see Bessie tomorrow."

Luke nodded with shining eyes. "Hanging out with you at Levi's is the best thing I do all week."

Levi's vision grew cloudy as he heard the confirmation he needed regarding Jonas's continued employment. For now at least, he had made the right choice by keeping Luke around the farm, regardless of his guardian's seedy behavior.

"I really need to get back to the meeting now." Hattie's shoulders slumped as a little bit of light left her eyes. "I'm looking forward to listening to what Greta has to say to me later. I'm in need of some encouragement."

Levi strode towards the door, determined to lessen the pull Hattie seemed to always have over him. "I'm going to get back to work too. Do you mind if Luke stays with Leah? He's helped me so much already. Being only six, I'd say he deserves a break."

She waved absentmindedly. "Of course. I'll see you tomorrow."

Levi shook his head as he stomped down the stairs outside of the cabin. His eyes narrowed, while he angrily hashed over his inward response to Hattie. He knew better than to get involved with a woman…and one who is nearly an *Englischer* at that! Pushing his thoughts aside, he began sanding the next beam. At least Hattie had made one positive contribution to Deer Springs. The town festival would hopefully jump start the schoolmarm's newly created aid fund, and pull the town to its feet.

Hattie sighed as she gazed out the window which was devoid of curtains for the fifth time in the past half hour. To say she was nervous about spending time with Marjorie was an understatement. She had been her closest confidant while in Bozeman. Her friend knew nearly everything possible about her past, and she couldn't wait to see her again. The thought of speaking with a friend forthrightly with no hints of secrecy filled her heart with relief.

She looked down at her clothing while the battery operated clock broke the silence as the seconds continued to tick by. Hattie wondered what Marjorie would think about her plain mourning garb. While in Bozeman, she had dressed like the local settlers due to her boss' request. But now, she was surely plain. How would Marjorie react to her Amish attire?

Hattie settled into a sturdy chair as she thought of Greta Miller. She was glad both her and Rose Graber were in her small circle in Deer Springs. Greta had sat with her for quite some time on the stoop of the school *haus*, as an early cool mist filled the air the night before. Her words had caught her off guard when she spoke fondly of Levi. *After my Jeremiah died, he helped us out so much. He encouraged me to sell my baking to the community, which has helped us get by. I don't know what I would've done without dear Levi. He has been the glue which holds Deer Springs together.*

Greta also gently explained the troubles surrounding their small community, and why they are wary of outsiders since Rhoda Greenloe left the scholars abruptly. She asked her to give Levi a measure of grace, since his previous *aldi* had fooled not only him, but the rest of Deer Springs as well. Greta spoke with such conviction that tears had spilled down Hattie's cheeks before their time of fellowship had come to an end. With a renewed sense of determination, she decided to always show compassion to others, even if not shown to her first.

Hattie's thoughts were interrupted as the sound of a sputtering engine wound its way around the school yard. Springing to her feet, Hattie took a deep breath as she peeked out the window once more. She had expected for Marjorie to arrive on the stage coach, but apparently she had purchased an automobile. This was unheard of on a teacher's salary. A smile brightened her face as she rushed to the door and swung it open, eager to meet her friend.

"Marjorie! I'm so glad you stopped by!" Hattie nearly yelled over the roar of the motor before it sputtered to a stop. Her friend opened the door with a squeal, and the two shared a warm embrace. Pulling back, Hattie looked over Marjorie, surprised by her change in appearance. Her once long auburn hair was cut into a fashionable bob, and her plum skirt had to be at least six inches shorter than the last time she had seen her. A long string of pearls hung nearly to her waist.

"Marjorie…you look so different."

"You look different too, Hattie. Why the black clothing?"

Her voice grew hushed. "These are my mourning clothes. I wear them to honor my *mamm*."

"Aw honey, I'm so sorry for the way everything has turned out for you."

She waved her hand dismissively. "It's alright. Don't worry about me, I want to hear about you. When did you purchase a car?"

"Oh, I just have so much to tell you. Talking about the automobile can wait. I've gotten married!"

Hattie placed her hand over her mouth, trying her best to hide her surprise. Had she lost her mind? "Married? But you weren't even courting anyone when I left Bozeman."

"Arthur swept me off my feet, and we married quickly. I wasn't even able to send word to you, since we headed to the church right after he proposed. That's why I wanted to stop by today. I felt like I would burst if I didn't tell you the good news as soon as I could."

Hattie felt a swoosh of air leave her lungs as she let out the breath she had been holding. "You didn't marry Arthur Parsons, did you?"

"The one and the same. Hattie, please don't be sore that I married him. I know he was keen on you for a while, but after you left town, he began to court me. I'm ever so happy."

Her brow scrunched in worry as she straightened her apron. Arthur Parsons was a wealthy ranch owner, who seemed to have remained untouched by the current drought. His land ran adjacent to a once-roaring river, which still produced enough water from the nearby mountain peaks to sustain his herd. While his wealth was enticing, his rudeness and pride was not. Hattie could hardly believe that her friend had not seen through his charm.

"I suppose Arthur gave you an automobile and the new clothing, *ja*?"

"He did. It's a Model-T." Marjorie patted the car's shiny black door. "It handles like a dream…except up hills that is. I have to drive backwards up steep embankments."

"Isn't that frightening?"

"Not after you get used to it." She flashed a sheepish grin in her direction.

The two women linked arms as they glided towards the clapboard home. Hattie ushered her friend inside before closing the door against the dry wind. She stood silently, wondering how she could gently broach the topic of her friend's marriage.

"Are you sure you got to know Arthur well enough before marriage?"

Marjorie sighed as she sank into the sky blue settee. "I'll admit that Arthur isn't the kindest man in town, but he offered me a sense of stability that no one else could. And he's not so bad once you get to know him. I've grown tired of worrying about what would come of my job as more and more settlers left the area since the influenza pandemic hit. Surely you can understand."

"I do understand, but I can't help but worry about you."

"Arthur is a prideful man, but he isn't an abuser. You don't have to worry about me having the same fate as your mother."

The room once again grew silent as Marjorie's words sunk in. She was right. Hattie couldn't continue to allow her own situation to color her view of other's marriages. This wasn't the fair or right thing to do.

"I apologize if I overstepped my bounds."

"No harm done." Marjorie glanced around the room, while craning her neck to peek through the doorframe. "Now where is this sister of yours? I'm dying to meet her."

"She's working on her homework in the next room. Levi will be picking her up shortly, and I'll be sure to ask her to stop and chat for a moment before she leaves."

Marjorie raised an arched eyebrow. "Is Levi your beau? And do you really think allowing your sister to leave home without you is the best idea? Are you sure that your uncle didn't follow her to Deer Springs?"

She chuckled softly. "So many questions. Where do I start? Levi is the local schoolmaster, and is the farthest thing from a beau possible. I'm not sure if my *onkel* followed her or not. Honestly, some strange things have been happening around here. More often than not I find myself wondering if Henry is behind it. The schoolmaster lives next door, and I trust him with my *schweschder* ...sort of. At least I think I do. Life in Deer Springs has been far from easy, and I'm hopeful Leah can have a *gut* time this evening."

Marjorie nodded sympathetically. "If you feel like you trust him, then go with your gut. You've been through so much, and there is no need for you to worry too much. It's not good for you." She crossed her legs, while a gem on her shoe reflected the light streaming in from the large picture window. "Life in Bozeman isn't perfect either. A strange character showed up in town for a few days not too long ago, and then left. He asked Arthur for a job before moving on his way. We found it odd since most folks are leaving Bozeman, and aren't trying to put down roots."

A chill ran down Hattie's spine. "The man wasn't Amish, was he?"

"No, he was just a regular old settler."

A sigh of relief blew through her lips. At least she could rest assured that Henry wasn't who Marjorie was talking about.

She leapt to her feet as a solid rap sounded at the door. "That must be Levi. Excuse me for just a minute."

The door handle felt hot in her palm as she twisted it open. All rational thought left her as she stared into Levi's deep chocolate eyes. His straw hat was slightly askew on his head, giving him a playful appearance. Hattie's eyes danced as she motioned for him to come in.

"So, this must be Levi."

He turned to Marjorie as a polite smile twitched on his lips. "And you must be Hattie's friend from town."

"The one and the same. Hattie didn't tell me that such a kind, attractive man lived just next door."

She coughed to hide the rush of embarrassment which had settled in her chest. Marjorie was always one to speak her mind, but this was too much.

"She *did* let me know that her life here hasn't been easy. I really believe she needs a break, and as her boss, it's your duty to make sure she's taken care of. What do the Amish do for fun?"

He clenched his hands by his side, proving that he was just as uncomfortable with this conversation as she was. "While we don't concentrate on the fun things in life, a different family does hold a singing in their barn every other week."

"How perfect. Do you think you could take Hattie to a singing sometime?"

"Enough, Marjorie." Heat swelled to Hattie's face as she rose to her feet. "My state of mind isn't Levi's responsibility, and I have no desire to attend a singing."

"I disagree. While it's completely understandable that you can't marry and have children like your mother, this doesn't mean that you shouldn't have fun from time to time. Going to a singing would be a harmless amusement. Arthur and I could even come and stay with Leah while you're gone."

"Speaking of Leah, let me fetch her for you, Levi." She breathed a sigh of relief as she stepped into her sister's bedroom while motioning for her to follow. All would be well again once the schoolmaster left.

"Leah's ready to go, Levi."

Leah skipped to his side and waved to Hattie while pulling her black bonnet over her *kapp*. "Thanks for allowing me to visit Bessie today." Her eyes lit up as she glanced in Marjorie's direction. "And you must be my *schweschder*'s friend from Bozeman. It's nice to meet you."

"I hope to spend some quality time with you soon, Leah." An amusing giggle escaped from her lips as she waved at the youngster. "For now, I hope you have a good time with your neighbor."

Hattie rubbed her temples as the door closed behind her *schweschder*. Settling into the settee with Marjorie, the two reminisced about their escapades in town for some time before saying a tearful goodbye. While giving a final farewell to her old colleague before she sped around the school *haus* with her auburn bob flowing behind her, Hattie wondered if meeting her very fancy friend would cause Levi to trust her even less than he did now. She bit the inside of her lip as an uncomfortable realization hit her square in the chest. She most likely would never be welcome in Deer Springs.

Chapter Nine

Levi whistled a word-less tune as he guided Dolly away from the station depot. After much deliberation, he had decided to request additional information from two of the women applying for the schoolmarm position. Ada Miller and Britta Stolzfus. Jonathan Philpot gladly took the inquiries, promising to deliver them to the Post Office in Bozeman the next morning. Levi had made certain the envelopes were addressed in such a way that no one could guess their contents. Guilt bit his conscience. Pushing all fear of being caught by the brethren aside, Levi avoided a few ruts in the road as he neared the school *haus*.

Surprised to see the light of an oil lamp flickering through the window at such a late hour, he pulled his mare into the school yard. Trouble seemed to follow Hattie wherever she went, and he wouldn't be surprised if something was now amiss in the school *haus*. He blew out his breath in both utter frustration and worry.

He quickly tied his horse to the hitching post before taking long strides towards the cabin. The door was hanging open by its hinges, and his breath caught in his throat as he stepped inside. Desks were turned on their sides, and a trail of papers were strewn across the length of the building. The words *YOU HAVE BEEN WARNED* were written in shaky handwriting across the blackboard.

Levi took a step back, drinking in the scene before him. Once his eyes adjusted to the dim light, his gaze trailed towards the warm glow of the oil lamp. Hattie was sitting on the worn wooden floor, her head resting in her hands as her brunette locks spilled over her shoulders nearly to her waist. The glimmering light caused flecks of gold to illuminate, making her look almost angelic.

He slowly walked towards her, stepping over the sea of school work littering the floor. Levi placed a worn hand on her shoulder before she jumped, and then rushed towards him. Gulping big heaping sobs, she leaned into his chest. Not knowing quite what to do next, he wrapped his arms around her nightgown as her slight frame shook with dread.

"What's going on here?"

Leaning back, she stared intently into his eyes. She pursed her swollen lips, as if she wasn't quite sure what to say next. "I heard a commotion when I was readying for bed, so I came over to see what was going on. I thought either a scholar might need some assistance or a member of the festival committee decided to drop off their last minute preparations. Instead, I found this mess."

Levi's heart skipped a beat as he thought of Hattie coming to the school *haus* alone without any form of protection. "With all of the issues around here, please realize that staying within the safety of your home is the best idea if you hear a strange ruckus."

"The problems around my home are directly related to me. I know they are. And now this mess is spilling into the school *haus*, and is sure to affect the *kinder* of Deer Springs. I'm not welcome here."

Levi gently stroked her cascading hair as she once again leaned into him with hiccupping sobs. It did seem like someone was intent on forcing Hattie out of her home. But who? While the church members in Deer

Springs were none too keen on her arrival, all signs seemed to point to an *Englischer* being behind all of this.

"Do you think Marjorie could have had something to do with this? She was just here yesterday?"

"*Nee*, definitely not. My friend would never hurt me in such a way. Her husband Arthur asked to court me some time ago, but I turned him down. He does have a few character flaws, but I don't believe he had anything to do with it, either."

Levi's ears perked when Hattie mentioned Arthur. He couldn't help but be suspicious of Marjorie the moment he laid eyes on her. She appeared even more worldly than most of the Bozeman settlers, with her shiny automobile and fancy clothing. While he knew it should come as no surprise to him, he was truly befuddled by Hattie's choice of friends. Regardless of what the schoolmarm thought, he believed the Parsons somehow played a role in the shenanigans which seemed to surround the schoolmarm wherever she went. He readied himself for this possibility.

"Well then, who do you suggest is behind all of this?"

"I'm not sure. I have an idea, but…"

"Hattie, if you have any inclination about who is causing these disturbances, you must tell me. As the schoolmaster, I have the right to know."

Sighing, she pulled back slightly. "I don't have any concrete evidence to go by. For now, I must continue on, for the sake of the town. I really must see the formation of the Deer Springs Aid Fund through to the end."

Disappointed, Levi righted a fallen desk. He had hoped that the vandalism of the school *haus* would have been the tipping point for Hattie, and she would decide to leave Deer Springs on her own accord. Instead, the guilt which tickled his conscience since he dropped off the new schoolmarm inquiries with Jonathan Philpot intensified. While staggering slightly, Hattie began to gather the mound of papers strewn across the floor. Levi started to place the rough-hewn desks into their rightful spots, wincing ever so slightly when he realized a few were in need of more serious repair. A cool breeze blew through the structure, alerting him to a broken window at the back of the building.

"Fall is settling on us quickly, *ja*?"

He nodded grimly as her soft words danced across the room. The seasons in Montana changed quickly, and sometimes without warning. The cool nighttime breezes which had picked up along with the snow capped mountain peaks were a sure sign that snow was on the horizon.

Levi watched as Hattie fluidly walked around the room. A feeling of sadness settled in the pit of his stomach. While he hadn't cared much for Marjorie's unexpected visit, he had been surprised to learn that Hattie wouldn't be able to have children since she was like her mother. Levi originally thought her flippant comment about not having a family when he was adding a lock to her door spoke only of her own desire to not have any *kinder*. Now he believed some sort of medical problem was likely to blame. To his knowledge, Hattie's mother only had two children, which was very uncommon amongst the Amish community. Perhaps the schoolmarm had inherited the same ailment. His heart hurt for her.

"It's no use, Levi. There is no way we can clean up this mess before the scholars arrive tomorrow morning."

"You're right. I will send word to the Bishop to cancel classes."

"*Nee*…wait. I have an idea. Would it be alright if we take the field trip to your farm tomorrow? I was hoping we could do so soon anyhow. We could meet in the school yard, and the scholars would be none the wiser. That way we can work on cleaning up over the weekend, and hopefully all will be well come Monday."

Levi stiffened as he took in the scene before him once more. Hattie had not only caused harm to come to the scholar's classroom, but to Rhoda's classroom as well. An uncomfortable tightness filled his chest as he stood frozen in place. The painful memories surrounding Rhoda flooded his mind as his eyes began to water.

"Well, what do you say? Would you mind if my class came by your farm tomorrow? If the scholars stepped foot into the school *haus* tomorrow, their parents would have even more reason not to accept me."

Just like that, sympathy for Hattie overcame his internal mourning for Rhoda. Her caramel eyes glistened, while filled with hope. Her lips parted slightly as she stepped to his side, as if she wanted to say more, but just couldn't.

"*Ja*, you can bring the scholars to my farm tomorrow."

She sighed with relief and took his hand in a brief clasp. Realizing the effect her closeness was having on him, he pulled back abruptly.

Hattie got back to work gathering papers. "By the way, I would like to let you know to please disregard Marjorie's mention of you taking me to a singing. As the schoolmaster, it's not your place to make sure I participate in trivial amusements."

Looking down, he considered what she was saying. Marjorie's questioning had been uncomfortable to say the least. But given Hattie's troubles, he couldn't help but think her friend was right. He looked around the disheveled school *haus* in disgust. While she didn't have much time left in Deer Springs if everything went according to his plan, giving her an evening to forget about her troubles would likely do her good, despite his hesitance.

"I could definitely take you to the next singing, Hattie. It might give you a chance to get to know the young people of Deer Springs better, too."

A dark pink pinched her cheeks. "I'll have to think about it."

He chuckled under his breath as he clasped the oil lamp and guided it towards the broken window to take a better look. She was turning the tables on him, for sure and for certain.

"My *daed* never did so well in social situations with my *mamm*. He would often become intoxicated and raise his hand in anger afterward. I don't know if going to a singing with you would be a *gut* idea."

Displeasure rose in the pit of his stomach. "I would never do anything to hurt you, Hattie."

She nodded curtly before holding her chin out stubbornly. "Nonetheless, I still need to think about it."

"Fair enough."

Suddenly, her eyes widened in fear. "Leah. I left in such haste when I heard the commotion that I forgot all about her safety. I must go to her."

Levi followed Hattie as she rushed out of the building. Ignoring the sting of cold air that slapped his cheek, he matched her strides as she headed straight towards her white clapboard home. The door slammed into the front of the *haus* after Hattie clamored up the steps, her bare feet causing a path of dust to swirl around them.

Waiting patiently on the porch, he gently rapped on the open door. "Hattie, is everything okay in there?"

She slowly appeared from one of the bedrooms, a look of relief on her face. "*Ja*, right as rain. Leah is sleeping soundly, and everything is as it should be."

Levi's eyes scanned the property, trying his best to verify that no one was lurking outdoors. One thing was for certain, he was growing tired of the trouble that followed Hattie Fisher wherever she went.

"Well then, I need to head home. See you tomorrow."

"Levi?"

He stopped in his tracks and turned towards her voice. "*Ja?*"

"*Danke* for your understanding."

Unable to answer, he threw his hand up in a wave before heading towards his rig. If only she knew what he was really thinking. He wasn't feeling the least bit understanding, but instead, was perturbed and incredibly confused.

Levi patted his black mare as he unhitched her from the rail. He had a long night ahead of him, between checking on his sheep and making sure his barn was prepared for Hattie's class. It wouldn't do if a scholar was hurt on a piece of equipment. Pushing Dolly forward, she settled into a steady trot while rounding the final bend towards his home. He hoped that the schoolmarm applicants would ask their Bishops to fill out his recommendation form quickly. They were his only hope for a return to normalcy.

"So, we're going to Levi's farm for a field trip today? I can't wait to introduce Mary to Bessie!"

Hattie smiled to herself as Leah shoveled a heaping spoonful of grain cereal into her mouth. Her eyes shined like liquid gold, which spoke volumes of her excitement.

"That's right. I'm glad you're looking forward to it. We'll meet the rest of the scholars in the school yard in just a few minutes."

Leah cocked her head in thought. "It's kind of strange for us to have a field trip so last minute and all. Is anything else going on?"

"Nothing that you need to worry about, dear girl."

Hattie faked a smile as she turned towards the dishes in the sink basin. She pulled a bucket of precious water from the floor and poured it over the growing pile. Wiping her hands on her apron, she bit the inside of her lip before getting to work.

She slathered the edge of her bar of lye with a bit too much force against a plate. Hattie was angry at herself for the mess in the school *haus*. Her greatest fear appeared to be coming to fruition right before her eyes. Most likely she hadn't adequately covered her tracks, and now her *onkel* had found them. Prickles of dread crept up her neck as she continued with the chore, and remained until the last dish was put away.

"Are you ready to leave now?"

"*Ja*, let me grab my bonnet and we'll be on our way. Since we aren't going to be working in the classroom today, you may leave your homework here."

Hattie couldn't help but grin as Leah let out another squeal of glee. Perhaps today wouldn't be so bad after all.

The Fishers straightened their *kapps* before placing their black bonnets on their heads and stepping out of the front door. The sweet smell of hay met their noses as they neared the school *haus*.

She gasped as they rounded the corner of the building. Levi's shiny ebony mare stood proudly in the yard, and attached to his harness was a wooden wagon filled with hay. Levi sat stiffly in the seat, with a sheepish grin filling his squared jaw.

"I thought the scholars might enjoy a hay ride to the farm today. It should be much more pleasurable than walking."

All thoughts of fear diffused from Hattie's chest as Leah rushed towards Levi.

"This will be so much fun, *ja*?"

"Most definitely." The schoolmarm crumbled onto the porch with relief. Hopefully with Levi's help, Leah would never realize that something was amiss in her classroom. She would hate to add anything else to Leah's already full plate. She had already endured too much turmoil in her short ten years as it was.

Little by little, pony carts began to fill the school yard as *kinder* arrived to further their education. The yard was buzzing with excitement as the realization hit that today wasn't to be just a normal school day. The boys and girls took turns patting Dolly and offering her treats from their lunch pails.

"Scholars, please gather around before we leave. I have a few instructions for everyone."

"Where are we going?"

Hattie held up her hand to silence the crowd as Mary Miller asked her question. "Levi Hilty has been kind enough to allow us to tour his farm today. We will learn about sheep farming, and perhaps a bit about building a homestead. I expect everyone to be on their very best behavior. You will be representing the Deer Springs Amish School in all you do. Now then, please deposit your books and homework on the porch and take a seat in Levi's wagon. We are going to take a hay ride to the farm. Oh, and be sure to bring your lunch pails."

"Can't we put our homework inside of the classroom?"

Hattie's lips pursed into a straight line as she tucked a stray strand of hair into her *kapp*. "Not today, Tommy. Please leave your belongings outside."

The children complied, and soon all were lined up like ducks in a row along the edges of Levi's wagon, each one eager to take in the view as Dolly trotted along. Hattie took her seat near the back, determined to stay away from Levi as much as possible today. She had grown to be a tremendous nuisance, she was sure of it. Despite her best efforts, she couldn't help but steal a peek at the driver. Surprisingly, his gaze was steadily focused on her, showing a measure of concern. She became lost in their warm silent exchange until he almost reluctantly turned away and gently slapped the reins across the mare's back, pushing her forward.

While being jostled towards the farm she realized just how much she would miss her class…and just how much she would miss Levi. She shook the thought aside with a laugh. Had her parent's relationship not taught her anything? No man ever deserved to be missed.

Hattie hugged her arms around her abdomen as the southern hills of Levi's farm came into full view. A spattering of white sheep dotted the dry terrain, along with a plain man standing to the side. Jonas. She sighed, resigned to the fact that most likely she would have to somehow deal with him today as well. Hattie looked to Luke, who had snuggled close to her. She gave his shoulder a squeeze as they entered the gate at the front of the property. She had no idea how he handled living with such a man.

Levi slowed the mare once they reached the tall, red barn. Its peak pointed towards the heavens, and the blue sky shone in contrast. Hattie grimaced as the wagon lurched to a stop. She wasn't sure if being the schoolmarm in this small town was the best choice after all. Her presence was now putting the school children in danger. If she had her way, she would either be curled up in bed or on a train with Leah heading far away from Deer Springs.

"Scholars, please line up a single file line once you depart from the wagon. Be sure to be extra attentive to what Levi says today, since there might be a short quiz about sheep farming come Monday."

Hattie's voice rose loud and clear over the groans of the school children as they hopped off of the wagon, two by two. The older *kinder* led the way, thoroughly interested in the inner-workings of the Hilty farm.

Levi motioned for the class to follow him into the barn, and Hattie once again took up the rear. She couldn't help but admire his strong shoulders standing tall over the children's heads, which was evidence of his good work ethic.

Once the class stood in the barn, he turned to face them. Hattie breathed in the fresh scent of hay while glancing into Bessie's pen. The ewe seemed to be resting peaceably.

"*Welkom* to my farm. As you can tell, I farm sheep, as do several of your fathers."

Bobbing heads raised up and down in understanding.

"At the moment, I own over five hundred Corriedale ewes. I am one of the first farmers in the area to raise this particular breed of sheep. Several years ago my ewes numbered over one thousand, but I've lost a *gut* many sheep to the drought. Others I've sold."

He paused for a moment as his eyes grew cloudy and his shoulders tensed. He let out his breath and snapped his suspenders before continuing.

"But this isn't the time nor place to speak of my woes. A successful sheep farm depends on keeping as many ewes as I have currently. If I lost any more, I could possibly go under. I make my living in three different ways. I sell lambs, wool, and milk."

A small hand shot up in the crowd.

"*Ja*, go ahead."

"What makes you the most money?"

Levi smiled at the dark headed boy. "I would have to say, wool. I sell the wool which is sheared during the spring to several different markets in the surrounding Bozeman area. The *Englisch* are usually more than willing to buy my product."

Hattie frowned as she tucked this bit of information away in her mind. If Levi was so opposed to dealing with her because he believed she was an outsider, why would he deal with the common settlers?

"Now believe me when I say my dealings with those in Bozeman are strictly business in nature. I prefer to deal with Amish customers."

She tried to hide her sarcastic scowl behind the head of a fourteen-year-old boy. Would Levi ever realize that those outside of Deer Springs are not all bad?

"Now then, please take a look around the barn. I expect everyone to be orderly, and to not touch any heavy equipment. You can find several milking stations to my left, and feel free to visit Bessie on my right. She was injured by a mountain lion about one week ago, and is healing nicely after sustaining a *gut* bit of blood loss. After we are done here, we will head to the fields to lay eyes on my flock, along with my sheepdog, Amos."

The barn began buzzing as the children dispersed, eager to study Levi's operation further. Hattie relaxed and leaned her frame against the edge of a barn door, her mourning dress gently brushing against the splintered wood. She closed her eyes, trying her best to stop herself from reliving the fear she experienced the night before. Her time in Montana was likely coming to an end, and she was having a hard time coming to terms with leaving her class after the town fundraiser came to a close. She felt a fresh set of tears spring to her eyes as she watched them rushing around the barn in excitement.

Her brow puckered as the pesky idea of attending the next singing with Levi entered her brain. While she didn't want to attend, the thought of clearing her name with the local young people was appealing. She would much rather leave town on a positive note, instead of the sour one which everyone seemed keen on embracing.

"How are you doing?"

She jumped as a rich voice tickled her ears. She opened her eyes slowly, and her vision focused on Levi. His shoulders slumped once again as if defeated as he leaned against the opposite door.

"I'm fine. Why do you ask?"

He raised an eyebrow. "You didn't seem like you were 'fine' when I left you last night. The vandalism at the school *haus* left you pretty shook up."

Heat filled her heart. "Who are you to determine whether I'm bothered or not?"

"I have eyes, Hattie."

The way her name rolled off of his tongue caused her to clench her fists by her side. He was treating her like a child, and she didn't like it one bit. Admitting defeat, she nodded her head slowly. "It did upset me to see the class room in such a state."

"Have you thought any more about attending the singing?"

She frowned, suddenly growing squeamish. How could he change the subject so quickly? "*Ja*, I have."

"And do you have an answer?"

Her caramel eyes flashed. "Why are you even asking this of me? What I mean to say is…we have nothing in common. I'm not sure attending a singing would be a *gut* idea. If I went it would only be to learn more about the young women in the district and to fellowship with Rose. Not to spend time with you. Do you understand?"

He grunted under his breath. "I'm not asking to court you, Hattie. Believe me. But I think getting your mind off of your troubles for a short time would be a *gut* thing for both you *and* Leah. From what you've told me about your life prior to arriving in Deer Springs, you were forced to grow up too soon and too fast. So what do you say?"

She was able to muster a single nod.

"*Gut.* We'll discuss the details later."

Hattie rubbed her parched throat as she pushed away from the door frame and walked back towards her class. She was so distracted in thought, the stealthy movement in the shadows of the barn missed her eye. Turning to Leah, she gave her shoulder a squeeze as they both patted Bessie's coarse wool. The thought of attending her very first singing at the age of twenty-two caused butterflies to dance in her stomach, regardless of being accompanied by a very disagreeable suitor.

Chapter Ten

Hattie placed her hand on the small of her back as she leaned over the short bureau which stood stoically against her bedroom wall. She dipped a white washcloth into a shallow bowl before cleaning her cheeks from the grime which had flown up from the wagon wheels of Levi's rig on the short drive from church.

While she had wanted to acquire her own horse and buggy in Deer Springs, there was really no need for it now. The benefit festival was to be held in less than one week, and Hattie figured she would turn in her resignation letter to Levi directly afterwards. She hated to put the town in the predicament of being without a schoolmarm once again, but she had a strong suspicion that Deer Springs would be more than happy to see her go.

At least the school *haus* had been adequately repaired, and the scholars had been none the wiser. They never made any indication that they suspected foul play. Levi had stuck to his word, and made the repairs quickly on the Saturday directly after the class' impromptu field trip to his farm. She frowned as she carefully pulled the pins out of her hair, determined to straighten the light brown fly-a-ways which tickled her cheeks. The field trip had left her more confused as ever about why Levi continued to employ Jonas. Even around a yard full of *kinder* he was uncouth and rude, and he slipped away on more than one occasion when he should have been doing his employer's bidding.

"Will Marjorie and Arthur be arriving soon?" Leah stuck her head inside the door frame, her eyes wide in anticipation.

"*Ja*, they should arrive any time now. Have you washed and put away the dishes from our afternoon snack?"

"I have. The blueberry muffins you baked this afternoon were *wunderbaar*, and I bet the young people at the singing will think so too."

Hattie raised her eyes upward, hoping that Leah might be right. During the afternoon meal after the church service that morning, she was all but ignored by everyone but Rose. The main topic of conversation was the upcoming baptism, but Hattie had remained quiet. As much as she had been looking forward to finally joining the Amish church of Deer Springs, she realized her and Leah would be on the move before she ever had the chance.

"Will you be home late?"

She patted her sister's head after she expertly replaced the straight pins in her coil of hair. "I highly doubt it. I'm only going to satisfy the wishes of Marjorie and Levi."

Leah shot her a look which indicated she wasn't entirely sure Hattie was being truthful before giggling and dashing out of the room. A frustrated breath blew through her lips as she straightened the pins in her skirt and followed her *schweschder* into the main living area.

A knot of worry settled in her stomach as she thought of what might come of Leah while she was at the singing. After her class room had been vandalized, Hattie was determined to become even more vigilant when checking her surroundings for signs of her *onkel*. She

128

wouldn't be able to adequately protect Leah while away at a singing, this was for certain.

"They're here!"

Leah's squeal echoed through the small home, causing Hattie to nearly jump out of her skin. Sure enough, the sound of a sputtering engine resonated throughout the room, indicating her friend's arrival. She had sent word to Bozeman earlier in the week stating that she had decided to go to the singing after all, and Marjorie had been more than happy to act as babysitter so Hattie could freely do so.

She opened the front door, waving for the Parsons to come inside as soon as their Model-T came to a stop in the yard. "Come on inside, and get out of this chilly air." The temperature had been steadily dropping all afternoon, and Hattie was quite certain that the first frost would be blanketing the Montana landscape come morning.

Marjorie jumped from the vehicle and rushed to Hattie to give her a warm hug. Arthur was slower to reach the door, and removed his bowler hat to doff her a curt nod before strolling inside.

Hattie sighed. It appeared as if Arthur hadn't changed one bit. While he was quite handsome with his sandy blonde hair, blue eyes, and rugged build, his features couldn't make up for his aloof nature which was often peppered with sarcasm and negativity. When he had something nice to say, it was usually about himself.

"Ooh, I'm so excited to be spending the evening with you, Leah. I've got all kinds of games and fun up my sleeve."

Leah brightened at Marjorie's promise. "I'm really looking forward to this evening. Hattie promised I needn't crack open a single book to study for my history exam this week!"

Marjorie flashed Hattie a knowing smile. "Always the teacher, aren't you? Although I'm no longer employed, I've realized that old habits die hard."

She pushed away the feeling of jealousy which had risen into her chest. While Hattie never wished to marry someone like Arthur Parsons, her desire to be a *frau* one day was strong. Her friend had attained a goal that she never would.

"I know I showed you around my home two weeks ago, but do you have any questions? Leah shouldn't be hungry, but if the need arises feel free to pull a snack from the ice box."

"How are you two doing in regards to food? I know times are tough around here, with the drought and all." Marjorie's wide eyes shined with sympathy as she tucked her short waved hair behind one ear.

"The Amish are a self-sufficient bunch, and we've never gone hungry despite the dry conditions. The women of the church share a small ration of their food with us as a form of payment for my services." She chuckled awkwardly, remembering the way the local women eyed her with distrust as they took turns bringing food from their own farms and community garden plot. If they could without being scolded by the Bishop, she was sure they would rather let her go hungry.

Hattie narrowed her eyes at Arthur, who was looking around the room curiously. A wave of suspicion washed over her, and she wondered if agreeing to go to the singing was such a good idea after all.

A sharp rap sounded at the door. Leah happily swung it open, revealing an uncomfortable-looking Levi. Hattie swallowed hard as she took him in. He was still wearing his for-*gut* clothes, and a slight hint of dark hair stuck out below his black felt hat. As much as she wished it not to be so, it felt an awful lot like they were courting.

The room began to spin at the thought and she clutched onto a chair tightly.

"Are you ready to go, Hattie?"

She trained her gaze on him as the words left his mouth. Strangely, he was looking straight past her and towards Arthur instead. The men continued to size each other up as she rushed to Levi's side.

Uncomfortable, Hattie fairly pushed Levi out the door. "*Ja*, I'm ready. Let's be going." Turning towards her *schweschder*, she engulfed Leah into a hug. "You be a *gut* girl for Marjorie and Arthur. Also, please stay put inside. Understood?"

"Of course."

Hattie managed a strained smile as the door shut behind her and Levi quietly led her to his waiting buggy. She had never seen this rig before, and it looked like it had been polished until it shined.

"I didn't know you owned a courting buggy."

He looked to the quickly dimming sky, while his strong neck rose from his collar-less shirt. "I haven't had any need for it lately."

She shuffled from side to side, growing increasingly more uncomfortable by the second. "I'm sorry if I gave you the wrong impression, Levi, but I have no intention of courting…"

"*Nee*." Levi interrupted her abruptly. "I do not wish to court you. It is simply expected of young people to drive these rigs to the singings. I didn't want to upset the Bishop if I chose to drive my enclosed buggy."

"Of course." Hattie stared at the ground as hot tears sprang to her eyes. Refusing Levi's assistance, she pulled herself into the buggy and scooted to the outermost corner.

"I didn't mean to offend you, but both of us know that anything besides a professional relationship is out of the question. Correct?"

"Correct." Hattie's teeth chattered as a cool breeze rocked the buggy slightly. Thankful that the darkening sky was sure to hide the blush of her cheeks, she wrapped her arms around her shivering frame as goose bumps raised on her arms. She was making a fool of herself, and she longed to bolt back into her home and head straight to bed.

Levi rolled his eyes as he jumped into the buggy. "Please scoot out of the corner and move closer to me. I don't want you to catch your death of cold on our way to the Miller's barn."

Reluctantly, Hattie inched closer to Levi. He reached under the bench seat and pulled out a thick lap blanket. He gently reached across her and tucked it around her side, causing her chill to subside.

Despite her trepidation, Hattie leaned into him. The warmth radiating from his body along with the wool blanket brought a sigh of pleasure from her lips. Perhaps tonight wouldn't be too painful, after all.

"Is this blanket made from your own sheep's wool?"

"*Ja*, it is. Greta Miller made it for me as repayment for some of the work I completed at her home after her husband passed away." Hattie caught his eyes shining by way of the lamp light which lit their way.

"Well, it's very nice."

"*Danke.*"

The two rode in silence for the remainder of the trip. Despite her newfound warmth, Hattie shivered when the Miller residence came into view. The church service had been held in Greta's home earlier, and as was tradition, she was hosting the singing in her barn as well.

"If you'd rather turn around and head home, I understand. After all, I'm sure you have many more pressing matters than to accompany me to a singing."

"I wouldn't have taken you here if I had other plans. Jonas should be keeping a close watch over my sheep right about now, so all is well."

Hattie couldn't help but notice the uncertainty in his tone. "Jonas isn't the most loyal of employees, is he?"

"He is not."

She squelched the question at the tip of her tongue as the buggy lurched to a stop. Why would Levi continue to employ a man with such terrible moral character? As much as she would like to ask, she figured it wasn't any of her business.

"Down you go."

Hattie sighed as Levi's strong hands pinched her waist as he gently lowered her to the ground. Her small feet crunched against the dry grass as she gently pulled away. She shifted her gaze while stumbling a few steps backwards.

"Are you ready?"

"As ready as I'll ever be."

As Hattie grabbed her contribution to the snack table from the buggy she became even more acutely aware of Levi's presence. As he gently pressed his hand into the small of her back, leading her towards the well-lit barn, her trepidation kicked it up a notch. She wished she was anywhere but there.

Levi's eyes squinted against the bright lantern lights of the barn as he ushered Hattie inside. He discretely glanced at the boards he had repaired for Greta Miller only one week ago. After Jeremiah had died, he had taken it upon himself to help the widow with her farm whenever he could.

"Where's the refreshment table?" Hattie's voice was as quiet as a mouse.

Levi pointed towards the far corner of the barn before leading the way to the spacious table filled with snacks. Jugs of root beer and water sat on a smaller table to the right, along with a mix-match of glassware.

He noticed her small hands shake ever so slightly as she placed her platter of muffins on the table. Shuffling his feet, he wondered if bringing her to the singing was the right thing to do. Once he had arrived to pick up Hattie, he realized that Arthur Parsons appeared to be even less trustworthy than Marjorie. Was he the one responsible for all of the trouble at the schoolmarm's residence? He was genuinely worried about leaving Leah in their less-than-capable hands.

Besides the fact of Leah's safety being at stake, watching Arthur sitting in the schoolmarm's home had sent prickles of jealousy up his spine. As much as he would like to deny it, he couldn't help but feel a spark of attraction towards Hattie. He knew far better than to go down that road again as the thought of Rhoda's betrayal doused his feelings like ice water. He hadn't attended a singing since his betrothed had left him, and the realization stung.

"I best be going to my side of the barn. The singing will start soon."

Levi turned on his heel and stomped over to the men's side of the barn. He turned to look at Hattie, who was frozen in place. A wave of sympathy shot through him as she meekly took her place amongst the young women, looking almost like a dejected child.

"I didn't know that the schoolmarm was your *aldi*. I guess it makes sense, since you're the schoolmaster and all. Rhoda and Hattie share many similarities."

He glared at the deep voice sounding from his right side. "Elias, I'm not courting anyone, and I would appreciate it if you kept your mouth shut."

"You could have fooled me by the way you are looking at the girl. You're making moon eyes at her, just like I do at Rose."

He let out a breath of frustration, wondering what he could say to make the younger man understand that his relationship with Hattie was strictly professional. "I don't know what you're talking about."

"I think you do. You have the look of a man that's in *lieb*."

Choosing to ignore Elias, Levi filed into place next to the other young men present for the singing. Too little too late, he realized that he was positioned directly across from Hattie. He averted his gaze when a small smile twitched on her lips. He certainly didn't want to give the wrong impression to the other young people in attendance. If Elias thought the two were courting, then others might as well.

In unison, the young people began to raise their voices in song. The tunes were much livelier than the solemn songs usually sung during the district's church services. Near the end of the hour, Levi couldn't help but realize how much he was enjoying himself. He had missed the feeling of fun and camaraderie which accompanied the singings. He had adopted the motto of "all work, no play" for far too long. A wide smile filled his lips as he snuck another glance in Hattie's direction.

Her caramel eyes followed him, lighting up warmly. He playfully wiggled his eyebrows at her, and felt satisfied as he watched her giggle. Marjorie had been right after all. The singing had not only done him, but Hattie *gut* too. They both deserved a break from the constant worry and tension which had filled their lives since she had moved to Deer Springs. While he didn't particularly want to be the one to accompany her to the Millers, he was glad she was there.

After a final song, the group was dismissed and the young men began to mingle with the young ladies. Levi's eyes narrowed as Adaline and Ruth Graber turned their noses up at Hattie before two boys no more than nineteen rushed to bring her a plate of snacks. He chuckled in spite of himself. Feeling jealous about the attention a couple of boys was showing to the schoolmarm was indeed laughable.

He clung to the shadows, hoping to give Hattie a bit of time to socialize before bringing her back home. She appeared uncomfortable at best as she took a dainty bite from a sugar cookie as several young men vied for her attention. Her eyes scanned the crowd, silently searching for something, or someone. Finally locking eyes with him, she mouthed *help me* while motioning for him to step forward. Chuckling at her predicament, he decided to wait just a few more minutes before coming to her rescue.

Levi strode towards the refreshment table, cordially nodding at Rose when she shyly handed him a glass of root beer and one of Hattie's muffins. His eyes rose in appreciation as he bit into the soft treat. Surprisingly, she was a superb cook. After taking a few swigs of root beer to wash the muffin down, he trained his gaze slowly around the lively barn. He looked at each face once, and then twice. Concerned, he realized that Hattie had disappeared. Berating himself for not going to her sooner, he abruptly sat down his cup before taking quick strides towards the exit.

He swallowed a gulp of air as cold as ice as he left the swarm of warm bodies and lantern light. Levi perked his ears, while hoping that a sound would lead him to her. He heard what sounded like a muffled voice coming from behind the line of courting buggies sitting neatly in a row. Ignoring all sense of decorum, Levi held his felt hat to his head as he rushed to the faint sound.

Rounding the edge of a wagon wheel at record speed, he put on the brakes before running into a couple huddled tightly together. Hattie looked up, fear shining from her wide eyes like a deer in headlights. At her side was Jonas, who was jeering like he had won a prize.

"Hattie...Jonas...what's going on here?" Levi's voice came out in a choke, as a feeling of relief pressed through him. The feeling was short lived once he realized that Jonas had once again forsaken his duties and left his sheep without the protection he had promised to give them. His eyes shifted from side to side, giving both parties the once over. Hattie didn't want to be alone outside with Jonas, did she? He pressed his hand against his temple as it began to pound.

"Jonas appeared at my side while I was inside the barn and insisted on showing me something out here. He took hold of my arm, and refused to let go. And now, he is trying to convince me to leave in his rig, but I'm not going anywhere." Her voice rose an octave with each word she spoke as she violently shook her arm free from Jonas' grasp.

"Is this true?" Levi stared down his employee while the scrawny man shifted his squinted eyes towards the gravel he was shuffling with his work boot.

"I was just looking to have a bit of fun, boss. You can't expect me to work all of the time, you know. Besides, you know as well as I do that this girl is a pretender. She's an *Englischer*, no doubt. Anyone who takes the time to fool all of us in Deer Springs doesn't deserve an ounce of respect."

Hattie gasped as she nearly flew to Levi's side. He reluctantly put a protective arm around her shoulder as he rehashed Jonas' assessment. In a way the man was right. He surely hadn't shown her the respect she deserved by going behind her back and looking for a replacement schoolmarm.

"Hattie, do you wish to leave with Jonas?"

"*Nee*, certainly not." She nearly spat out the words as her eyes narrowed.

"Well then, you heard the lady. Jonas, I expect you to respect her wishes and head home. I'll see you bright and early tomorrow morning." He glanced around the rig, searching for Jonas' charge. "By the way, where's Luke? He was with you at the farm before I left for the singing."

"As I've said before, Luke is none of your concern." Jonas pressed his lips into a jeering grin before he stepped into his buggy. He flicked the reins, signaling his malnourished horse to shakily trot forward.

Levi swallowed a ripple of emotion as he worried for Luke's well-being. Where was the boy? Was he safe? Little by little, he had begun to view the child as his own. It was hard not to do so when the tot spent so much time at his farm, and his guardian was a sorry excuse for a human being.

"Were you really going to let me leave with Jonas?" Hattie turned her pert nose up at Levi as her rosy lips formed into a pout. He wished he could tuck a stray tendril of chestnut hair behind her ear as she took a step closer on tiptoe. "Let me tell you something, Levi Hilty. If you think I would ever give a man like Jonas the time of day, you do not know me at all. While I'm not interested in men…well, at all…if I was, Jonas Beiler would be the last man on earth I would give my attention to. Have I made myself clear?"

He smiled as he gently grasped her shoulders and held her at arm's length. "I know, Hattie. I just figured that it would mean more coming out of your mouth than mine, so I gave you the opportunity to explain your feelings. I wouldn't have let you leave with that scoundrel."

"You wouldn't have?"

"Never."

She relaxed, and crumpled once more into his side. He stiffly patted her mourning dress, while wishing he could remove himself from this awkward situation.

"I think it would be best if we left so I can check on my sheep before I bring you home since we will be passing by there first. Is this a problem? Would you rather socialize for a bit longer?"

"I've had my fill of 'socializing.' Other than Rose, my only real interactions were with a few boys and Jonas. I doubt the young ladies of Deer Springs will ever truly trust me. And after my run in with Jonas, I'm ready to head home to my Leah and warm bed."

He gently pushed away from her and took a few steps back. Fighting back the urge to engulf her in his arms was becoming more difficult by the second. She looked so afraid and broken, and yet he realized that at the same time she would be the end of him. He could never risk opening his heart to anyone ever again.

"Well then, let's be on our way. Would you like to grab your contribution to the refreshment table before we leave?"

"I'll just pick up my platter at a different time. I'm sure Greta won't mind."

Levi couldn't help but feel disappointed as he helped Hattie into his rig. He wouldn't have minded eating another one…or three, of her delectable muffins on the way home. Being a bachelor had its disadvantages, the lack of home-cooked meals being one of them. He never went hungry, but his food was far from tasty.

Levi gently tapped the reins against Dolly's back after he tucked Hattie in once more against the cold. He hurried the horse into a trot, wishing to arrive at his farm in record time. He hoped with his whole heart that Jonas' negligence hadn't caused his flock any harm.

Chapter Eleven

Hattie couldn't help but allow her teeth to chatter as she was rocked to and fro while Dolly quickly trotted towards home. The temperature was surely hovering around freezing, and she berated herself for not being better prepared. She should have at least grabbed the cape her mother had lovingly made for her long ago which was now tucked safely in her bureau. The beautiful wool blanket kept her legs toasty and warm, and she was thankful for this small mercy at least.

Instead, she was forced to seek warmth from Levi's side, which made her terribly uncomfortable. As another cool blast of air rocked the rig, she pressed herself even closer.

"Are you all right?"

"*Ja*. Don't worry about me." Hattie was trying her best to not be perturbed at the man who nearly allowed Jonas to carry her off into the night. She had been scared out of her wits when Jonas' icy fingers slid around her arm when she wandered towards the edge of the barn to avoid the awkward conversation several boys had tried to involve her in. Her hopes of connecting with other young women were dashed, as most formed cliques while whispering insults in her direction. While she had thoroughly enjoyed raising her voice in song in the

Miller's barn, she could have done without the remainder of the night. Dealing with Levi, Jonas, and Arthur in the same evening was quickly sending her into an emotional tailspin.

"I wouldn't be surprised if we received frozen rain tonight."

Her ears perked in curiosity. "Really? It has been so long since we've had rain, and I'm sure the crops would benefit greatly from it."

He smiled wryly. "It's probably too late in the season for most crops to profit from it. I would like to see a bit of rain, though."

Hattie settled back into the seat, returning to her disappointment. She sat in silence, mulling over the question which she wished to ask of Levi more than anything. He turned the courting buggy into the lane which led to his farm. He then jumped from the rig and looked to the nearby field before giving a satisfied nod and heading into the barn.

With a sudden push of courage, Hattie lept from the buggy and followed Levi inside of the barn. He stood in a lone corner, carefully lighting an oil lamp before setting it on a bench.

"What are you doing here? Give me just a minute, and I'll drive you right home."

"I have a question to ask you, and I don't think it can wait another minute."

"Go ahead." Levi continued walking around the barn completing his tasks, before stopping at Bessie's pen and taking a better look at the ewe.

She rolled her eyes, perturbed by the way he brushed off her concern. She took a few tentative steps closer, and hoped the tightness in her throat would ease.

"My question is about Jonas. Why don't you fire him? He is a sorry employee, and he doesn't deserve the paycheck."

His shoulders slumped as he took a deep breath. "Luke."

"Luke? What do you mean, Luke?"

"Jonas *is* a sorry excuse for an employee. But I am keeping him on board because of Luke. Jonas doesn't take *gut* care of the boy, and if Luke is given the opportunity to spend time with me each day, I can make sure he is getting at least one decent meal, along with a bit of fun. I was once an orphan myself, and I understand what it feels like to be unwanted."

Hattie sucked in her breath as a hint of compassion shined from her eyes. She wouldn't wish the feeling of loneliness on anyone. "I didn't know you were an orphan."

"I was. My parent's died in a barn fire when I was only three. I wished I could have saved them, but I couldn't." A look of anguish crossed his features. "I was forced to live with my *aenti* and *onkel*, and my aunt made life quite miserable for me. *Aenti* Katie was once in *lieb* with my *daed*, but he chose to marry my mother instead of her. I believe she blamed me for her heartache. I was treated like a hired hand until I reached manhood and was able to strike out on my own. As soon as I heard about the Homestead Expansion Act, I packed my bags and was on my way to Montana at the ripe age of seventeen."

"Oh Levi, I'm so sorry. The barn fire, nor your *aenti's* treatment was your fault. I believe you are a *gut* man for paying Jonas just so you can keep an eye on Luke. Not many people would do such a thing. You have a kind heart."

He slowly shared a lop-sided smile as he continued to stroke Bessie's wool. "*Danke.*"

Hattie sank to her knees and let the ewe's wool tickle the back of her hand. "When do you cut the sheep's wool?"

"Don't you mean, 'shear' them? Weren't you listening to me at all during your class' field trip?"

She shook her head and smirked at his teasing tone. "You're right. I was a little distracted during the field trip." Besides being distressed by the school *haus* vandalism and Jonas lurking nearby, simply being around Levi seemed to cause her to lose her train of thought. A man never quite had this effect on her, and she didn't like it one bit. She knew that she must stay focused on Leah's safety, it should be her only priority.

"I shear my sheep in the spring. It is an exciting time around here, and many members of the community stop by to help."

"I would love to own a blanket like the one you keep in your courting buggy. It is so soft and warm."

"Well then, come spring, I'll ask Bessie if she can help make that happen. She's almost well enough to be put back to pasture."

As soon as the words left his mouth a pained expression crossed his face. Staring at him peculiarly, Hattie shrank back, realizing that her blanket would likely never materialize since she would be far from Deer Springs by then.

The two sat in awkward silence as a cool breeze entered the barn through the open doors. Hattie breathed in the crisp air, and cocked her head to peer out of the door. "That smells like…"

"Snow."

Sure enough, tiny flakes descended from heaven and helplessly clung to the dry blades of grass outside of the vibrant red structure. Hattie clasped her hands with glee as she turned to take in the beautiful sight.

"I didn't think it would snow so early in the season."

"Neither did I, but the weather in Montana is very unpredictable. It will probably switch over to rain soon."

"I'm going to enjoy it while I can." Hattie closed her eyes, and thought of the many fun-filled winters she shared with her *mamm* and Leah in Lancaster County. While her *daed* was sleeping off his latest hangover, the three would have a grand time building snowmen and sipping hot chocolate by the fire. She wished for such times again.

"Hattie?"

She opened her eyes, realizing she had accidentally placed her hand over Levi's while stroking Bessie. Shivers shot up her spine while she tried to pull away, but just couldn't no matter how hard she tried. He turned his palm over and gently grasped her hand in his. She leaned into him, feeling his heartbeat against her ear as the gentle pattering of snowflakes sounded on the metal roof above them. She decided to forget her troubles for only a moment, since tonight marked the only singing she would ever attend.

Before she realized what was happening, Levi gently pulled her closer and enveloped his arms around her slight frame. Happiness filled her from the top of her head to the tips of her toes. She leaned into him, and gazed into his eyes as he tipped her head up ever so gently. Surprised by the feelings rolling inside of her, she gasped for air before slowly pulling away.

"Levi...I think I need to go now."

Disappointment shadowed his face as he nodded. "*Ja*, I think you're right. Everything seems right as rain around here and we best be going." His voice was thick with emotion.

Hattie wobbled slightly as she rose to her feet and used Bessie's pen to steady herself. Levi moved quickly to offer her support, but she reluctantly stepped away with a deep sigh. She had given him the wrong idea, and she needed to begin righting this wrong immediately.

Hattie had taken a few tentative steps towards his rig when a loud crash sounded inside of the barn. Her eyes rose in alarm as she whipped her head around, the strings of her bonnet slapping her cheeks.

She stood motionless as a puff of smoke blew through the air as flames licked the edges of the building. A fire had started! Hattie shook with fear as she stood motionless, feeling absolutely helpless as the flames quickly devoured the dry straw lining the floor of the barn. Bessie bleated pitifully, as she weakly pawed at her stall.

Hattie nearly sank to her knees as Levi ran towards the blaze. She quickly got her wits about her, and rushed towards the well pump. Pumping as hard as she could, she filled a bucket of water before sprinting back to the barn.

She breathed a sigh of relief as Levi emerged, holding a frightened Bessie in his arms. He gently steadied her feet a good distance away from the building before turning to Hattie with pain shining in his eyes.

"The barn most likely will be a total loss, and will be taken quickly since it is so dry. Let's concentrate on saturating the grass around the barn so it will not spread across the field. And please join me in praying that this snow will change into a rain shower. This will be our only hope."

Hattie nodded quickly before lugging the heavy pail closer to the barn, wincing as the heat caused the snowflakes caught on her bonnet to melt and run down her neck. She turned and ran, sad for Levi's loss. In light of learning about his parent's death, she knew this would be very hard on him.

The two continued to rush pails of water towards the structure while Hattie prayed with all of her might that her beloved snow might turn into a soaking rain. Slowly but surely, the snow turned into sleet, and then a rain that misted over the landscape. Soaked, shivering, and cold, Hattie continued with her task until the ground closest to the barn was thoroughly drenched.

"Hattie, that's *gut* enough." Levi clung onto her shoulders and forced her to stop. "The barn is but a smoldering pile of ashes now, but the field and the house will be saved."

A feeling of uneasiness crept over her. There was no good reason for the fire to start in such a way, and she had a sinking suspicion that it was due to her, yet again. "Why do you think the fire started?"

His eyes darted around the field uneasily. "I hate to say this, but I think it was a case of arson. There is no way my heavy oil lamp could have tipped over on its own. Someone was in the barn with us."

She curled her arms around her abdomen, breathing in the scent of smoke which had permeated completely through her cape dress. "I must go to Leah...now."

She nearly choked on her words as she scrambled through the field towards her home. Locking her emotions in a shell of ice, she ignored Levi's calls for her to return and kept running into the darkness as quickly as her feet could carry her. Disregarding the trouble lurking nearby, she climbed over the barbed wire fence on the property line. Hattie had no time to lose. Leah could be in grave danger.

"So boss, what's the plan for today? With your barn gone and all, I can go home if you'd like." Jonas shot Levi an impish grin as the words slipped off of his tongue. Luke stood stoically by his side, while his head was turned almost 180 degrees so he could stare at the barn rubble with wide eyes. Only Levi's metal equipment could be salvaged within the wreckage, and he intended to see just what he could save once he was sure the area was free of hot spots.

"*Nee*, you are needed here. Please leave Luke with me and tend to the sheep in the field. Amos is keeping watch as we speak."

Jonas gave a curt nod as he meandered off with a spring in his step. The man's lack of sympathy did not surprise him. Nothing but Luke caused him to hold his tongue as a smile spread across his employee's face. Jonas' uncouth manners were wearing on his last nerve, and despite the poor youngster, he wasn't sure how much longer he could handle keeping him employed.

"What happened to your barn?"

Levi bent down to the child's level and placed a hand on Luke's shoulder. "It caught fire last night. Thankfully, no one was hurt, and it can be rebuilt."

He watched as a glint of torment crossed his features. "I don't think I should hang around here anymore. *Onkel* Jonas says I'm nothing but trouble, and maybe I caused the fire to start."

Levi pulled the boy into a hug, while remembering how his *Aenti* Katie used to tell him the same thing. He had been haunted by the barn fire his parents had been killed in for nearly all of his life. His *aenti* did her best to keep the dreadful memory alive, whispering in his ear that he would never amount to a *gut* Amish man, all while making references that the fire was his own fault. If his *daed* had not asked for his *mamm's* help while making him a toddler bed in his workshop, then they would still be alive.

As Levi aged, he realized that the Amish usually do such a thing when a new *boppeli* was on the way, and while he had no concrete proof, he believed this was probably the case. His own barn fire did nothing but bring up painful memories from the past that he would like to leave buried. He hadn't been strong enough to save his parents then, and he definitely wasn't strong enough to support a *frau* now. Rhoda made that clear when she headed east on the train, leaving his broken heart behind.

"You're not any trouble, Luke. Please don't believe that. I'm sure *Gott* has a *gut* plan for you, and I would like nothing more than to be here beside you when you figure it out."

"Really?" Luke's eyes shined with hope as his light blonde bangs swept across his forehead underneath his straw hat.

"Really. Now run along and fetch a snack from the kitchen."

Luke's footsteps thundered through the expansive home towards the root cellar. While Levi was irritated at Jonas, this little conversation solidified his decision to have an excuse to keep the boy around. Luke needed an advocate, and Levi intended to fulfill that role.

He leaned against the door frame as the smell of ash and burnt wood wafted to his nostrils. Levi was still in shock by the implications of the fire the night before. His eyes narrowed in suspicion as he surveyed the landscape. Someone was behind the fire, he was sure of it. But who?

In his opinion, the likely suspect was Arthur Parsons. He hadn't liked the looks of the man the moment he laid eyes on him, and he had close access to the property the night before. But what were the man's motives? Was he still in *lieb* with Hattie, even though he had married Marjorie? He had been suspicious that one of the schoolmarm's past suitors was responsible for the newfound trouble in Deer Springs from the beginning.

When the fire erupted, he had been concerned for one thing and one thing only. Hattie's safety. Levi had made a dire mistake in letting himself get too close to her the night before. She wasn't the girl for him, and he knew better. Still, the tender look she shot his way got the best of him, and he allowed himself to let down his guard. He vowed to never do so again. At the same time, he sorely realized that he was not treating her with the respect she deserved by going behind her back and trying to hire a new schoolmarm when she was in his arms.

Levi stepped into the kitchen and rumpled Luke's hair as he grabbed an apple off of the counter and took a bite. His eyes scanned the space, looking for the envelopes bearing the return addresses of the bishops representing Ada Miller and Britta Stolzfus. They arrived not long ago, but since the fundraiser planning was in full swing, he had forgotten to give them a *gut* look over. Picking up Luke's discarded hat, he found the two neatly addressed envelopes which he had torn open in haste before the singing. Unfortunately, he would have to write his apologies to the bishops and begin the application process yet again. This time with full disclosure to both the community and Hattie.

The sound of horses' hooves sounded through the open front door and into Levi's ears. He had sent word into town about his current predicament this morning, and he hoped a few able-bodied men had arrived to help him survey the damage. The Amish helped others within their community as much as they could, and a barn raising would likely be in his near future.

He took a final chomp out of the apple before throwing the core into his waste can. Taking long strides, he headed towards the door before jumping in surprise. Levi had expected a few younger men to be stopping by, but instead, Bishop Graber took a wobbly step out of his buggy once his horse had pulled close to the hitching rail.

Rushing to help the older man, Levi took the reins and firmly tied them to his post. "*Gut* morning, Bishop. What brings you out to my farm today?"

"I heard that your barn burned last night and I wanted to see the damage for myself." His wrinkled face squinted against the bright sun as he whistled low. "It's all but gone, *ja*? I'm thankful the rain came when it did. Otherwise, your grass and flock would likely be damaged as well."

Levi couldn't quite find his voice as the Bishop continued to survey the rubble.

"I would say let's schedule a barn raising this week, but since the fundraiser is in a few days we should probably wait just a bit longer. Will that serve you well?"

"*Ja*, just fine."

"*Gut*, it's settled then." The Bishop slapped his back good-naturedly as he turned towards the house. "Do you mind if I rest my back for a spell before heading home to my *frau*? Riding in a buggy is not *gut* for my old bones."

Levi nodded cordially as he led the way towards his home. As much as he would like to deny it, he felt the sting of resentment towards his elder. Besides insisting that he keep Hattie on as the schoolmarm, the fact that he did little to protect orphans like Luke from the likes of Jonas caused him to question the man's judgment. He wished instead of coming inside he would return to his rig and be well on his way.

When the elder stepped inside he headed towards the kitchen instead of sitting in the front room. "I heard Luke has been hanging around since Jonas is your hired hand. Do you think he'd mind fetching us something to drink?"

"*Nee*, of course not." Levi settled into a chair as his head began to pound. A feeling of uneasiness settled over him like a blanket. The kitchen had grown quiet, and his ears perked as he heard the sound of paperwork thumbing through someone's fingers.

Uneven footsteps once again entered the room. "Levi, what is this all about?" The Bishop's brow tightened in concern as he waved a stack of applications through the air.

Dread filled Levi's stomach as he shot to his feet. "Where did you find those?"

"In your cabinet. I noticed the schoolmarm recommendation letters on your counter, and decided that they warranted a closer look. What have you been doing?"

He hung his head in shame. "I knew that Hattie Fisher wasn't a *gut* fit for our community, so I decided to take matters into my own hands and search for a replacement."

"How dare you deliberately go against my wishes?"

Embarrassment twisted through his insides. "I didn't think you were being reasonable when you instructed the Fishers to stay in Deer Springs. With all due respect, I was also concerned when you disregarded clear signs that certain church members need discipline, like Jonas Beiler. I figured you might not be thinking clearly since so many of Deer Springs were taken by influenza last year or are affected by the drought."

Bishop Graber hung his head in silence for a moment, before raising his eyes in clarity. "Levi, I understand your concerns, but you do not know what I know. You have not seen the pain I've seen as overseer of the community. You do not know the extent of Hattie Fisher's plight, or her pain."

Levi's ears perked in curiosity.

"You are right about one thing. I have been too lenient on Jonas Beiler. While I need to rectify that, it is none of your concern. Think about your own sins.. I have seen the sin of secrecy and disobedience today, and they need to be dealt with. I will bring the matter before the brethren, and then before the church. I hate to do this, since you are one of the most respected members of our community. You bring out the best in everyone around you. You are a *gut* man Levi, and I would like nothing more for you to remain in our fellowship. But for you to do that, a confession is in order. Hattie has done nothing to cause me not to trust her, and she has almost completed her baptism classes. She will become a fully functioning member of the Deer Springs Amish Church soon. You must remember that."

The Bishop's voice grew louder with every word, and his face turned red as a tomato while he began shuffling to the door. He turned and waved the paperwork in his hand, before tucking the applications deep into his overcoat. "Please go to *Gott* in prayer, Levi. We will be in touch."

Levi's face blanched as the Bishop stepped out of his home. What had he done? Instead of helping the community by finding a new schoolmarm, he had only made a mess of things. Just like he always did.

He could barely swallow as a soft rap sounded at the door. Had the Bishop forgotten something? Levi's head felt like it was swimming as he rose to his feet and answered the knock.

Instead of the burly old Bishop, Hattie and Leah stood before him. The two almost blended into one as their black cape dresses meshed together when leaned into each other's side. He stared into Hattie's face, which was a mistake. While her wide caramel eyes and rosy lips reminded him of his current predicament with the Bishop, they also brought to mind his ill judgment the night before. He forced his gaze to his feet.

"We just wanted to check on you. How are you doing?"

Her soft words reeked with compassion, and Levi shuffled from foot to foot as he inched farther from the door…farther from Hattie.

"Fine."

"Do you have any guesses as to who started the fire?"

He didn't catch the wobble in her tone as she clutched Leah tighter.

"*Ja*, I bet it was Arthur Parsons. It makes perfect sense that he is to blame since the clues around the debacles at your *haus* point to an *Englischer*. As you know, *Englischers* are nothing but trouble."

"*Nee*, Arthur was with Marjorie the entire time. How dare you even think of such a thing?" Her voice grew more pointed as her golden eyes narrowed.

"Well then, who do you suggest?"

"Dear one, run along and play with Luke please." Leah dashed inside, eager to find her playmate.

"I don't know for certain…but I do know that Arthur remained with Marjorie while she was babysitting. When I arrived home, I found Leah asleep on the couch. Both of the Parsons recounted the sound of shuffling from outside of my sister's window, and they felt more comfortable with her sleeping in the main room. Whoever set the fire in your barn was likely at my home first."

"Hattie, what is going on here? I believe you know more than you are willing to let on."

Her cheeks grew pink as she clutched her hands at her side. "I'm sorry I've been a burden to you. You won't have to worry about me for much longer."

The implications of her words left him as he recalled the Bishop's warning. She was a burden all right, and now even his church membership was on the line because of her. He needed to escape her prying stare as quickly as possible.

"Don't worry about me, I'm just fine. While you're here though, I wanted to let you know that I apologize for holding you in the barn last night. I hope you weren't given the wrong impression with my boldness. I'm truly sorry."

Her hands clenched into fists as she slowly backed away. "You're right, it was a mistake. Don't worry about it...I will stay out of your hair from now on."

She called for Leah to come, and just like that, they were gone. Levi's shoulders slumped as the gravity of his situation weighed down on him heavily. Hattie might as well be sore at him now, since the second she found out about his indiscretions in front of the church she might never speak to him again.

Chapter Twelve

"*Wie geht's?*" Greta Miller tossed a grin to Levi as he stood on a ladder while attaching a newly-made fundraiser banner to freshly stained beams. They had been carefully placed in the ground the evening before.

"*Gut.* How are you?" Levi returned her greeting with a half-hearted smile.

"*Ach*, I'm right as rain. I was just thanking the *gut* Lord for sending Hattie to us when He did. She has given me and my *kinder* such hope for the future. Who knows? Perhaps we will all have a fine life in Deer Springs after all."

Greta meandered away slowly, leaving her words which stung like a bee behind. While Hattie's fundraiser was likely to offer much-needed help to many of the Amish in the community, his bad choices made him believe that his future was dim.

He hadn't spoken to Hattie in a number of days. As the hours ticked by he realized that the last thing he wanted to do was to hurt her. The Bishop's admonition rang through his ears, and he wondered what Hattie might have gone through which brought her to Deer Springs in the first place. He had been so concerned about her initial appearance and his own problems that he hadn't given a second thought to what she might have endured. And for that he was sorry.

His broad shoulders clenched from exertion as he tightened the banner's rope before alighting the ladder. Levi realized that for the first time, he felt badly for any pain he had caused the schoolmarm. It was time to make things right.

Taking a swig from his ration of water, Levi surveyed the pasture. The residents of Deer Springs swarmed around him, many families setting up either game or bake sale booths. A dunking booth sat in the corner along with a large platform dedicated to the Deer Springs Aid Fund.

He looked this particular booth over with a sense of awe. Hattie had been true to her word, and the sole focus of this festival was to raise money to help her hurting Amish brothers and sisters. Flyers about the aid fund stood neatly stacked on the table, along with a locked jar for accepting donations.

His breath caught in his throat when he first saw a glimpse of Hattie. Her hair was tucked neatly into her *kapp*, and her mourning dress was pressed to perfection. Her face radiated with concern as she leaned close to Greta, who was gesturing wildly. An understanding smile parted her lips as she pointed to her right and the older woman went on her way. Despite the distrust most of Deer Springs shot in her direction, Hattie seemed to really care for the community. This both confused and intrigued Levi at the same time.

Reluctantly, he began taking long strides towards her. As much as he would like to avoid her, Levi realized that he must ask what he could do next to help. Since Hattie was the woman in charge, to her he must go. His stomach tightened as he wondered if he had the courage to let her know about the secret schoolmarm applications and to apologize.

His throat grew dry as he made his approach. Her back was turned to him, and his fingers shook as he tapped on her slender shoulder.

"Levi, I wasn't expecting you here. What can I do for you?" She looked at him matter-of-factly as the strings of *kapp* danced slowly in the wind. Hattie took a step closer to Leah, who was sitting quietly inside of the tent, completing her homework.

"Of course I came to the fundraiser. Did you think I would stay at my farm, twiddling my thumbs?"

She pursed her lips tightly. "Maybe."

"If you expected me to do such a thing, you don't know me very well."

"No, I don't. After all of this time, I don't know you at all."

The two locked gazes as the crowd continued to grow by the second. A man bumped arms with Levi, forcing him to bow out of their staring contest.

"Miss Fisher, is that you?"

"*Ja*, it is. How is Walter doing?"

Hattie gazed shyly at a man who was dressed in cowboy attire from head to toe. Surely he was from Bozeman. Levi's eyes narrowed. Was this another one of the schoolmarm's suitors?"

"He's swell, except for the fact that he misses his favorite teacher. You were one of a kind, and Walter learned so much from you. My wife and I also noticed a huge improvement in his attitude under your tutelage. Are you teaching in Deer Springs now?"

She quickly nodded.

"Well, they are lucky to have you. Your teaching methods are top notch. I'll let Walter know that you are here, and he'll be sure to say hello."

"*Ja*, I would love to see Walter again. I'll keep my eyes open for your son."

157

The two exchanged a wave before the man sauntered off.

"Who was that?" Levi realized that he had been holding his breath, and he let it out with a bit too much force.

"That was the father of one of my former students. As much as I enjoy teaching in Deer Springs, I do miss my class in Bozeman. His son was one of the troubled youth I mentored in my spare time." A wistful expression laced with pain flitted across her face.

In a moment, he was transported back to his barn as the soft snow began to fall. He wished he could take away her sadness, and fought back the urge to cup her cheek in his hand.

"Well then, why don't you return to Bozeman?"

"I could never do that now. For Leah's sake, and for my own. My heart has longed to return to my roots for some time now. I could never give up being a part of an Amish community again."

Sighing hard, he realized he had nearly done just that while going behind the Bishop's back. Would he be able to confess completely before the church during the next Lord's Day gathering? Would the congregation offer him forgiveness?

His chest tightened as he realized that now wasn't the time to apologize to Hattie. He didn't want to give her another reason to worry when the fundraiser was almost ready to begin.

"Well then, what should I do next?"

Hattie looked dazed as she shook her head in confusion. "What are you talking about?"

"The fundraiser. Today you're in charge, and I need to know where my help is needed."

She frowned fiercely. "Please take a moment to relax, and then I would appreciate it if you could man this booth while I check on the other vendors. Does this suit you?"

"Suits me fine."

Hattie rolled her eyes while letting her breath out in a huff. "*Gut.*"

Levi couldn't help but choke back a smile at her curt words. She was feisty alright, but he was slowly realizing that her take charge nature was appealing. Very appealing.

A sharp squeal turned Levi's head in haste. Annie Zook stood behind the Deer Springs Aid Fund booth, her face flushed as she placed a hand over her mouth in shock. "Did you see the size of this donation?"

Curiously, Levi's boots crunched over the dry grass towards Annie. After the night of early snow and rain, the weather had returned to its regular dry pattern. A cool breeze brushed against his smooth cheek as he stepped forward.

"What are you talking about, Annie?"

"A very large sum of money has been dropped into the donation bucket. Why, it's over ten times the amount of money we had hoped to raise during the entire day. I wonder who could have done such a thing." She fanned her face with her apron as she laughed in delight.

Levi scanned the crowd, which was quickly becoming filled with *Englischers* from Bozemen. Was one of them the mystery donor? Perhaps Hattie was right to invite the settlers living in the nearby town to the festival.

"I don't know."

"Neither do I, but whoever it was is a very generous soul."

Levi quietly slipped away from the normally-ornery woman. How very strange it was to see Annie Zook being thankful. Perhaps he had been wrong about Hattie...the festival was off to a wonderful start, and it was all due to her.

His eyes slid into slits as a loud commotion rang through the crowd. A nearby cowboy let out a holler, and the women around him laughed wildly. Maybe he had been too quick to judge the outcome of the fundraiser after all. The *Englischers* from Bozeman were bad news, and the cause of Hattie's trouble could be lurking nearby. Levi broke into a run towards the source of the noise.

Hattie placed a protective arm around Leah as the two watched one of the older scholars become the dunk tank's first victim. The surrounding crowd roared with laughter as the wet teenager climbed back to his seat with great fanfare.

"Do you think you would like to take a turn in the dunk tank?"

Leah's face grew white as her lanky frame sank into her *schweschder*. "*Nee*, certainly not!"

Hattie threw back her head in laughter. "Fair enough, dear girl."

The two continued to meander through the crowd, making sure that each vendor was adequately staffed and had the needed supplies. Before leaving the Aid Fund booth Hattie had managed to slip her donation into the jar unnoticed. Grateful tears sprang to her eyes. Despite her poor reception in Deer Springs, she was more than happy to help the community in their time of need. Her mother's inheritance had made that possible.

Hattie's countenance fell when she saw the way Leah interacted with the friends she had made at the school *haus* as they walked around the festival grounds. The girl wouldn't be happy about her decision to leave Deer Springs, but for her safety, they must. She had already made contact with an Amish community in Missouri, and was finalizing plans for their departure. Fear prickled on her neck. She knew with almost complete certainty that Henry had found them, and they must make their escape soon.

Besides worrying about the vandalism at the school *haus*, Hattie now also felt an immense weight of guilt concerning the fire in Levi's barn. Not only was her presence bringing trouble to her own home, but now she was negatively affecting the entire community. Except on one count, that is. She sorely realized that at least one positive turn had come from the fire. She would be forever thankful that the fateful blaze had interrupted her evening with Levi. She must never allow herself to be found in a similar predicament again.

Hattie had done her best to avoid the schoolmaster at all costs this morning, and yet he had still found her. She hoped no one noticed her annoyance when he insisted on helping today. Levi would be much better off if he remained far away from her, and Hattie planned to eagerly stay away from the Aid Fund booth for the remainder of the festival if he was around. It was hard to deal with the constant reminder of her incompetence that his face brought to mind.

"Hattie, it's your turn in the dunk tank now!"

Mary Miller tugged on her sleeve, her cheeks spread into an impish grin. Leah nodded knowingly and grabbed her other arm and began pulling her *schweschder* towards the main attraction.

"*Nee*, the dunk tank is set up for the *kinder* to enjoy. I couldn't possibly participate." Hattie's cheeks grew warm as they pulled her closer. It would hardly be proper for her to be sopping wet in front of the entire community.

"Please…for us?"

She looked past Mary's pleading eyes and across the sea of scholars which were planted firmly next to the dunking booth. It had been painstakingly filled with buckets of water from the underground spring nearby. Normally the Bishop would not allow water to be wasted in such a manner, but he gave his consent for this special occasion. Her class meant so much to her, and since she was leaving soon, she needn't worry about what type of impression she left on the community any longer. Besides, most folks would probably relish seeing her in such a state. Hattie reached down to pat Luke's head as she reluctantly took a step forward. Hattie abruptly realized that she would miss both him and Levi more than she cared to admit.

"*Ja*, alright. Let's get on with it."

The class erupted in a cheer as she took hold of her skirt and climbed to her seat. Once she reached the top, she berated herself for not admonishing Leah to stay close by during her turn. Frowning, she squinted into the crowd of *Englischers*. Her *onkel* could hide easily amongst the throng of festival-goers.

Nellie Stover took a step forward, holding a clutch of balls to her chest. Her muted green cape dress caused her emerald eyes to shine beneath her taut auburn hair. "Don't take this personally, Miss Hattie. We all would love the chance to dunk our favorite teacher, and it is all in *gut* fun."

She gasped, surprised by Nellie's words. Had her class grown fond of her? Both the teenagers like Nellie and the youngsters like Luke stood in a semi-circle around her, while whooping and hollering with glee. She had been so consumed by the rejection of local parents that she didn't realize she had made a good impression on the youngsters. "Do you really mean that?"

"*Ja*, I do." Taking a step back, Nellie threw the first ball towards the target. It barely missed, and whizzed into the coniferous forest behind the fundraiser.

She smiled. "I'll aim closer next time."

True to her word, she lined up the ball in her hand before releasing it with skill. It hit the center of the bullseye perfectly, and Hattie gasped in surprise as she sank into the tank of icy water.

She couldn't help but grin as the cheers of the *kinder* reached her ears once she broke the surface. She giggled as she grasped at her head to verify that her hair was still properly covered. Once this important detail was taken care of, Hattie rubbed her eyes, looking through the fogged glass of the tank while searching for Leah.

A familiar face flashed close to the tank, and Hattie shrank back in fear. Could her eyes be playing tricks on her? She rubbed them swiftly and looked closer.

Hattie let out a shriek as she began scrambling towards the ladder. She climbed the rungs two by two, hoping to escape the tank before it was too late. Her ankles seared with pain as she jumped to the ground, while deciding to forego the ladder which led to the ground entirely.

She gulped for air as she straightened, before letting out another shriek as a warm towel enveloped her.

"Hattie, whatever are you doing? What's wrong?"

She glanced upwards as terror gripped her features. She shook violently as a desperate cold reached the marrow of her bones. Levi stood next to her, solidly balancing her with his strong arms. "My...my *onkel*...my *daed's* brother...he's here! I must find Leah!"

His eyes narrowed. "Why would your *onkel* be in Deer Springs? Where is he?"

She lifted a shaking finger as she shrank behind his tall build.

"The older man wearing the cowboy hat and plaid shirt, there? The settler from Bozeman?"

"*Ja*, that's him." She swallowed the bile which had risen to her throat as her knees knocked together as she looked Henry over. Other than his clothing, he was just as she remembered him. His ragged face looked just like her *daed's* which was no surprise since they were twins. His lanky build slid through the crowd, as a crooked grin punctuated his features. His brown eyes were faded and his dark hair had grayed considerably from his youth. Simply seeing him took her breath away. Hattie was instantly transported back to her childhood, which was filled with both agony and fear when her *daed* and *onkel* became enticed to their strong drink.

Levi's eyes narrowed. "I thought you told me your *mamm's* family was *Englisch*. But now you have pointed out your *daed's* brother, who is clearly *Englisch* as well. You've been lying all along, haven't you? You aren't Amish at all."

Hattie clutched her throat, her voice having left her. As much as she would like to, now wasn't the time to argue her case. She was as surprised as Levi to see Henry dressed this way. Her *onkel* was born and raised Amish, and was living as such even as he tried his best to gain custody of Leah. Something wasn't right, and she intended to get to the bottom of it. But for now, all that mattered was that her *schweschder* was found safely. If her *onkel* intended to kidnap Leah, he must go through her first.

She shook loose of Levi's grasp and dropped the towel to the ground, despite the coolness of the day. "Leah!" She took in a deep breath, and yelled with all of her might. Her eyes darted from her left to her right, but she was nowhere to be found amongst the crowd of Amish and common settlers. She broke into a run, frantically rushing through the crowd. "Leah!"

The crowd grew quiet as they looked at her strangely. Wrenching sobs coursed through her shivering frame as she continued her search. Hattie reached the edge of the festivities, reluctantly turning from the calming evergreen forest which beckoned her to flee in fright. She would have if Leah was firmly in her grasp. She gasped as a strong hand wrapped around her forearm from behind, causing her to stop in her tracks.

"Are you Miss Hattie Fisher?"

She turned, and was suddenly face to face with a large man with steely blue eyes. His rugged jaw looked grim as he looked her over. She gazed at the dry ground and allowed her eyes to take him in, from his tall boots covered in dust to his wide-brimmed hat. At his chest sat an official badge, indicating his position of authority. She breathed a prayer for help as she finally gazed at the big Montana sky which was as clear as a bell, much unlike her clarity of mind at the moment.

Hattie shrank into herself, unsure of her fate as unanswered questions swirled through her mind. "*Ja*, I am."

The man grimaced while slowly pulling a pair of handcuffs from his back pocket. "I hate to be the bearer of bad news, but you are under arrest."

The crowd around her gasped as he gently pulled her arms behind her back before locking the handcuffs tightly around each of her tiny wrists. Hattie hung her head in shame. "Why am I being arrested? What have I done wrong?"

"You are headed to debtor's prison."

"To debtor's prison? There must be some sort of mistake, you see I…"

"What seems to be the problem, officer?"

Levi stepped next to Hattie, shooting her an incredulous look. Alarm filled his features. Her cheeks burned with embarrassment as she shuffled her practical shoes across the dust. Levi's grim countenance hurt her heart as he shook his head with red cheeks. What he must think of her now.

She continued to scan the crowd as Levi and the officer became deep in conversation. Everything moved in slow motion, and the cheerful fundraiser banners lost their sheen. Their words garbled together as her world started to spin. Hattie commanded herself to focus as her eyes darted across the field once again to search the crowd for Leah. She began to fully understand what was happening as her eyes shot up in surprise.

"It's a trap! It's all a trap! My *onkel* is here, and I believe he wants to kidnap my *schweschder*. He has arranged for me to be arrested so he can get away with her. Please let me go, and I'll lead you to the true suspect."

Levi laid a hand on Hattie's shoulder. "*Nee* Hattie, it isn't a trap. The officer here has a valid reason to arrest you. Now, you need to comply and I'll follow you to Bozeman so we can get this sorted out. As the schoolmaster, you are my charge."

"Come along, ma'am." The officer firmly began to pull her towards his waiting automobile.

"*Nee*, I must find my *schweschder*!" She dug in her heels, while realizing reluctantly that fighting against a police officer would likely cause her more harm than good. "She is in grave danger!"

The officer ignored her pleas and tightened his grip as he pushed through the crowd. Hattie locked eyes with Rose, who was staring at her incredulously with a hint of fear and mistrust.

"Rose, please look for Leah! She's in danger!"

The woman shrank into Elias, who had placed a supportive hand on her shoulder. The two locked eyes before Rose looked back to Hattie and nodded affirmatively.

"*Ja*, we'll try to find her."

Hattie held the soft promise close to her heart as she continued her walk of shame towards the police car. She tried her best to swallow the fear which had taken up residence in her chest, but in her heart, she knew the truth. Henry had done his due diligence, and Leah was as good as gone.

Chapter Thirteen

Levi did his best to ignore his irritation as he followed the trail of dust left by the Bozeman police. Automobiles were much faster than his horse and buggy, and for once in his life he wished he had been blessed with a quick way to town. He slapped the reins across his mare's back, guiding Dolly down the rutted road at a quicker pace. Levi hoped his mare would make the trip to town without any problems. He couldn't wait around for Jonathan Philpot's coach at a time like this.

Embarrassment about what had just transpired at the fundraiser seethed through him. He could hardly believe that Hattie had lied to him for all of this time about her Amish upbringing. One look at Henry Fisher proved it all to be a joke. What would cause her to act like she was someone she was not? His deception paled in comparison to her own.

To top the morning off, his charge was carted off to debtor's prison in front of the entirety of Deer Springs. She had brought shame not only to herself, but to him as well. A familiar, slow burning resentment seared inside of his chest. The officer clearly stated his case to him while Hattie was in another world. She had failed to pay off, or even make the necessary payments on, her mother's farm after her death. Officials of Pennsylvania sent word to

Bozeman that she was wanted and was expected to be sent back East as soon as possible.

Levi tried to keep his wits about him as he rounded the bend and the town of Bozeman came into view. A line of small businesses along with a few less-than-desirable establishments dotted the landscape. He tried his best to calm his mare as she wound her way around an assortment of both carriages and automobiles which were zooming around town too fast for his liking.

"What did you think about Hattie's *onkel*, girl? Do you think Leah is truly in danger?" Levi absentmindedly spoke to Dolly as his jaw clenched against the unrelenting traffic. While the schoolmarm had proven herself to be a liar, he couldn't deny the look of honest fear which had stained her features when her *onkel* came into view. Her eyebrows had raised like the nearby Rocky Mountain peaks. But why would Leah's own relative be a threat to her? It didn't make any sense.

He coughed on a mouthful of dust as a group of cowboys galloped through the center of town. By all appearances Henry Fisher seemed to be one of them. Hattie had a lot of explaining to do. He would likely never regain what little trust he had in her again.

Once his buggy neared the end of town he spotted the Bozeman Police Station on his right. Its brick facade framed a modest sign indicating he had reached his destination. The police car that had brought Hattie to town sat squarely at the entrance as a mocking reminder of what a fool he had been to hire her.

Levi pulled past the police station and jumped from his rig to attach it to the nearest hitching post. He quickly brushed down his mare and offered her a snack before trudging towards the double doored entrance. As the schoolmaster, Hattie was still his responsibility, even in this. He must fully understand her actions and give an account to the community. If not, he would surely be shunned during his confession.

He shuffled his feet and wiped his hands across his plain gray pants at the door, hoping to clean himself of the muck and mire his body had accumulated during the long journey to town. As a whoop from saloon-goers across the street rang in his ears, Levi was thankful that Deer Springs was secluded away from the noise of Bozeman.

A jingling bell tinkled over his head to announce his arrival when he swung the door open. He blinked his eyes as they slowly grew accustomed to the dim conditions inside of the station. Levi stepped up to the stark counter, feeling terribly out of place in this strange environment.

"Can I help you?" A short, stout man craned his neck above the counter, looking at Levi suspiciously. He raised one thick eyebrow in amusement. "We normally don't see the likes of two Amish folks in the station in a single day."

Levi shuffled his feet, fighting the urge to back up and leave the station far behind him. He eyed the man's badge, which was emblazoned with the name *Smith*. "*Ja*, I'm here to see Hattie Fisher. She was arrested earlier today at the festival in Deer Springs which was to benefit the Influenza Aid Fund."

"I'm not supposed to let civilians associate with our prisoners."

He bit the inside of his cheek as he thought of Hattie being labeled a 'prisoner.' He wished the Bishop would have followed Levi's instincts and sent Hattie off immediately instead of subjecting the town to her foolishness. "She is the schoolmarm in Deer Springs, and I am the schoolmaster. I must see her and try my best to figure out what is going on here."

The officer's brow furrowed. "If you're only a few minutes, I'll see what I can do. Please follow me to the back of the building."

Levi pulled at his suspenders as he followed the man through a set of swinging double doors. They passed by a handful of dank cells before the hallway widened into a larger room. A sweep of cool air brushed across the cinderblock walls and caused him to shiver. He never dreamed that Hattie would be a resident here.

"There she is. She should be booked and in her cell shortly, but go ahead and talk to her if you must."

His eyes followed the deputy's finger and darted to the side of the room. Cold metal chairs stood in a neat row. He swallowed hard to combat his unbelief when he finally spotted her. Hattie sat quietly between two burly men who looked like they had been put through the ringer. All three held their hands behind their backs, with handcuffs digging into their wrists. Hattie's *kapp* sat askew on her head and light brown tendrils of hair lapped at her shoulders. Her wide golden eyes spoke with depths of pain. She was quite a sight, and looked sorely out of place.

"I wish you wouldn't have come. I don't want you to see me like this."

"I had to come, Hattie. I must get to the bottom of your arrest for the town's sake. You have been living a lie, and as hard as this is, I'm thankful it is now out in the open. You have a lot of explaining to do."

She looked at him in unbelief as her rosy lips drew into a tight line. Tears began to pool in her eyes, causing their caramel hue to lighten.

"This fellow isn't bothering you, is he?"

Levi startled back as the man sitting to Hattie's left let out a low growl. "We don't take kindly to men being rude to ladies, do we Jeb?"

The other man with a sandy crop of hair nodded his head knowingly. "That's right, Leroy."

"Boys, don't worry about me, I can handle Levi Hilty here." Hattie's chin shot up in defiance as she stared the schoolmaster down. "Please worry about your own troubles and I'll tend to mine."

"Hattie Fisher, your cell is ready."

The stout officer motioned for Hattie to stand and follow him. "Right this way."

Levi awkwardly stepped around the troublesome twosome who remained in the back room while following Hattie towards her cell. The deputy roughly grabbed the keys by his side as he took her wrists in his hands. With practiced precision, he loosened the cuff's hold before motioning for her to step foot into the tiny cell. She quietly followed his instructions as small tears squeezed from the corners of her eyes. Hattie meekly took a seat on the cot which lined the edge of the wall as the man shut and locked the cell with finality.

"I'll give you just another minute, but you must speak to Miss Fisher through the bars." The deputy patted Levi's shoulder in sympathy as he headed back towards the reception area. "I'm sorry I had to lock you up, ma'am."

She nodded quietly while looking down into her open palms. Levi noticed the last beams of sunlight streaming through the tiny window above her, causing her exposed skin to radiate brightly through the dust.

"I'm going to ask my question again, and this time, I expect an answer. What is going on here?"

Her eyes shot up indignantly. "Why should I waste my breath? I know without a shadow of a doubt that you wouldn't believe me."

He huffed out a grunt, annoyed by her continued avoidance of his question. She must be guilty if she wasn't willing to be forthright with him. He was reminded of Rhoda, and the way she always liked to do the same. Up until her last day in Deer Springs, she would always sidestep Levi's questions or ideas. Hattie was obviously just like her. He was a terrible judge of character, most likely because he lacked strength of character himself.

"Whether I believe you or not is beside the point. I must hear your side of the story. Now."

She shuddered before leaning into the cot and muffling a sob into the thin pillow. "I'm not sure if I could think clearly enough to tell you my story now if my life depended on it. All that I can think about is my Leah and her safety. I'm afraid she is gone forever."

Befuddled, Levi leaned against the cool metal bars which kept Hattie from his reach. There she goes talking about Leah again. Could she really be in danger? His brow shot up as he put a few small clues together. He had thought that the problems at Hattie's home, the school *haus*, and his barn were all somehow linked to past acquaintances from Bozeman. To a past courtship or romantic relationship. He was so suspicious of the schoolmarm, that he never feared Leah's safety might be in jeopardy. But was she the cause of all this trouble the whole time? A heap of worry fell onto him as he remembered with fondness the many hours little Leah spent beside him at his farm. He couldn't bear the thought of harm coming her way.

"I need you to collect your thoughts, Hattie. This is important."

"*Ja*, I know it is. I just fear we are too late."

He wished he could reach through the bars and gently shake some sense into her. "It will only be too late if you refuse to cooperate and let me know what is truly going on here." He spoke his words quietly, hoping that his persistence would bring her back to reality. He needed to know the root of the Fishers' problems immediately.

"You know who was causing all of the trouble around Deer Springs, don't you?"

Her eyes narrowed as she wearily sank against the wall. "*Ja*, I surely do. In fact, without a shadow of a doubt now."

"Details, Hattie. I need details."

She signed at his impatience as she hiccupped against a rising sob. "If I tell you my story, will you do whatever you can to help us? I know we shouldn't make vows, but Leah's in a heap of trouble. Will you give me your word?"

He swallowed hard, wondering if agreeing to Hattie's request would be wise. His continual absence of judgment and own lack of strength caused him to question this very simple question. Would he be able to help her, and besides that, should he if he could?

Setting aside his trepidation, he nodded slowly while glaring at the cinderblock wall. "You have my word."

Hattie squeezed her eyes shut as she once again leaned against the pillow inside of the dark jail cell, wilting inside. She could hardly believe this was happening. The tall officer was fairly quiet during the drive to Bozeman, but she was able to pry the cause of her arrest out of him.

Apparently, the funds she had forwarded to her *mamm's* bank in Lancaster had been intercepted before reaching the institution. After sending an abundance of late notices to her past address in Bozeman, the bank reluctantly turned the case over to local authorities, who called for her arrest. She had all of her mail forwarded to her new address in Deer Springs, and yet the late notices from Lancaster Community Bank never reached her hands. Her brow wrinkled in disgust. Someone had intercepted the late notices as well, and she believed she knew exactly who was behind both forms of trickery. Henry Fisher.

"Hattie? Are you alright?"

She reluctantly opened one eye as she peered warily at Levi. She could hardly believe that she was stuck in such a predicament, and in front of her employer no less. She gulped back the lump which had formed in her throat as she thought of her *schweschder*, who was probably doing far worse than she. Levi had promised to help her if she told him her story. Would he keep his word? Numbness crawled across her limbs.

"I'm waiting."

"I know, I know. Please give me a moment to compose myself." She took a ragged breath as she wiped her face with the back of her hand. She breathed in deeply, inhaling the cool wetness of the jail cell before she began.

"I must start at the very beginning for you to truly understand the gravity of my concerns. Does this suit you?"

He tapped his foot impatiently while nodding quickly. She looked away from his chocolate eyes, fearing she would lose her train of thought.

"Well then, it all started when my *mamm* was just a young woman. She was an *Englischer*, and her father owned a large lumber yard in Philadelphia. As I've told you before, her family was very wealthy and could offer her anything she ever hoped for, and yet she longed for a simpler way of life. She often found herself wandering the countryside near Lancaster County whenever she could break away from her social obligations in Philadelphia society."

"How does your story relate to all of this, Hattie?" Levi motioned across the interior of the police station to emphasize his words.

"I'm getting there. During one of her secret excursions, she came across my *daed*, Joshua Fisher, who was an Amish man. Once he realized her wealthy connections to the large lumber yard in Philadelphia, he swept her off her feet. Unfortunately, she didn't realize that he was simply leading her on to access her large dowry and family connections. He and his twin *bruder*, Henry, were trying to get their building business off the ground. She seemed to be the ticket to success they were looking for."

Levi leaned against the cinder blocks as he crossed his arms in front of him. His eyebrows pushed together, as if deep in thought.

She took a deep breath before continuing. "My *mamm* converted to the Amish faith and took her kneeling vow in order to marry my *daed*. It wasn't long thereafter that she discovered his plan, along with his addiction to alcohol and abusive habits. She was a strong woman, and decided to do whatever she could to keep her dowry and inheritance out of his hands. Once she gave birth to me she set up a trust at the local bank bequeathing all of her funds to me and any subsequent children upon her own death. My *daed* was livid to have his dream of my *mamm* funding a successful business slip away from him, to say the least."

"Hattie, I'm so sorry you and Leah had to endure all of this."

She waved his concerns away. "Don't be. We've all had our troubles in life, *ja*? Let me continue on, then. My *daed* and *onkel's* business floundered in their unsteady hands, and they believed all of the blame fell squarely on my *mamm's* shoulders. We all paid heavily for their troubles and financial worries. You see, they took out several sizable bank loans which they never could pay off. We were literally drowning in debt. After my *daed* died due to his alcoholism, my *mamm* was left to pay off his debt. Specifically their farm. The many years of abuse had taken their toll on her, and she was very frail, and unable to work. She also was unable to touch her own money, since it was allocated solely to my *schweschder* and I and locked up tight in Lancaster Community Bank. I felt to blame for her predicament, and eagerly answered an advertisement for a teacher's assistant job out West when I saw the call for help at the local ice cream parlor."

"But why is your *onkel* after Leah?" Levi removed his hat to scratch the top of his head.

"Almost one year ago, my *mamm* died. She didn't die of natural causes, but was murdered. She died due to a blow to the head, and was found in a nearby *Englischer's* field." She traced the outline of a cinder block with her finger, mustering up the strength to continue. "Almost directly after her murder my *onkel* petitioned the court to grant him full custody of my Leah. I fought it of course, and by *Gott's* grace I was named my sister's guardian while still living in Montana. Henry was none too happy, and his correspondence through the court was downright threatening. His persistence along with some of his words has led me to believe that he was responsible for my *mamm's* death, and now he is after my Leah. I had hoped Deer Springs would offer us a form of refuge, but I obviously wasn't careful in covering my tracks once I decided to move."

Her final words came out in a soft whisper, before the gravity of her sister's predicament caused her to shoot to her feet and begin pacing the small stall.

"Levi, we must do something! I had paid off the debt in full once I was given access to my *mamm's* inheritance, but someone intercepted it before it reached the bank. I do not belong in this prison cell. My *Onkel*

Henry is no *Englischer*, and yet he was dressed as one today for a reason I haven't yet figured out. My *schweschder* is in danger, and I must find her!"

Hattie leaned against the cool metal bars as she wrapped her fingers tightly around them. Her skin prickled as warm hands enveloped her own. Eyes wide, she looked up at Levi as deep concern shone from his face. He was so close that she could feel his breath tickle her cheek.

"If what you're telling me is the full and honest truth, then something must be done. But I'm sorry to say, I'm not the one to do it."

"What are you saying? You said you would help if I told you everything I knew. You don't plan on going back on your word, do you?"

His eyes clouded over as he gently squeezed her hands before slowly pulling away. I'm not strong enough to do any *gut* here. I've let more people down in my life than I can count, and I can't be trusted to help you like I ought."

She thought back to the many times Levi had proven his worth to anyone who needed him in Deer Springs. Despite his distrust, he had always been there for her and Leah. The way he put up with Jonas just to have access to Luke never ceased to warm her heart. She toyed with the strings of her heart-shaped prayer covering as she leaned away in thought.

"Whatever are you talking about?"

"My entire childhood I never could do anything right. My *aenti* made sure that I remembered my failings at every turn. And she was right. As soon as I moved West and met the woman who I thought was to be my *frau*, she left me. If you trust me to find and help Leah, I will just let you down, too."

Her mouth hung open as his words sank through her.

"Levi, I know you've been hurt in the past. But you must realize that your *aenti's* and Rhoda's actions only indicate a lack of strength on their part. I believe in you, and in your ability to help me."

He shuffled from side to side, looking awfully uncomfortable as he blew out a ragged breath. She slipped her arm through the bars, and held her outstretched hand towards his.

"Please Levi, you must try. I won't hold you accountable if Leah is not found. I have a sinking suspicion that Leah is in Henry's grasp as we speak, and if there is a chance he is still in the area..."

Her voice trailed off as he raised his face to hers with a renewed sense of certainty. He reached through the bars and grasped her small hand in his own.

"I don't know if I can help, but I will try my best to find Leah. The thought of her being in danger hurts my heart. I've grown to care for the girl."

Renewed hope shot through Hattie. "Really, Levi?"

"Really."

She prayed a silent prayer for a fruitful search as she pulled away from his grasp. "I will speak to the deputy about getting this all sorted out as soon as possible. I still have a sizable part of my inheritance left, that is, if it hasn't been wiped out by Henry. I'll see if the money can be wired to clear my name as soon as possible."

"In the meantime, I'll head back to Deer Springs and see what I can do. They couldn't have gone too far within the course of a day."

"Please hurry. If we only had an inkling as to where Henry might be hiding. I highly doubt that he planned my *schweschder*'s abduction all on his own. He must have had an accomplice."

As soon as the words left her mouth Levi's eyes widened in understanding. "*Ja*, I think you're right. And I might know just where your *onkel* is hiding."

Hattie jumped as the thick door leading towards the lobby swung open and Deputy Smith stepped close to her jail cell.

He looked pointedly at Levi. "I hate to say this, but your time is up. I hope you found the answers you were looking for because you must be on your way."

"You're just the man I hoped to see. There has been a possible kidnapping in Deer Springs, and I'm in need of your help."

The officer's eyes widened in surprise. "A kidnapping, you say? Deer Springs is usually as quiet as a mouse. Follow me to my office so I can make a quick report before we are on our way."

Hattie's eyes trailed across the outline of Levi's back as he followed the deputy down the hall. She was ever so thankful that the schoolmaster would have an officer along to help. She was also grateful for the speed of a police automobile. They would surely arrive at the Amish community in less than half of the time it would take Levi's horse and buggy.

She sank onto the cot, hoping another officer would be available to help her sort out her wrongful imprisonment shortly. While she hoped that Levi could apprehend her *onkel*, she would not rest until her *schweschder* was safe in her own arms. She hoped they were still in Deer Springs, and that Levi would know just where to find them.

Chapter Fourteen

Adrenaline pulsed through Levi's veins as he clutched onto the side of the automobile. His knuckles turned white with determination as the police car edged closer and closer to Deer Springs. The weather had once again grown cold, and snowflakes dotted the windshield as the vehicle sputtered along.

"How are you holding up back there?" Deputy Smith's words were garbled as he navigated a sharp curve. "I'm sorry you are riding in the back like a criminal."

"I'm as well as can be expected." Levi settled into the seat, wondering what Hattie must have felt like while in this position only a few hours ago. After listening to her story at the police station, Levi felt even worse about seeking out a new schoolmarm behind her back. He grumbled quietly to himself. *How was I supposed to know about the troubles which led her to Deer Springs in the first place?*

Yet another bump jarred his senses. "It won't be much longer until we arrive, *ja?*"

The officer looked rattled as he pushed the pedal to the floor. "Nope, not long at all. Hopefully we will be able to apprehend the criminal before he leaves town with the girl. Are you sure you know where to find him?"

"Pretty sure." It didn't take Levi long to put the pieces of Hattie's puzzle together once he heard her story. Henry must have found a place to stay in Deer Springs which was near to the Fisher's *haus*, and he suspected that he knew just who was harboring the suspect. Himself.

Deputy Smith turned his automobile to the left once he entered the township of Deer Springs and he continued to speed down the main thoroughfare through town. After passing the local mercantile and several farms, he slowed once the school *haus* came into view. Turning off his headlights, he crept up the remainder of the road before cutting his motor near the gate which led to Levi's home. The two men jumped out of the car and began to climb the hill on foot, hoping Henry had not realized they were closing in on him.

Levi led the way as his heart pounded in his throat. Leah must be found safe, or he would never forgive himself. By now, the ground was blanketed by a quiet white covering, but it held none of the beauty which was evident when he held Hattie tight in his barn.

He slowed once he topped the hill and then trudged on towards the valley below. Nestled quietly into the hillside sat a small outbuilding, which he had built to eventually house a handful of employees. Just as Levi suspected, a flickering light shined from the window of the bunkhouse, letting him know that it was presently occupied.

The two men hunched down while the officer drew the gun which had sat by his side in its holster. Levi walked slowly as Deputy Smith motioned for him to remain quiet. The officer crept towards the door while Levi held back. He watched his shoulders rise and fall in determination before he raised his leg and kicked the front door with all of his might.

"Hands up, everyone, hands up!" Deputy Smith's voice bellowed from his stout frame as he charged through the door which was hanging by a hinge. Levi jumped into action, and followed directly behind him. He kicked aside a plethora of open bottles as he waded into the bunkhouse.

Utterly disgusted, he wrinkled his nose. His once clean outbuilding was now littered with garbage, and soiled clothing was strewn about. Obviously Henry had been using it for quite some time. He forced his gaze away from the mess while he searched for Leah. Was she still there, or was it too late?

A quiet yelp sounded from the rear of the bunkhouse and the two men wasted no time scurrying towards the noise. Levi knew that the rear door would be an easy escape, and he berated himself for not being mindful enough to secure the back exit while the officer broke through the front. If they escaped, it would be all his fault.

Not wasting any time, Levi spun around in his tracks and headed back through the front door. He nearly fell to the ground as he turned the corner at the rear of the bunkhouse, watching as puffs of his warm breath billowed into the air like smoke. He grabbed the back edge of the building, trying to propel himself forward as fast as he could.

Levi could hear the door knob rattling as he jogged past the embankment and towards the back door. Thinking only of Leah's need, he wedged himself into the doorframe and braced himself for impact.

The door opened with force as a dark figure crushed into his body. *Thump.* Ricocheting off of him, Henry Fisher fell back into the dim light of the bunkhouse.

"Levi, please help me!" Leah cried out past her capture as her pleading eyes caught on his. She laid sprawling on the cool ground of the soddy structure.

Having broken free from Henry's tight grasp, she scrambled into a corner and curled herself into a ball.

Sorrow pulsed through Levi as he realized Hattie had been right. Both she and Leah had been through so much, and he had only made things worse by not trusting her. He fought the urge to run to Leah's side, and instead continued to block the exit.

"So boss, it looks like you finally caught onto us. It took you long enough."

Levi glared past Henry's head and stared directly into Jonas' jeer. "How dare you take advantage of my kindness? I offered you and Luke a way to better yourself, and this is how you repay me?" His jaw twitched as he surveyed the back room. "Speaking of Luke, where is the boy?"

"I'm right here." The towheaded child peeked out from behind an overturned table. "I'm sorry Levi, I knew my *onkel* was up to no *gut*, but he made me promise not to tell." His voice grew soft as he cowered a little lower.

"It's not your fault, Luke. Don't hold yourself accountable." Levi felt the pain he had experienced as a young *kind* fly through him yet again. After verifying that Deputy Smith had taken up the rear and there was no way of escape, he zeroed in on Hattie and Leah's *onkel*. His jaw twitched as he took in the scrawny excuse of a man. His shifty eyes spoke volumes. Levi planted his feet firmly into the ground and prayed Henry wouldn't make any sudden moves.

"So, we finally meet face to face. You've given me a lot of trouble, you know."

Henry's words came out in a raspy gravel. Confusion squeezed his stomach as he returned the man's glare.

"What do you mean, 'I gave you a lot of trouble?' Don't you understand the pain and suffering you've put Hattie through?"

"*Ach*, who cares about Hattie? The child has brought nothing but problems since she came along and my sister-in-law decided to take my money and give it to her. Do you know how much debt I'm in now?" He grinned slyly while tipping his cowboy hat. "I have the chance to finally live the *gut* life if I can keep possession of this youngster here since Temperance is out of the picture. In case you didn't figure it out already, I was behind that too. The police blamed her death on an *Englischer*, but I was the one who killed her before dragging her body to a far off field."

Levi clutched the side of the doorframe as Leah began to cry. Luke scooted over and gently laid a hand on her shoulder.

"I followed Leah here on the train and Hattie was none the wiser. I had planned to quickly snatch both girls, but you made it impossible. Your protection was more than I could handle on my own, and I knew I needed an insider's help. I asked Hattie's friend to hire me in Bozeman, but he saw right through me. At least I was able to find some clothing which would help throw you off my track while I was in town. When I figured it would be better for me to stay close to Deer Springs anyhow, I found *gut* 'ole Jonas here wandering around outside during some sort of meeting at the school *haus*."

"During the open *haus*." Levi's thoughts flew about as he tried his best to determine the crux of the problem.

"*Ja*, that's right. He did a mighty *gut* job of getting hired on by you so quick like. I offered him part of the large chunk of change I intercepted when Hattie made the bank transfer to pay off my twin's debt if he could deliver the girls to me. He came close during the singing. I was ready to snatch Leah from her bedroom window when I got word that Jonas failed to bring me Hattie. I decided then and there that setting your barn ablaze might be fun.

After all, it was so close to home." He stood to his feet and patted the side of the soddy appreciatively.

"You'll never get away with this."

A sly smile curved his crooked jaw.

"Watch me. This isn't over yet. I won't rest until I get my hands on *both* of the Fisher girls."

With that, Henry sprung towards Leah while she screamed in fear. Levi jumped into action. With long strides, he quickly closed the gap between himself and the child before he folded himself over her in protection. A shot rang out while shattered glass fell to the ground. Deputy Smith bellowed for Henry and Jonas to stay put and hold their hands up.

Prickles of sweat soaked through Levi's skin as footsteps clambered out the exit. The room grew quiet as he regained his breath. He coughed through the gunpowder as he slowly lifted his body away from the quivering child. "Leah, are you alright?"

"*Ja*, I think so. I never would have guessed that my *Onkel* Henry was such a scoundrel." She shook violently. "I want Hattie."

A small figure crumbled into his side. "Luke, I'm so glad you're still here."

"Jonas left me, just like my *mamm* and *daed* did when they died. Who's gonna take care of me now?"

Levi grew silent as he listened closely. The frigid wind blew in a flurry of snowflakes, but aside from the whistling breeze all was quiet. He rose to his feet and clutched both youngsters by the hand before stepping carefully over piles of trash and sticking his head through the back door. The snow was falling hard and heavy, and he couldn't make out the figures of Henry, Jonas, or Deputy Smith through the white haze.

"What's gonna happen next, Levi?"

"I don't know, *kinder*. I just don't know."

With a tight grasp on both of the youngster's arms, he quickly trudged away from the crime scene and brought them to the safety of the police car. He joined them after ushering the two into the back seat and firmly locking the door. He was glad to bring Leah back to Hattie, but several problems remained. Her *onkel* was still at large, Hattie was in jail, and how would he ever explain to her that he had been harboring the enemy all of this time?

Hattie wrung her hands together as the day broke. She had barely slept a wink on the terribly uncomfortable cot, but she knew that sleep would have still eluded her if she was sleeping inside of the most comfortable hotel in all of Montana. After giving the deputy in charge her bank account information and asking that he wire the information to the police station in Lancaster, she paced her small cell until finally collapsing onto the cot in pure exhaustion. Hattie realized that until her *schweschder* was found safe and sound, she would likely get no rest.

"Miss Fisher?" Deputy Miller stepped next to her cell and skillfully unlocked the door before swinging it open wide. "We just received word that the needed funds were in your bank account, and the transfer is imminent. You are free to go."

Relief spilled over her as she rose on shaky knees. "*Ach*, I'm so happy to hear it. I need to return to Deer Springs as quickly as possible."

"Well now, I'm not sure if you will be returning to Deer Springs anytime soon. There was quite a snowfall last night, and I doubt your buggy could make the trip."

Her brow furrowed in desperation. She must try to make her way to Leah, if she hadn't already been taken out of the area. "What do you suggest then? My *schweschder* is in trouble, and I want to do what I can to help."

"I doubt there is anything you can do, miss. If you'd like, you are more than welcome to stay put…in the lobby that is, until Deputy Smith returns with word about the kidnapping. He left over fifteen hours ago, and even with the treacherous road conditions, I suspect he will be back shortly. I apologize for not sending reinforcement to help in the search, but we are short staffed as it is. The sheriff along with most of our officers are away to help with the recovery effort after the mining accident in Butte. Deer Springs is usually such a peaceful place, and we aren't used to having to supply officers to your area."

"It's alright. Thank you for filling me in." She shook back a sob as she clasped her hands over her face. While Levi had vowed to help find Leah, she couldn't help but wonder if he had truly gone through with it. He didn't seem too keen on the idea when she pleaded for his assistance the night before.

Deputy Miller shot her a pained smile as he led her towards the lobby. She glanced out a small window wistfully. The town had turned quiet and was blanketed in a winter wonderland, while it was still only mid-fall. Was Leah enjoying the scenery, or was she already farther south by now? She clumsily slid into a chair as the world around her grew numb.

A few hours later, the sputtering of an automobile engine perked her ears. The town had been quiet all morning. Could it be? Hattie pushed back from her chair, and wiped her sweaty hands on her black every day apron. Standing on tiptoe, she looked out of the foggy window. Sure enough, a worn police car was driving down the street. She trembled in trepidation as it came to a stop directly in front of the station.

The passenger side door jarred open and Hattie held her breath, hoping beyond hope that Leah would emerge. When Levi stepped out of the door on shaky legs, an involuntary sigh of gratitude rushed through her. Dark shadows creased the bottom of his eyes and his clothing was blackened with mire.

Slowly, he reached his hand inside, offering someone assistance. Hattie's eyes grew wide as Leah stepped out, in the same condition as Levi. The girl rushed towards the police station, and Hattie swung the door open wide, beckoning for her to come in.

Light shined from her eyes. "Hattie!" The young girl's squeal held both a mix of fear and delight as she flew into her sister's arms. They fell into each other while the schoolmarm led her to the row of chairs and they sank down in exhaustion. Hattie righted her sister's lopsided *kapp* while stroking her hair.

"There, there dear one. You're safe now."

"I was dazed when *Onkel* Henry grabbed my arm and dragged me away at the fundraiser. At first, I didn't even recognize him. I was so scared when he clasped his hand over my mouth."

She paused to shudder violently. "After I realized it was our *onkel*, I thought that perhaps he was trying to surprise us. But I quickly found out he had other plans in mind. He and Jonas were talking about taking me to California, and I tried my best to escape. Then they tied me to a chair so they could pack. If Levi hadn't come to save me, I would be long gone by now. Why would our *onkel* do such a thing?"

The child let her tears flow freely as Levi and Luke quietly stepped into the police station. She couldn't help but wonder what role the schoolmaster played in Leah's rescue. He had saved them…yet again. Her caramel eyes followed his every move as he wearily fell into a chair on the opposite side of the room. How could she ever repay him?

"So Jonas had something to do with this?"

"*Ja*, he did."

Hattie fumed inside as her suspicions of his sorry nature were confirmed yet again. "I expect our *onkel* and Jonas will be led to their cell at any moment. We can step away for a time if it would be too difficult for you to face them again."

"They won't be led to a jail cell, Hattie. They got away."

She clutched her *schweschder* tightly as the blood flowed from her face. "They got away?"

Leah nodded forlornly. "They did. I hate that they weren't caught, but right now I'm just so thankful I'm not on a train headed to California that I don't even care."

Hattie grew silent as a shiver ran down her spine. It was difficult to relish her sister's safety when she knew danger was still close at hand.

Deputy Smith pushed through the front door while dusting snow from his boots. "Hattie, I'm happy to see that you've been released. Did you get your financial problem worked out?"

Hattie smiled in spite of herself. Over the past twenty-four hours she had formed quite the comradery with the officers at the Bozeman Police Station. "*Ja*, I did. I will never recover the funds which were originally stolen, but at least I am no longer under arrest."

"That's good to hear." His face turned grim as he stuffed his hands deep into his pockets. "I wasn't able to apprehend the suspects. They made a run for it during the snowstorm, and I lost them. After searching for a good two hours, I returned from the woods to start the long drive back to Bozeman. It took much longer than usual due to the snow."

"*Danke* for trying. I know the conditions must have been difficult for you." Her voice grew soft as she pictured her *onkel* and Jonas alone in the Montana wilderness. Would they leave well enough alone, or circle back and try to kidnap Leah again?

"Once I realized they were long gone, I knew we had a few things to talk about before going any further. The police report for Leah's kidnapping is no longer valid since she is again in your care. If either you or Levi officially file a police report for the vandalism he caused to your property, I'll be able to obtain back up as well as a warrant for their arrest. What do you say?"

Hattie gazed down at Leah as she memorized her sister's every feature. "I...I don't know if I can do that. I do not wish any form of revenge on my *onkel*, I only want him to leave us be. As an Amish woman, I've committed to live a life of non-resistance. I'm not sure if obtaining a warrant for Henry Fisher's arrest would be the right thing to do. After all, my Leah is safe with me now, at least for the time being." Pursing her lips, she kept her eyes from Levi's questioning look. "It is not the Amish way to persecute or repay evil for evil, so leaving Deer Springs for *gut* is our only choice."

Deputy Smith flinched as he ran his hand through his patch of wild hair. "I'm not sure if that's the best idea, Miss Fisher. Without a warrant from your testimony, there is only so much I can do. Regardless of what you decide, we will be patrolling the area as soon as the snow thaws. Your uncle has given me reason to believe that he's dangerous, and we don't need the likes of him in Deer Springs nor Bozeman."

A sudden look of understanding dawned on his face while he snapped his fingers. "Wait just a minute. Please excuse me while I wire the Lancaster Police. I think they just might issue a warrant for Mr. Fisher's arrest if you are not willing to file a report."

The deputy shuffled away quickly as Levi cleared his throat. She stared him down, surprised by the spark of excitement she had felt when he first entered the police station. Shutting down her beating heart, she decided to voice the serious question which must be asked.

"So, Jonas left the boy?"

Levi looked down at Luke, who was leaning into his shoulder. His heavy eyes could stay open no longer, and his eyelashes kissed his cheeks as a soft snore brushed from his mouth. "*Ja*, he did. I can believe it, and yet it still surprises me. He doesn't have to worry about a place to go, though. He can stay in my home for as long as he'd like."

A warmth spread through Hattie's abdomen as she stared at the two men, one strong and tall, and one frail and small, sitting before her. Levi was a *gut* man after all, and Luke was lucky to have him. How could she ever thank him for saving her Leah?

"Until Henry is found, I would like for you and Leah to remain here in town. Perhaps we can arrange for you to stay with your friend Marjorie for a time."

Hattie raised her eyebrows in surprise. "He very well might never be found, and Leah and I should probably be on our way out of town before he has the chance to follow us again. I just need to stop by our home to pick up a few necessities first."

Levi squeezed his eyes shut in frustration. "You don't understand, Hattie. Deer Springs is much too dangerous for you right now. Your *onkel* was lurking right under your nose."

"What are you saying?"

He opened his eyes wide and implored her to keep her gaze steady on him. "I don't know how to say this, but I was harboring your enemy all of this time. Henry enlisted Jonas to help him attempt to kidnap Leah, and then he took up residence in my very own bunkhouse. I'm sorry Hattie. I didn't know."

The room began to grow dim. "Is that all?"

"No, there's more. Henry admitted to killing your *mamm*, which is why Deputy Smith is hoping to receive a warrant from Lancaster. And he wasn't interested in kidnapping only Leah. He's been after you all of this time, too."

She choked back a mix of anger, fear, and frustration as he rose to his feet.

"I have no time to lose, and I'm going to see if I can wire the Parsons immediately. I believe Luke will be safe here. Would you mind keeping an eye on him while I'm gone?"

She nodded silently.

"*Gut*. I'll be back as soon as I can."

He offered her a farewell nod before the door slammed shut behind him. Hattie felt fear press around her as she took in the two youngsters left in her care. She had been such a fool. How did she not realize that her *onkel* had been staying right under her nose, ready to pounce on both she and Leah as soon as he had the chance? While she didn't believe Levi had anything to do with it, the fact that her *onkel* was hiding on her employer's property still stung. She wouldn't be able to forget the irony in Henry's betrayal for quite some time.

"We're always going to be together, right Hattie?" Leah drowsily asked. She felt the child grow heavy as her head rested on her shoulder.

"I hope so, dear one. I hope so."

Chapter Fifteen

"Have we almost made it?"

"*Ja*, Arthur's ranch is just around the next bend."

Levi sat straight as a stick next to Hattie as he led Dolly through the muddy slush. They had been forced to stay at the police station until the snow and ice lining the hills which climbed towards Deer Springs had adequately melted. He had feared that by now, Henry and Jonas were far from the area, although they were traveling by foot. There was no telling what the two scoundrels were capable of.

"How long before Leah and I can come home? I doubt Henry is still hanging around, and I want to leave Montana as quickly as possible."

His heart pinched at the thought of the two of them leaving, and he couldn't help but chuckle to himself when he realized that is exactly what he wanted all along.

"What's so funny?" Hattie eyed him cautiously as she threw her gaze into the back of the buggy for the tenth time since they had left the Bozeman city limits. She was definitely taking her duty as Leah's watchful *schweschder* seriously.

"Don't worry about it." It wasn't the time nor place to tell the schoolmarm what was troubling him. Her mind was fully occupied with worry concerning her *onkel*, and rightly so.

"I'm looking forward to staying with Marjorie and Arthur for a spell. We had such a *gut* time when you two were at the singing. And I've never been inside a fancy home before. I wonder what it will be like." Leah's eyes shined in anticipation despite her predicament. Levi was glad the girl had something to look forward to after her harrowing ordeal at his bunkhouse.

"I'm glad you had fun with Marjorie and Arthur, and I'm sure they will enjoy seeing you again, too."

"*Ja*, Levi should take you to another singing sometime so the Parsons can stop by again."

Hattie visibly flinched before staring straight ahead with a faraway look in her eyes. "I doubt I will ever attend another singing. Let's discuss something else, please."

Levi's grip tightened on the reins as he noticed her growing discomfort. While he hadn't been too keen on taking the schoolmarm to the singing either, in the end, it had been...rather nice.

Whenever he accompanied Rhoda to the Deer Springs singings, she had made sure all attention was on her. Hattie carried herself completely differently, and her quiet humility was like a breath of fresh air on a warm summer's day. Despite her humble and kind nature, she wasn't afraid to stand for what was right, and be a voice for justice and truth. He sighed within himself. The more he learned about Hattie, the more she intrigued him.

His thoughts were interrupted when he spotted a large home rising in the distance against the backdrop of snow-capped rocky mountain peaks. "Is that Arthur's ranch?"

"The one and the same. I stopped by on occasion since some of his hands had *kinder* who were in my class when I was a teacher in Bozeman. I was able to connect with the scholar's families on a more personal level when I made home visits."

He shook his head in astonishment. Of course the schoolmarm had to give him yet another reason to admire her. Leaving Hattie, Leah, and Luke behind at the Parson's homestead was going to be difficult, but he had serious business that needed to be tended to.

Levi's wagon wheels sliced through a mixture of sludge and snow as he urged his mare to curve into Arthur's long driveway. He eyed the home before him in awe. The large building was constructed completely out of hand-hewn logs. Four separate rock fireplaces sat at each corner of the house, and dainty tendrils of smoke puffed out of each one. Three automobiles were visible inside of the closest barn, which was a good indication of the wealth that abounded on this large ranch.

"So, Arthur wanted to court you some time ago?"

"*Ja*, but I always refused. While I believe Arthur to be harmless, he had an air of pride about him that I found very distasteful. Wealth has a way of doing that to folks, I guess. Besides, finding a husband has never been on my to-do list. I guess I'll be a spinster for the rest of my life, since I'm just like my *mamm*."

He winced as his wheels squealed to a stop next to the hitching rail closest to the home. He hated to think that Hattie's fear of not being able to produce a large Amish family would keep her from wanting to marry. Her kind heart and strong spirit would be a tremendous benefit to any Amish man.

Hattie alighted from the buggy and reached inside to assist Leah. The girl took her hand and jumped quickly to the ground as a swirl of thin snow cover puffed up around their feet. They exchanged a knowing smile as she planted a firm kiss on the girl's forehead.

"This reminds me of our fun times in Lancaster, *ja*? Do you remember sledding for hours on end before I left for Montana? I know you were such a young *kind*, and your memory might not serve you well."

"I do remember Hattie. Do you think we can sled here at the ranch?"

"We'll have to see dear one, but I'll be sure to ask Marjorie. The snow is melting quickly, and we might not get our chance."

Levi saw through Hattie's shaky smile as he realized what she was doing. He agreed that keeping Leah's mind off of her *onkel* and Jonas was the best thing to do, and he decided to keep the conversation going.

"How about you, Luke? Do you enjoy the snow?"

"I surely do. And do you know what my favorite part is? Snowball fights!"

With that, Luke formed a snowball in his small hands and threw it at Leah who squealed with delight. The adults humored the fun until they reached the stairs leading to the front door of the massive home.

"Leah, *kumme* here. Now please." Hattie's gaze darted quickly from side to side as she motioned for her *schweschder* to join them on the front porch.

Levi frowned inside, sorry for her distress. Worrying about her sister being taken from her at any moment must be such a large burden to bear. He shuffled his boots, mustering a bit of courage to ask Hattie an important question.

"Do you think Marjorie would mind having an extra mouth to feed…I would like to leave Luke with you for the time being."

Hattie's mouth puckered in disgust. "What are you saying? I thought you planned on tending to Luke like he was your own. You are quick to back away from your *gut* intentions, aren't you?"

He sighed in exasperation. "*Nee*, I have full intentions of caring for the boy for the rest of my life if need be. But I have some business to tend to in Deer Springs."

"What business do you have that would keep you from watching the boy? I don't understand."

"Dangerous business. I do not want to put Luke in harm's way."

She pulled Leah close to her side, while her eyes brightened in surprise. "What are you saying?"

"I'm saying that I plan on accompanying Deputies Smith and Miller to Deer Springs to help them look for Henry and Jonas."

"You can't be serious. Leah is safe now, and they are dangerous. Why put yourself in this predicament if you don't have to?"

He sighed while gazing across Arthur's ranch. When he came face to face with Henry in his bunkhouse he couldn't help but feel repulsed by everything he had put Hattie through. The young schoolmarm had done nothing to deserve this man's wrath, and Levi knew he must do everything in his power to stop him from ever hurting her again. It was the least he could do since he had been harboring her *onkel*. He turned to her, and traced the outline of her soft features with his eyes. Come next week, he would be asked to stand in front of the church and confess his own shortcomings to Hattie. He had been such a fool to let his own past stain his opinion of Hattie before he truly got to know her.

"I just must. Please don't try to understand my reasoning."

She squeezed Leah's shoulders gently before sinking into one of the wide rocking chairs gracing the front porch. "I know what it is. You're upset because Jonas and Henry were using your bunkhouse all of this time. I'm begging you to not worry about that. It's just a little soddy after all, and I'm sure the people of Deer Springs would be more than happy to help you clean it up and rebuild if necessary when they are raising your new barn."

Hattie didn't understand his intentions at all. It was her he was worried about, not his bunkhouse, or even his burnt barn. Rather than explain further, he took a step towards her and gently rubbed his thumb against her cheek.

"I will be leaving Luke here with you then. I'll be back as soon as I can." His voice was thick with concern as he pulled away and turned towards the stairs.

"I don't understand you Levi Hilty. Not one bit." Hattie bit down hard on her lower lip. "But may *Gott* be with you."

Levi picked up his pace as he descended the stairs. Leah hurried after him, and insisted on giving him one last hug. His footsteps carefully avoided the patches of ice and snow the snowstorm had left in its wake. He glanced one final time at the Fishers and Luke before pulling himself into his buggy. Levi grimaced when he realized that somewhere along the line he had actually grown fond of the schoolmarm and her *schweschder*. His feelings didn't matter though. Once Hattie realized he had done his best to send her away behind her back she would want nothing to do with him.

Levi's jaw clenched as beads of sweat fell from his brow. He clawed over a fallen log as he continued up the steep incline, his breathing becoming more labored as he climbed in elevation. He swallowed back the fear that came along with entering mountain lion territory. Levi was on their turf now, and he didn't like it one bit.

After leaving the Fishers and Luke behind at the Parson's ranch, he hastily rode back into Bozeman to hitch a ride with Deputies Smith and Miller to Deer

Springs. When the sun reached its highest point in the sky the temperature increased enough to encourage a major thaw. The police car chugged up the hills leading towards the Amish community with relative ease, and after stopping at Levi's home, the officers and he began to search on foot. The police men had offered to loan him a firearm, but he quickly refused. While he hoped to find Leah's captors, he knew his faith made inflicting bodily harm on them out of the question.

"Do you see any sign of them?" Deputy Miller yelled across the forest a good one hundred yards away from Levi.

"*Nee*, not a one." His fists tightened in frustration as he surveyed the landscape. Henry had been terrible at covering his tracks when he was stalking the Fishers. Levi had hoped they had been careless and done the same today, but no such luck. There was no sign of them.

"I think we should look in a different direction. We've searched this area pretty thoroughly."

Levi nodded in agreement as he followed the officers down the steep incline. He nearly lost his footing as he tried to descend the hill a bit too quickly, anxious to find Henry and Jonas as fast as possible. His heart burned in anguish when he realized what likely would happen to Hattie and Leah if the scoundrels were not found. As it was, leaving them behind at the Parson's ranch was one of the hardest things he ever had to do.

The sun began to set as the threesome continued down the hill. Levi squinted his eyes, gazing towards the valley where Bozeman rested. He wondered what Hattie was doing. He hoped with all of his heart that she was still safe.

"Men, I think we might have to call it a day. The search likely won't be very fruitful once night falls."

"Can we at least make a full circle around the outskirts of my farm before we head back to town?"

Levi's abdomen filled with dread at the thought of not leaving every stone uncovered before calling off the search for the night. The bunkhouse looked as if it had remained empty since the night before, but unlike Hattie, he had a suspicion that Henry wasn't too keen on leaving Deer Springs without the Fisher women.

"Okay, but let's make it quick. My stomach is growling something fierce."

Levi tried his best to ignore his own hunger pangs as he followed the officers around the edge of the hillside. He grimaced as he heard the soft bleating of his flock as his farm came into view. He could make out spots of white as they nudged their noses towards the wet grass while seeking to fill their bellies. His face pinched with worry as he wondered how his sheep were fairing. He had left them to fend for themselves over the past few days, and without the safety of a barn in the snow no less. But he had no choice. Hattie and Leah took precedence over his beloved flock.

"I think I've spotted some fresh tracks!" Deputy Miller tilted the brim of his hat backwards as he leaned closer to the ground. Levi lengthened his stride and closed the gap between them hastily. Could they be on to them?

Fresh boot prints lined the ground, digging deep into the muck. "*Ja*, that was them, all right. I don't think anyone else would be walking on the hillside directly behind my farm."

"Gentleman, let's keep moving. We don't have any time to lose."

Levi heeded the officer's words seriously as the three fanned out across the hillside. Disappointed that time was ticking against them, he rubbed his squared jaw in agitation as his eyes scanned the ground with quick precision.

The men hurried along with their search, and Levi sighed as they once again reached his fence line. Perhaps the scoundrels wouldn't be caught after all. There must be something more that they were overlooking…

Instead of scanning the hill once again, he focused his gaze directly along the stretch of cleared ground which surrounded his barbed wire fence. What if Henry and Jonas decided to circle around the furthest edge of his property to lie in wait? It was definitely possible. His eyes widened as a patch of color caught his eye many yards away. Could it be?"

"*Schnell*…hurry!" Levi motioned for the deputies to give chase as he raced towards the object. He pumped his legs faster, willing for them to propel him as quickly as possible.

His heart pounding, he slowed once he reached what appeared to be a patch of fabric. He lifted it up curiously, as the frayed plaid edges danced in the cool breeze.

"It looks like it came from the shirt Henry Fisher was wearing." Deputy Smith's brown eyes creased in concentration. "But why would his clothing be torn up like that?"

Without saying a word, Levi's eyes darted into the coniferous tree line. There he found his answer. He raised a shaky finger and pointed at the gruesome discovery. "Mountain lion."

Hattie paced in front of the roaring fire as Marjorie took turns playing a game of checkers with Leah and Luke. Once verifying that all of the doors were tightly locked, she did her best to act like nothing was amiss, for the *kinder's* sake. But the truth was she could do nothing but think of Henry and Jonas, who possibly were lurking nearby. She felt like such a fool for not realizing it sooner.

"King me!" Leah squealed out in gladness. Marjorie feigned disappointment while she did as the girl instructed.

"You are a much better checkers player than I, and it just isn't fair."

"Oh Marjorie, I'm sorry you feel that way. I'll try to go easy on you."

She caught her friend's teasing wink before she continued to play the game. Arthur sat quietly on a settee while reading the latest edition of *The Bozeman Gazette* while smoking a pipe. Hattie appreciated the way the couple opened up their home to them on such short notice. Even Arthur had offered an apology for their ordeal as he swung his doors open wide and beckoned for them to enter with a smile on his normally sour face.

She wiped her sweaty palms on her dress as the minutes continued to tick by. How long did the police intend to conduct their search? Surely if the men were not found by nightfall they would head back to town until the next day. Her brow puckered as she remembered the way Levi insisted on being involved. It was foolish of him to seek revenge for the damage to his property. Things were just that…things, and he wasn't living up to the *gut* example Bishop Graber gave to the congregation each day.

Hattie had been confused by the strange prickles she felt when Leah had rushed to his side before he left the Parson Homestead and went on his way. Should she allow her *schweschder* to grow close to him? After all, they would be leaving Deer Springs soon if their uncle wasn't found.

"Well, will you take a look at that? It looks like the police are here to pay us a visit." Arthur stretched his long frame to stare out the window as headlight beams shined into the living area. "I wonder if they have any news."

Hattie jumped away from the roaring fire and hastened towards the front door. Relief ran through her once she saw Levi's tall build step out of the police car out of the corner of her eye. Confused by this reaction, she shook her head in bewilderment. Despite the fact that he had saved Leah, she still couldn't allow herself to care about the well-being of any man.

She shivered as a blast of cool air blew into the home as she swung open the door. Her eyebrow lifted. Levi was making his way onto the porch alone. What could this mean? Wouldn't it make more sense for the deputies to speak to her?

"Hattie, could you please step outside for a moment? I have something I need to speak to you about."

"But I couldn't leave Leah inside without me. Give me a minute and I'll fetch her."

He gently clutched her shoulders and pulled her onto the porch while quietly closing the door behind her. "Please trust me and give me just a minute of your time. Leah's safe now, and I think it would be best if you hear what I have to say alone."

He wanted her to trust him? She stiffened and leaned back, ready to dart back inside at a moment's notice. Didn't he understand that she could never open her heart to trust again after all she had endured? Despite her confusion, she perked her ears to hear what he had to say, while expecting the worst. Henry and Jonas had likely slipped away, just as she had suspected.

"Like I said earlier, you have no need to fear for Leah's safety any longer. At least as far as Henry is concerned." He paused to hang his head while he reached forward to give her hand a squeeze. She fought the urge to pull away as her fingers were enveloped by his warmth. "We found Henry and Jonas."

Relief washed over her like a flood. "That's *wunderbaar*. I prayed for an outcome such as this, but never thought it would actually happen. Are they locked up tight in Bozeman?"

He winced slightly. "Not exactly. We found them in quite a bad way near my far fence line. Apparently, they were circling back around to kidnap Leah again. And this time, I doubt they would have been satisfied with capturing only Leah. Henry was after your funds, too."

Anguish lined his chiseled features. "What I'm trying to say is, before they had the chance to come after you again, they crossed tracks with a mountain lion or two. I take it the creatures didn't take too kindly to them wandering around in their territory. They are dead, Hattie. You don't have to worry about them any longer."

A sob broke loose from her throat as she leaned into her chest. Pure relief rushed over her, along with a hint of sadness. While she longed to experience the freedom which accompanied the absence of Henry Fisher, he was still her *onkel*. News of his death brought back a sea of emotions similar to when she found her *daed* passed out on the sweet hay of their barn after his final drinking binge.

"There's more, Hattie."

"I don't know if I'm strong enough to handle more."

She heard a quiet chuckle resonate through his chest against her ear. "I'm quite positive that you are strong enough to handle just about anything life throws your way. You are the strongest woman I've ever met."

"Do you really mean that?"

"*Ja*, I do."

She swallowed a sigh as she nodded in resignation. "Well then, go ahead and tell me whatever it is you have to say."

"Your *onkel* is at the coroner's office in town right now, and the police are asking for you to come and officially identify his body since you are the next of kin."

She took in her breath sharply. Hattie would need all the strength had today, this was for certain. "If I must, I will go."

He squeezed her hand tightly, and she felt recharged by his encouragement. "*Gut*. I'll ask the Parsons if they mind keeping an eye on Leah and Luke while we're gone. And please don't worry. There's no need to fear for your sister's safety any longer."

Hattie stood on shaky feet as Levi slipped into the home. She felt lightheaded at the task before her. How was she ever going to handle seeing her *onkel* in such a way?

A few moments later, Levi stepped foot on the porch once more. "Are you ready? Arthur and Marjorie said they would gladly watch the *kinder* while we are away. This shouldn't take long."

Hattie mechanically followed him down the steps and into the waiting automobile. A mix of both happy and sad tears clouded her vision as the car slowly made its way into town. The group was silent since the gravity of the situation was apparent to all.

Deputy Miller pulled the Model-T to a sputtering stop in front of the coroner's office. Hattie winced as she stepped into the small building.

"Right this way, Miss Fisher. All you need to do is indicate that the deceased is indeed Henry Fisher."

Hattie followed Deputy Smith into a small back room. Her face blanched as she leaned against a wall to steady her shaky frame.

"Miss Hattie Fisher, do you identify this man as your uncle, Mr. Henry Fisher?"

"*Ja*...I mean yes, I do."

The officer looked at her sympathetically. "That's all I need. Thank you so much for your time, ma'am. You are free to leave the room now."

The room began to spin as she clutched the door and yanked it open with all of her might. Hattie quickly exited the building, where she promptly leaned over the sidewalk planking and lost her dinner.

She was still trying her best to catch her breath when she felt a soft touch on her shoulder. "That must have been awfully hard. Are you alright?"

"I'll be alright before long. Please just give me a minute." She tried her best to erase the gruesome site of her *onkel* from her brain. Levi wasn't kidding when he said he was found in a very bad way.

"I want...*nee*, I need to get back to my Leah."

Levi nodded in understanding. "Come along, then. I'll bring you to her as quickly as my rig can carry you."

Chapter Sixteen

Levi looked over the pile of fresh lumber stacked in neat cords next to the heap of ashes and rubble which used to be his barn. He gazed into the crisp blue sky as he dragged his rake across a pile of ashes, searching for any salvageable metal parts. All signs of an early winter had passed, and the day beckoned for him and Luke to come outdoors.

"I found something!" Luke held up the heavy latch which Levi had used to secure the barn when it wasn't in use.

He stopped to pat the boy on his head. "*Gut* job. I definitely will be able to put that to use in the future."

Levi watched the orphan with a contented smile as he continued to search the rubble with a large rake. While he would like to officially be named his guardian before the church, his fate wouldn't be certain until Levi confessed to trying to hire a new schoolmarm behind everyone's back. His stomach filled with dread while he wondered what would happen to the boy if he was shunned. Most families in Deer Springs had too many mouths to feed during the drought as it was, and would be hard pressed to take on another *kind*.

He looked across his pasture towards the schoolmarm's home. He could hardly believe that just a short time ago he had hoped for Hattie to be well on her way, and now he yearned for just the opposite. Levi hadn't talked to her since her ordeal. He knew she needed a *gut* amount of time to heal. But with Sunday fast approaching he realized that he must confess his transgressions to her as soon as possible. It would never do for her to hear of his shortcomings without warning during the next church gathering.

"Levi, are you my *daed* now?"

His heart lept into his throat when he stared down into the boy's shining blue eyes. He had tried his best to be the fatherly example the child so desperately needed over the course of the past week, but he wasn't truly his *daed*...at least not yet. He didn't want to give the boy any sense of false hope before the brethren made their decision once his confession was heard before the church.

"Nee, I'm not your *daed*. But hopefully, I will take on that role very soon."

"I'm so glad I'm not with Jonas anymore. I was always hungry and sad unless I was at your *haus*. I'm so happy now. *Danke* so much for taking me in."

Joy spread inside of Levi as he realized he had finally seen a glimpse of what he had been searching for for so long. A family.

"Don't mention it Luke, the pleasure has been all mine."

The two continued to work until the sun rose high in the sky. After a quick lunch break, they sipped full glasses of lemonade on the front porch.

"So, what do you say? Do you think we should get back to work? We need to prepare the ground before raising the barn."

"Would it be alright if we stopped by to visit Leah for a little while first? I've missed her so much since we've returned home from Bozeman. I've only seen her at the school *haus*, and I used to spend time with her and

Bessie every day. I miss them both now that Bessie is well enough to be with the rest of the flock."

He hung his head in defeat while realizing Luke's request wasn't too much to ask. In fact, he had planned to find the time to speak to Hattie briefly today anyhow. "*Ja*, I guess we can do that. Let's get on with it."

After taking a final swig of lemonade, Levi led the way into the kitchen where he sat the dirty cups into the sink basin. He let his gaze linger at the spot where the schoolmarm applications used to sit. Like his concern for Hattie's safety, the wretched pieces of paper were long gone. After the Bishop had confiscated them from his home, he hoped to never see them again.

"Come Luke, let's head to the Fisher's home."

The boy ran ahead of him, leaving the front door wide open. Levi shook his head at his exuberance as he quietly clicked the door closed. With a mix of reluctance and excitement, he followed the boy towards Hattie's quaint clapboard home.

As soon as he reached the fence line dividing the two properties, Levi realized that Luke had already found Leah and the two were happy as clams while eagerly searching for large pinecones amongst a patch of thick grass. He smiled in spite of himself when he looked towards the window and saw no sign of the schoolmarm's worried face. She obviously had loosened her grip on Leah since she needn't worry about the threat of her *onkel* any longer.

"I'll be inside if you need me."

"Okay!" Luke barely looked up from his search when he acknowledged his farewell.

After rapping quietly at the door, Levi crossed his arms in anticipation. He was prepared for the worst since he didn't believe Hattie would take his confession well. But why should she? He'd brought this problem onto himself.

The door creaked open and she slowly stuck her head outside. His breath caught in his throat as he took in her fresh face. She looked younger somehow. He winced when he realized that her terrible burden had likely caused her to be riddled with constant worry. Watching her struggle to identify her deceased *onkel* had been one of the hardest things he'd ever had to do. Surprisingly, it was far harder than losing Rhoda.

"*Hullo*, Levi. What brings you here today?"

"I hope I'm not intruding, but I need to speak to you about something. It's rather important."

Uncertainty clouded her eyes before she nodded and lifted her hand in acceptance. "Please come in."

Levi quietly filed in behind her, before plopping onto a wooden chair. He snapped his suspenders, wondering where he should begin. Once he realized his first concern was her well-being, he figured that was a natural place to start.

"How have you been?"

She laughed quietly, and her soft voice sounded like music to his ears. "I've been better, but thankful that I no longer have to worry about my wretched *Onkel* Henry."

He nodded, hoping she would continue.

"There are many important decisions which must be made regarding the future of Leah and I. While I know I can remain in Deer Springs without fear of Henry, the fact still remains that most people in the town do not like nor trust me. Watching me be arrested at the town fundraiser didn't help with this circumstance." She laughed once more underneath her breath. "Besides, now that Henry is gone, Leah and I have the option of moving back to our beloved Lancaster once again. How I would love to be surrounded by my *mamm's* cherished treasures once more. For now, all of her items are being stored in a distant relative's barn. I haven't brought this up to Leah yet, but I'm seriously considering a move back home."

His world stopped as the realization that both Hattie and Leah might be leaving Deer Springs soon hit him in the chest like a ton of bricks. With Henry gone, Levi had assumed they would stay. He smiled at the irony of it all. It was funny to think that at the town festival Levi was still determined to find a replacement for the schoolmarm…just in the proper way. As soon as he learned the absolute truth about Hattie's past his heart changed its tune. He wanted nothing more than for the Fishers to remain in Deer Springs permanently.

Swallowing the frog in his throat, he opened his mouth to speak. "I understand your desire to move back to Lancaster, and I'll support any decision that you make. After my confession, you might not believe me, but I would like nothing more than for you and Leah to stay in Deer Springs permanently. You are the best schoolmarm our scholars have ever had."

"I'm not so sure about that." She cocked her head to the side as the strings of her *kapp* brushed against her slender shoulders. "What confession are you talking about, Levi? I doubt you've made many mistakes in your life, let alone one big enough that it deserves a confession."

"*Nee*, you are sorely mistaken. I hate to say this, but I'm afraid my mistake will make your decision to either remain in Deer Springs or leave for Lancaster easy for you. And I believe your choice will not be to my liking."

Hattie's back straightened in surprise. "*Ach*, I'd appreciate it if you'd just tell me what's the matter. I can hardly stand the suspense any longer."

Embarrassment blew through him. "After the Bishop made his decision to keep you on as the schoolmarm against my wishes, I decided to take it upon myself to find your replacement immediately. I placed an employment advertisement in several papers around the country seeking a qualified Amish teacher. After a *gut* amount of applications rolled in, I asked two qualified women to send in a recommendation from their respective Bishops. Before the fundraiser I realized the error of my ways, and decided to stop the hiring process. But it was too late. Bishop Graber discovered my secret and has requested that I confess before the church on Sunday. I plan on doing so."

Hattie sat in silence for a moment, and he wondered what she was thinking. Would she ever forgive him?

"I made a grave mistake, Hattie, and I've come to ask your forgiveness. Please forgive me."

"So this whole time you've wished for me to leave? Even when you helped find Leah?"

"*Nee* Hattie, by then I realized how wrong I was. Please believe me. Will you forgive me?" He dropped to one knee and held his head down in contrition.

Hattie gasped as her hand flew to her mouth. "It is our way to forgive, and therefore I will forgive. Please get up off the floor."

He rose to his feet and grasped her hand in appreciation. "Thank you so much Hattie. I just had to make things right with you before Sunday. I hope you understand."

She looked flustered as she quickly pulled her fingers away. "Don't mention it."

"I must be going because a lot of work needs to be done to prepare the ground for the barn raising next week. Would you mind if I allowed Luke to continue playing with Leah for a while in your yard? He was itching to return to his favorite playmate."

She waved her hand absentmindedly. "*Ja*, that's fine. I'll see you later."

Confusion creased his brow as he analyzed Hattie's strange reaction. While she forgave him with her lips, had she in her heart? Only time would tell. Unfortunately, he had a problem that was only amplified with each passing day. What would he do with his growing feelings for Hattie? He finally felt like he was becoming whole after Rhoda's rejection, and now his kind and beautiful neighbor might be moving across the country.

He let the wind calm his fears as he stepped once again onto his property. Hattie was a strong and independent woman, and he must put his feelings aside. His growing care for her must not affect her decision to either leave or stay in Deer Springs. This was only the right thing to do. Besides, come Sunday he might be shunned and asked to leave the community for *gut*.

Hattie brushed a stray wisp of chestnut hair from eyes as she admired Leah's tenacity. Her *schweschder* had finished sewing her second cape dress of the day, and was ready to eagerly begin her third.

"It will be so nice to wear colored dresses again, *ja*? It is almost the one year anniversary of our *mamm's* death, and we will be free to wear what we please."

She folded her hands quietly in her lap as she contemplated the fact that her *mamm* had been gone for a full year. It hardly seemed possible. Hattie rose from her papers and gently ran her fingers over the plum cotton fabric. She was so thankful to be free from wearing fancy clothing since she had now fully returned to her roots.

A grin tilted her lips. "Our mother wouldn't want us to mourn forever. I believe she would much prefer to see us in cheerful colors, *ja*?"

"That's right."

As the treadle sewing machine quickly stitched straight lines though the fabric by way of Leah's pumping foot, Hattie wondered if the time was right to broach the subject of their future. She knew that it was only right for her *schweschder* to have a *gut* say in where she wanted to live.

"Leah, now that I no longer have to worry about Henry, we are free to live wherever we please. In fact, we can move back to Lancaster if you'd like. What do you think about that?"

The girl's brow scrunched as she stopped sewing abruptly. "I've never really thought about moving again. I really enjoy living in Deer Springs. Can't we stay?"

"Well, I guess we can. But life in Deer Springs is much harder than in Lancaster County. We wouldn't have to worry about the drought, or lack of food. Doesn't that sound appealing to you?"

"Sure, it does. But I've made so many close friends here, and I couldn't stand the thought of leaving Luke and Levi. They are mighty *gut* people, *ja*?"

Hattie moved to her window while deep in thought. Levi's Corriedales were grazing near the property line, and she caught sight of both Levi and Luke keeping watch nearby. She looked away shyly before taking another peek. Levi's strong arms were holding a staff to his side as he played the role of overseer. He truly was a *gut* shepherd.

She pressed her forehead to the cool window pane as she remembered his confession not so long ago in this self-same room. A man had never apologized to Hattie and it threw her for a loop. Levi had proved to her time and time again that not all men were like her *daed* and *onkel*, but she still didn't know if she could believe he was trustworthy. Knowing that Levi had tried to replace her without her knowledge stung, but his decision to make things right spoke highly of his character.

She smiled to herself while he ruffled Luke's hair good-naturedly when the wind caught his hat from his head. Not only was he hardworking, Levi was also wonderful with *kinder*. Hattie hoped that his home would be filled with a whole passel of children one day.

"What are you thinking of, *schweschder*? I sure hope you are making the decision to stay in Deer Springs."

"Leah, while I will definitely listen to your input while deciding questions about our future, there are several variables to be considered. Most people in Deer Springs do not trust me."

"But why, Hattie?"

"It's complicated." She sighed, thankful that Rose and Greta had taken the time to hear her out once she returned home from identifying her *onkel*. Their friendships ran strong, but the rest of the town had avoided her like the plague since her arrest at the Deer Spring fundraiser.

"It's only as complicated as you'd like it to be. Why don't you come clean about our past to everyone? Maybe then they will understand."

She pondered the simple advice. Was she really making her problem more confusing than need be? What was holding her back from sharing the truth now that her *onkel* had passed away? Pride? Fear?

"I believe you are wise beyond your years. *Danke* for the advice, Leah."

"There is one other thing I'd like to talk to you about. After learning about the inheritance our *onkel* was trying to steal from us, I wondered why you even kept it in the first place. Shouldn't we be relying on *Gott* and our community to see us through instead of money?"

Hattie's brow crinkled in thought as she poured a cup of *kaffi* in the kitchen. She took a slow sip while contemplating her sister's wise words. While she always was willing to help those in need by donating portions of the fund, she admitted she didn't want to see it dwindle entirely.

"I guess deep down, I feel like our inheritance is our last connection to *Mamm*. But I've been holding onto the wrong thing, *ja*?"

"I think you have. Money will never be a true connection to our mother. All that matters is that we hold our memories in our hearts. If we give the inheritance away, we won't ever have to worry about someone coming after us for the wrong reasons again. Wouldn't that be nice?"

A light went off in Hattie's head as she gazed out the window once more. If she donated her entire inheritance, then she needn't worry about a man feigning attraction to her for the wrong reasons. She would be free to pursue a relationship if a man proved himself trustworthy.

"Leah, I'm going to step outside for a bit. Please continue on with your sewing."

Her decision to stay put made, Hattie grabbed her cape before slipping out of the small home and purposing her steps towards Levi's flock. She didn't go far before the clip clop of horse's hooves alerted her to a visitor. Surprised to see a man arriving on horseback, she cautiously threw up her hand in greeting until fully recognizing the rider.

"Jonathan! What brings you here?"

He slowed his steed and dismounted quickly, while his breath came out in steady puffs. The middle-aged man reached inside his coat pocket and pulled out a letter. "I forgot to deliver this to Levi earlier in the day, and I wanted to bring it to him in case it was important. Would you mind walking it over? I need to get back to my coach real quick like in order to return to Bozeman on schedule."

"That's no problem. I'm headed to speak to Levi right now."

"Great, thank you Miss Fisher."

Jonathan awkwardly mounted his stallion before nodding cordially and riding off into the distance. She eagerly anticipated a short visit with Levi as she quickened her step and padded into the tree line. Hattie began to hum a tune from the singing as she nonchalantly looked down at the letter in her hand. Surprised, she paused when she noticed the fancy script of a woman's hand jotted across the envelope. Hattie's eyes quickly scanned the return address. *Rhoda Greenloe.*

Levi was still corresponding with Rhoda? She held back a surprised gasp as she reached the clearing and neared the fence. Perhaps things still weren't as they seemed after all.

"Hattie, it's nice to see you!" Luke bounded over to the fence, eagerly pointing to a sheep. "Do you see Bessie over there? She's right as rain. I'm so glad the barn didn't burn until she was almost completely healed."

"*Ja*, I'm thankful for that, too." She tightened her lips and stared at Levi. "*Hullo* there. I bet you're glad the barn will be raised again next week. There's no telling when we'll have another snowfall."

"That's right. I'm hoping that everything will go well at the church meeting and the barn raising can go on as planned."

Hattie clutched onto the letter tightly as the ache in her heart picked it up a notch. She had hoped to announce that she and Leah were staying in Deer Springs. But now what Hattie had to say didn't seem so important. She offered a feeble nod in response before holding her head high and thrusting the letter under his nose.

"Here. Jonathan brought this by and asked that I deliver it to you. So here you go."

As soon as he removed the envelope from her grasp she turned to leave. He gently clutched onto her wrist, drawing her closer. Her cheeks pinked while her heart skipped a beat.

"Hattie, wait. I had a few things to ask of you…" His voice sank into silence once he noticed the return address.

"I see you are still corresponding with Rhoda. How nice."

He shook his head in confusion as her voice met his ears. "I don't know what this is about. I haven't heard from Rhoda since she left."

"Maybe she wants to make amends."

"Maybe."

She frowned at his short response while turning to walk away. "Like I said, I must be going."

"Have you made any decisions regarding your future yet?"

Hattie stopped in her tracks and eyed him suspiciously. "Why do you ask?"

He shuffled his feet from side to side, looking like a shy school boy. "I care about both you and Leah."

She bit back a retort and stood in silence instead, pulling her cape to her chilled skin a bit closer.

"I have spoken to Leah and we've decided a few things, but I still have to work out several minor details. I'll let you know as soon as our plans are set in stone."

"Sounds fair enough to me. I hope you have a nice evening."

Unable to reply, Hattie took to the cover of the forest. While she had begun to see Levi in an entirely new light, the discovery of Rhoda's letter put a damper on things. Hattie thought she had finally found a man who she could open her heart to. Had she been wrong?

Hattie determined one thing was for certain. Levi Hilty or not, she was going to do everything in her power to remain in Deer Springs, for Leah's sake.

Chapter Seventeen

Uncertainty propelled Levi's feet forward as he dragged towards the Graber's home the following Sunday. His time had come, and he was ready to confess his sin to the church and get this whole mess behind him. He prayed that the rest of the congregation would be as forgiving as Hattie had been.

"I'll be asked to speak in front of the church for a time, and I expect you to be a *gut* boy while I'm not able to keep a close eye on you. Do you understand?"

Luke scrunched his brow as he broke into a jog to keep up with his long strides. "Why are you going to speak in front of the church today? You aren't one of the ministers."

"You'll find out soon enough. *Kumme* now."

Candles lit a welcoming glow from the windows of the wide Graber home. The *haus* was large due to several additions made to better accommodate their large brood. He hoped the Bishop would show mercy to him in his very own home today.

His heart nearly stopped when he watched Hattie and Leah step out of Greta's buggy. He had offered to bring the two to church today as always, but Hattie had demurely refused. He wondered if her reluctance to ride with him had anything to do with Rhoda's letter. Truth be told, he almost fainted when he opened the correspondence and realized that his previous *aldi* had answered his call for employment.

Apparently, her fancy life in Chicago hadn't gone quite as planned. He rolled his eyes while thinking about the way he promptly used the application as fodder for his wood stove without any remorse whatsoever. Hattie had shown him that he was looking for both strength and acceptance in all of the wrong places.

Levi filed into the Graber home behind Luke and slid into a stark backless bench. Without thinking, he trained his gaze towards Hattie, who was sitting on the woman's side of the open room. Her cheeks were flushed pink from the cold wind. Even in her stark black dress, he didn't think he'd ever seen a prettier sight.

Only a few minutes later, the brethren exited the room in a single file line to meet before the service began. Levi's face grew somber as it settled towards the front of the whitewashed wall.

In unison, the congregation rose and together raised their voices in several songs from the *Ausbund*. The ministers returned to the room stoically while the congregation was singing *Das Loblied* as was their tradition. The church members and unbaptized Amish alike then settled in for two different sermons preached in High German. As the third hour neared its end, droplets of sweat formed on Levi's brow despite the cool temperature in the room. He wished he could turn around to lock eyes with Hattie who was sitting in the section allocated for unmarried women. Her deep caramel eyes had a way of calming his nerves.

After Pastor Zook finished speaking, Bishop Graber stiffly rose to his feet and shuffled to face the congregation. "If you are not a member, I ask you to step outside. We must take care of a bit of serious business. Levi Hilty, would you please step forward?"

He mechanically followed his instructions, while silently asking God for the strength that only He could give. Levi's expression remained somber as he stood next to the Bishop. Hattie stepped from the bench with the other unbaptized young adults and *kinder* with folded arms. His heart pinched as he watched her stand near the open front door.

"In one month's time, we will gather together for a much happier occasion. Several young people have been attending baptism classes, and I'm glad to say that it looks like our church district will welcome several new members come November."

Levi caught Hattie's eye and noticed how they took on a shine. Could this possibly mean she intended to stay in Deer Springs? He hoped it might be true.

"But today, we must put thoughts of the future aside and concentrate on the important matter at hand. It recently came to my attention that Levi Hilty has been hiding something from all of us. Please take heed to his confession, and afterwards we will vote on whether he should remain as a fully functioning member."

Levi's throat grew dry as he saw Luke press into the schoolmarm while she offered a warm squeeze to his side. He had so much to lose if he didn't adequately confess and repent.

"While I'm standing before you to confess a specific sin, first I must take care of a few other issues which are weighing heavily on my conscience."

Whispers began to rumble through the crowd as the members looked at each other curiously. Bishop Graber raised his hand to silence the church and motioned for him to continue.

"First of all, I would like to apologize to the entire community for hiring Rhoda Greenloe as the schoolmarm a few terms ago. I showed terrible judgment of character, and I realize Deer Springs suffered when she left town without notice. When she left, I began to question the motives of outsiders in general, which was wrong. It was Rhoda who wasn't *gut* for our community…who wasn't *gut* for our *kinder*. The *Englisch* have nothing to do with her lack of character. I'm deeply sorry for my poor judgment."

Hattie clasped her hands to her face as a quiet sob sounded from her throat. Pushing away from the open door, she hurried her steps towards the nearby pasture. Even in her haste, her motions flowed with grace. Rose jumped up from her bench and rushed to follow once she noticed the commotion. Levi wished he could do the same, but knew if he had any hopes of remaining a church member in *gut* standing he must finish his confession.

His ears burned as he wondered what Hattie could possibly be thinking. She probably was ashamed of what had just come from his mouth…ashamed of him. He reluctantly realized that his growing care and love for the schoolmarm would likely never be returned.

"Secondly, I let my fear of making the same mistake twice affect the way I treated our current schoolmarm, Hattie Fisher. I fear that my guarded and unenthusiastic welcome caused many of you to distrust her as well. Over the past few months, Hattie has proven me wrong, and we should all be very grateful that she chose to teach in our meager school. She is a *gut* Amish woman, and if I've given anyone cause to think otherwise, I beg your forgiveness."

Bishop Graber nodded appreciatively. "You have come to the correct conclusion regarding Hattie. *Danke* for taking the time to right this wrong as well. Deer Springs, you would do well to heed Levi's words. Do not be so quick to judge a book by its cover."

Silence scorched through the room as Levi felt a soothing calm, glad that he had done his best to vindicate Hattie's name.

"Now onto what I was asked to confess this morning. I apologize from the bottom of my soul for trying my best to find a replacement for Hattie's position without seeking the approval of the Bishop and community first. While I was concerned that Hattie wasn't the right person for the job based on her *Englisch* appearance only, I also allowed my negative experience with Rhoda to stain my impression of Hattie without getting to know her first. My actions were wrong. I repent of them fully, and ask for your forgiveness. I would like nothing more than to remain as a fully functioning member of the Deer Spring Church District."

Somber faces surrounded him as Bishop Graber clasped his shoulder after standing for a moment in silence. "I appreciate your heartfelt confession. Levi's transgressions have reminded me that accountability is a *gut* thing, and I will do my best to not overlook problems in the community, even if we are currently going through hardship. Jonas' death taught me a lesson, too."

"Let's take a moment and put it to a vote. All those in favor of keeping Levi in our fellowship with full privileges please raise your hand."

As a sea of hands shot up across the room, Levi lowered his head in humble gratitude. It looked like he might be able to become Luke's official guardian, after all.

"Are any opposed?"

The room grew silent as hands were folded in laps throughout the home.

"It's decided then. Levi, may you go in peace and sin no more."

"There is one other thing I would like to discuss since I have the floor if it's alright with you."

"Speak your case."

Levi took in a deep breath before he began. "As you all know, since Jonas Beiler has left us I've been looking after young Luke. I have thoroughly enjoyed caring for the boy, and with your permission, I would like to become his official guardian."

The Bishop nodded thoughtfully. "You are a *gut* man, Levi. You have borne the burden of helping the less fortunate in our community like a true Amish man. You interact well with the child, and I would like nothing more than to see you two joined as a family."

Levi nearly burst with joy as he motioned for Luke, who was curiously peeking inside of the room, to join him. The boy bounded to his side, and wrapped his arms around his middle in a hug.

"Let's dismiss and enjoy our fellowship meal. *Danke* for everyone's willingness to settle this pressing matter."

Levi stood at the front of the room and extended his hand in fellowship to a line of church members. He couldn't help but hope that Hattie might slip back into her place, but she stayed away. He tried his best to remain focused on the matter at hand, but his thoughts kept drifting back to her.

The smell of pickled beets and shoofly pie reached his nostrils as he turned to Luke. "I'll be outside if you need me. Please go ahead and eat your fill when it's your turn."

"Okay, *Daed*."

Tears filled his eyes as the youngster quickly stepped out of the room, no doubt to find Leah. He could hardly grasp the idea that he finally had a family, albeit small.

After he received the last firm handshake of fellowship, Levi slipped out of the room unnoticed. He donned his jacket before stepping outside into the cool air. He was determined to find Hattie, and do what he could to make things right. He felt a pinch of discomfort when he realized that she hadn't heard his full confession before the church. While it was true that he had scratched the surface of his betrayal while at her home, it was only right for her to know his true heart on the matter.

He spotted two small females huddled on the steps of the nearby *dawdi haus*, their heads together as if in deep discussion. Levi carefully avoided a patch of ice as he took a tentative step forward. It was high time to confess not only his wrongs, but also his love to the talented schoolmarm. While she likely would not return his affection, he knew that if Hattie remained in Deer Springs, he wanted nothing more than for her to be his.

As he grew near, Rose Graber lifted her head with flashing blue eyes. Hattie's gaze stayed focused on icy ground while her friend squeezed her shoulder and rose to her feet.

Taking careful but purposeful strides, Rose reached him quickly. "Levi, I think it's best if you leave Hattie alone for now. She has a lot on her heart and mind and wishes to be left in peace."

"I don't think you understand. I must speak to her…"

"I do understand, but listen to me. She just truly realized some pretty deep feelings, and she doesn't know what to do with them. Hattie's heart is in a rather precarious place, and she has some important things to mull over. I understand it's difficult, but she's asked that I send you away while we are talking things through." With a wink so small he almost missed it, Rose left him standing stoically in the yard to return to her friend.

Yielding with an uncomfortable sigh, Levi trudged back into the Graber's home. Hurting Hattie was the last thing he wanted to do, and he surely had done so by allowing Rhoda's betrayal to distract him for so long. While it might kill him to do so, he made the decision to keep their relationship strictly professional while she held him at arm's length.

Hattie sighed with contentment as she wrote yet another *A* on one of her scholar's assignments. Since her arrival in Deer Springs, her class had progressed beautifully. She was so grateful for the opportunity to positively impact the *kinder* in the community.

Nearly one month had passed since Levi's confession before the church, and she had yet to have a private conversation with the man. At Rose's request he had left her alone after the fateful church service, but to her dismay, he continued to do so. He had quietly and dutifully taken it upon himself to help her beyond any matter of rhyme or reason around her home over the past month. But through it all, Levi had made sure to be long gone before her class dismissed and she retired for the evening. She had watched the strength and joy he had experienced while parenting Luke from afar, and her fondness had grown for him with each passing day. *Nee*, it was more than only fondness, it was love.

Hattie jumped with a start as the front door of the school *haus* swung open. Luke and Leah had been building a snowman with her sister's new kitten Marmie, and they were probably hoping to warm up for a spell.

"Are you busy?"

A flurry of emotions jumped to her throat as a rich baritone reached her ears. She would know that voice anywhere. Hattie had memorized the sound when she first rushed to the school *haus* in that dreadful red dress. A variety of overwhelming feelings washed over her. In this moment, she realized that a life of *lieb* with Levi might truly be possible.

"*Nee*, my tasks can wait. What do you need?"

He shook the snow from his boots before entering the building. She admired his strong and steady gait as he took a few steps forward.

He cocked his head appreciatively. "Your dress looks nice. Are you out of mourning for your *mamm*?"

She shrugged her shoulders as she studied her frock. "I guess you can say that. While I will always remember her, it was time to move out of our mourning clothing. It's what she would have wanted."

"I think that's a *gut* idea. You look lovely. How's the chinking holding up?"

She blushed, flustered by the continued small talk and flattery. Embarrassment that only a few short months ago she had asked him to keep the gaps in the log cabin open wide, she grinned sheepishly. What a miserable late fall and winter it would have been. "*Gut*. In fact everything at the school *haus* has been going wonderfully. I would be glad to give you a full report. I've been quite surprised that the schoolmaster hasn't paid me a visit in such a long time."

She couldn't help but feel the wound that ran deep as she reminded him of his absence. Why did he continue to avoid her?

"I've been quite sure of your competence, and didn't feel the need to pay you a visit until now. I hope I've given you enough time to sort through your future. I hate to bother you even now, but I realize you were considering a move to Lancaster. With your inheritance, you could move anywhere, really. Before the next semester begins, I need to know if you plan to stay. I'm sure you understand."

She read the pain in his eyes, confused. Did he care about the decision she made?

"I guess I've made your decision easy for you, with all I've done. Why, you couldn't even stand to look at me during my church confession. Not that I blame you."

He leaned in closer, tipping his black felt hat away from his eyes to stare deeply into hers. "In case you were wondering, the letter from Rhoda was actually an application to receive her old job back. Apparently things aren't going as well as she had hoped in Chicago. I made quick work of it, and it acted as kindling for my cookstove that night."

Hattie choked back a tear, surprised by what he was saying. Didn't he understand that the reason she charged away from the Bishop's home was because just like listening to him explain Rhoda's letter now, watching him confess in front of the church was too much? The pain from her past began to slip away at that moment, and she didn't know what to do with herself. She put the fear that he had reopened his past relationship to rest once and for all.

She pushed aside her school papers as she rose to her feet. "*Nee*, it's not that. When I heard you speak in front of the brethren, I realized that I was beginning to let go of the pain from my past, and it scared me. I also could tell how hard your confession was for you, and I couldn't stand to see you in such a way."

He shook his head in bewilderment. "Even after all I've put you through, you still regard others as more valuable than yourself. You're unbelievable, Hattie Fisher."

She cautiously allowed herself to savor the comfort of Levi's closeness. If only he could see that he meant so much more to her than she ever dreamed possible.

"I'm not unbelievable."

"It was a compliment. I've never meant a woman more wonderful, strong, or beautiful as you. I mean that."

Hattie nearly choked as her heart jumped in her throat. What could he be saying?

"You never answered my question. I really need to know your plans for the New Year. Surely you can see my dilemma."

She rubbed her sweaty palms on her muted cornflower blue cape dress as her eyes took on a shine. "It looks like I'm in desperate need of a job, and if it suits you, I would like to stay on as the schoolmarm right here in Deer Springs. Besides, I plan on being baptized into the church come Sunday. It would never do for me to leave so quickly after making this commitment before the brethren."

He looked at her appreciatively. "While there is nothing that I would like more, do you mind if I asked why you and Leah decided to stay here? With your inheritance, you easily move both your home and church membership back to Lancaster."

"After consulting Leah, she let me know that she sees Deer Springs as her home now. And after thinking it through, I agree with her. I'm not sure what you said before the church during your confession, but the community has welcomed me with open arms since that time. *Danke* for that." Hattie thought of the number of humble apologies she'd received from the parents in her class. She made sure everyone knew the complete story of her past shortly afterwards, and the newfound parental involvement in the small school *haus* was astonishing. A smile tugged on her lips.

"I just righted my wrong. It was the smart thing to do."

She swallowed her pride while gazing at the soft snowflakes falling outside of the thick paned window. Should she be so bold as to tell Levi how she had grown to have feelings for him? "I also must admit that both

Leah and I would be saddened to leave you and Luke behind. We truly care for you."

His hand trembled as he stopped in his tracks and clutched the nearest desk. "You would? Not just Leah, but you would as well?"

"*Ja*, more than you will ever know."

With a look of determination, Levi strode towards her and clutched her small hands in his. She sighed with contentment as a shaky smile slowly filled his squared jaw.

"I would like nothing more than for you to stay in Deer Springs, Hattie. Not as the schoolmarm, but as my *frau*."

Her frame began to quiver as she stared into his clear, chocolate eyes. A subdued caution filled her countenance. "Do you truly know what you're saying? While I would like nothing more than to be a mother to dear Luke, I wouldn't want to marry for anything less than love…I want you to love me, Levi. Do you?"

"I've grown to love you more than I've thought it possible to love another human being." He pulled her closer, and she felt his heartbeat in her ear as she crushed into his side. "I'm forever grateful that you came to Deer Springs. And don't you ever worry about us having a small family, like your own. Marjorie mentioned that you would never have a large family since you were like your *mamm*, and we can handle any medical problems together. In fact, I would be more than satisfied to share my home with only you, Leah and Luke for the rest of my days."

She chuckled slightly as she happily breathed in his soothing scent. "Marjorie said that only because I vowed to never marry due to my inheritance. Just like my *mamm*, I thought I would never know if a man loved me or my full coffers, and so I opted to not put myself in the same position. I'm not aware of any medical problems I might have. Lord willing, I would be able to bear a fair amount of children."

Hattie caught her breath as she pulled away from his arms. It was time to give him the true test of his love. Would he still want to marry once he knew what she had done with her inheritance?

"There is something else I should tell you. The reason I need to remain employed is because with Bishop Graber's help and blessing, I'm in the process of donating my inheritance to worthy causes. Not just part of my inheritance, but all of it." Her lips drew together as she tried her best to read his expression. "Half of it is going to the Troubled Youth Program at Bozeman Preparatory School, and the other half to the Deer Springs Aid Fund. I hold both of these *Englisch* and Amish organizations close to my heart. Also, after paying off my *mamm's* farm in Lancaster once and for all, I decided to donate it to a family in need. If my lack of money would cause you to not want to marry me, I need to know now."

"Sweetheart, I love you, money or no. Don't you understand that?"

Her heart sang with happiness as he pulled her close once more. She let out a contented sigh as he pressed a gentle kiss into her forehead.

"So, what do you say? Will you marry me?"

"*Ja* Levi, I would be honored to become your *frau*."

He let out a whoop before lifting her above his head and spinning her around. She giggled with delight as he gently set her down and wrapped his strong arm around her shoulder. Hattie thanked *Gott* for keeping her and Leah safe while leading them to Levi. He had placed an amazing, trustworthy man right under her nose. She finally was to have the family she'd always wanted, but never thought would materialize. They joined hands before rushing outside to tell the *kinder* the *wunderbaar* news.

Epilogue

"Today's the day *schweschder*, aren't you excited? I will be gaining both a *daed* and *bruder* in just a few short hours. I can hardly wait!"

Hattie hushed the butterflies dancing in her stomach as she turned to give Leah a wobbly grin. She smoothed a wrinkle from her royal blue wedding dress and crisp white apron before giving an answer.

"*Ja,* more than you'll ever know, dear one."

She sighed in contentment as she waited with her *Newehockers*, the attendants in the small wedding party, in one of Levi's upper bedrooms before the ceremony began. Hattie peeked out the open window as a bright spring breeze caressed her freshly scrubbed forehead. She was amazed by the number of buggies and automobiles alike which were parked neatly in rows across Levi's vast pasture. Why, all of Deer Springs as well as half of Bozeman must have come for the festivities. Levi had affirmed he was more than happy to welcome a *gut* many *Englischers* into his home while mailing invitations. He now completely accepted Hattie's *mamm's* past, and he often encouraged his bride-to-be to visit the Troubled Youth Program in Bozeman.

"It's so nice that Levi sent for all of *Mamm's* furniture to be brought to our new home as a surprise.

Isn't he grand?" Leah rumbled her freshly sewn cape dress slightly as she flung herself on her old bed from Lancaster.

Hattie choked up as she surveyed the room which was to belong to her *schweschder*. Levi had outdone himself by secretly filling many of the rooms of his *haus* with her once-*Englisch mamm's* treasures. She had never felt so loved and at home as he shyly gave her the grand tour the night before.

"*Ja*, he is. While it was hard to wait through the winter to marry, I'm glad now that we did. It will be *wunderbaar* to begin keeping house with all of the comforts of our old home, and it was so very important to me to be able to finish out the year as the schoolmarm here."

She smiled, thankful that Bishop Graber had allowed the couple to postpone their marriage past the regular fall wedding season. While she wanted nothing more than to become Levi's other half, given the events of the fall it was nice to take a breath and have something to look forward to as Levi's barn was raised and she completed her commitment to the school *haus*. Hattie choked up a little just thinking about it. While she could hardly wait to fulfill her dream of becoming a *frau* and *mamm*, she would miss the scholars with all of her heart.

"Are you ready to become Hattie Hilty? It's almost time for the ceremony to begin." Rose, who along with Leah were to stand by her side, gently touched her arm and began leading her towards the door.

Hattie's eyes rose in surprise as her heartbeat picked it up a notch. Was she truly ready for this? Taking one last glance out the window, she wondered at the newly born lambs which frolicked along the hillside with their mothers. Levi's freshly painted barn stood straight and tall against the landscape, offering a welcome retreat for her soon-to-be husband's flock. A contented sigh filled her frame. Spring was a time of new beginnings, and she was ready for hers.

Placing one foot in front of the other, Hattie was led by Leah and Rose to the bottom level of the home. The wall partitions separating the rooms in the lower level had been removed, offering a huge expanse for the guests to the wedding. The room grew quiet as her presence was made known, and Hattie caught her friend Marjorie giving her a quick wink as she clutched Arthur's arm by her side. Hattie tunneled her vision towards the front of the room, searching for her Levi. With renewed determination, Hattie clutched her hands together and began to walk steadily towards her groom.

His shuffling feet steadied when he first caught sight of her. Transfixed, he stood straight and tall as he turned towards his bride. All of Hattie's fears took wing as she admired her handsome, trustworthy man. His new collarless suit had been pressed to perfection just the night before, and his boots shined with muster. She could hardly believe that soon, they would belong to each other.

Once she reached the Bishop, who was standing near Levi's wide stone fireplace, she turned to Levi. The Amish took wedding ceremonies very seriously, and Hattie planned to say her vows with full sincerity when the time came. They took their seats together, holding their backs straight.

After the end of three-hour service, Levi and Hattie met privately with the ministers for about forty minutes, where they received admonitions and blessings concerning their impending marriage. Hattie's eyes shone with joy once they returned to the congregation. There, they committed to love and cherish one another for the rest of their lives during the five minute wedding ceremony.

Levi clasped her hand as they ascended the staircase together, ready to have a few precious moments alone as man and wife before joining the wedding festivities at the *eck*, a special corner table set aside especially for them. Shivers of happiness rushed up her arm as he squeezed her fingers while leading her into the master bedroom.

"I've been waiting for this day for a long time. I'm so thankful you are finally my *frau*." He wrapped his strong arms around her. She felt dizzy with excitement as she listened to his words slip off his tongue. She had been anxiously waiting for this day, too.

"*Kumme* now, I have something to show you." Levi gently pulled away and led her to her very own hope chest from Lancaster which now graced the foot of his bed.

"I still can't believe you arranged for all my *mamm's* things to be brought here from Lancaster. It must have cost a fortune."

"Anything for you, my dear. I guess one perk of waiting until spring to marry is that I was able to arrange for your things to be taken out of storage and brought here by train and stagecoach. This never would have been possible during our harsh winter."

Hattie nodded in agreement as Levi pulled the clasp on the trunk and reached for a passel of papers. He smiled sheepishly while motioning for her to step forward. "While Deer Springs will be losing the best schoolmarm possible, as the schoolmaster, I would like my lovely *frau* to be given the honor of choosing her replacement. I asked the Bishop to forward the teacher applications back to me, and the choice is yours, sweetheart. No one knows our scholars better than you."

She giggled as she took the applications from his outstretched hand. "*Ach*, I would be glad to give my opinion of the applicants, but the final decision is truly up to you."

"*Nee*, I would like nothing more than for you to be as involved as you wish in the running of the Deer Springs Amish School. I know the scholars mean so much to you, and I don't want our marriage to stand in the way with your involvement. Of course, I hope many *kinder* will join the ranks of Leah and Luke before long. You are the best *mamm* I could ever hope to give my children."

Tears misted her vision as he reached once more into chest and pulled out a large woolen blanket.

"This isn't much, but Bessie wanted to give you a wedding gift, too. After the spring shear, I brought her wool to Greta and asked her to make a blanket for you. I hope it's to your liking."

She brushed her fingers against the special gift, at a loss for words. "I couldn't ask for anything more."

"You've made me the happiest man alive, you know that don't you? I promise to love and cherish you forever, Hattie Hilty. You never need to worry about that."

She sighed with happiness as Levi gently wrapped the blanket around her shoulders and pulled her towards him. Hattie tilted her head towards his as his lips gently brushed against hers. When he finally lifted his kiss, he softly rubbed his hand across her back. Hattie had never felt so loved, wanted, and content. Surely she was home.

If you enjoyed this book, please be sure to review online and share with your friends!

Thank you!

ALSO BY NICOLE CRONE

Her Island Summer

Marine biologist Sarah Andrews is forced to rely on her old boyfriend when the Tybee Island Marine Rehabilitation Center is badly damaged during a storm. When Colby Mansfield arrives to pick up the pieces, he can't easily forget how Sarah broke his heart to pursue her career a decade ago. When yet another misunderstanding threatens to tear their budding relationship apart, will Sarah build a wall around her heart? Or will she open her eyes to the integrity of the man standing right in front of her?

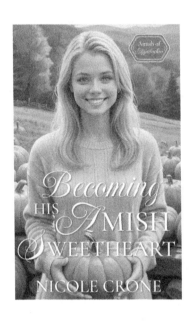

Becoming His Amish Sweetheart

After Amelia Taylor's twin brother died in a farming
accident, she couldn't wait to leave small town life
behind. That is, until she met Abram Miller at her
family's pumpkin farm in the Appalachian Mountains.
Abram came back to his Amish upbringing three years
ago after pursuing a music career, and still hasn't been
able to convince his family he's here to stay. He'll teach
Amelia how to enjoy life again, while she'll threaten his

commitment to the Amish church. Could an Amish man and and *Englishe* woman ever share real love?

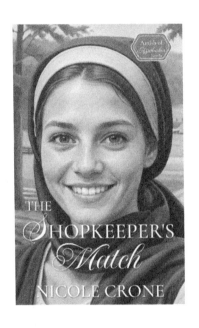

The Shopkeepers Match: An Amish of Appalachia Novella

Two are better than one in the quaint, Amish community of Clear Creek...

When Lydia Yoder's family leaves to take care of her ailing grandparents, it's her chance to prove she can handle running their general store in the Appalachian mountains. When shopkeeper Matthew Lapp comes to lend a hand against her wishes, it looks like Lydia's hopes are dashed. With the biggest shopping day of the year looming, will they learn to work together before it's too late? More importantly, is there more to their relationship than meets the eye?

About the Author:

Nicole Crone has enjoyed learning about Amish culture for two decades now, and enjoys writing fiction about this way of life. Researching 1920s Montana was a lot of fun, and she hopes you enjoyed this novel.

Nicole is an avid fan of clean, sweet romance novels, and has a bookshelf full of them. She started writing a novel herself at the ripe old age of ten, and has been hooked ever since.

Nicole enjoys writing fiction novels from her home in the North Georgia mountains. She has been a contributing writer at Year Round Homeschooling, and her articles have been featured at For Every Mom. When Nicole isn't writing, you can find her gardening, reading, or homeschooling her children.

You can visit Nicole at her website, https://www.nicolecrone.com.

Made in the USA
Monee, IL
04 October 2024